THE
SPHERE
WARS

JOSEPH ARBOUR

◆ FriesenPress

Suite 300 - 990 Fort St
Victoria, BC, Canada, V8V 3K2
www.friesenpress.com

ISBN
978-1-5255-1891-1 (Hardcover)
978-1-5255-1892-8 (Paperback)
978-1-5255-1893-5 (eBook)

1. Fiction, Technological

Distributed to the trade by The Ingram Book Company

TABLE OF CONTENTS

DEDICATION

To my lovely wife Edith who continues to encourage and support me in my writing. Thanks for your patient reading and insightful feedback on my drafts. To my two daughters Dr Victoria Arbour and Dr Jessica Arbour who continue to be such an inspiration in my life.

JULY 1ˢᵀ, 2090

Pugwash, Nova Scotia, hadn't seen this type of gathering since the very first of the Pugwash Conferences called for by Albert Einstein and Bertrand Russel. Leaders from the surviving nations had gathered to map out a new world order. The meeting was concurrent with a gathering of the remaining world's leading scientists, charged with developing an international agreement that would prevent science from ever again being manipulated for political and military gain. Those attending hoped that the world had learned a lesson.

The new Demi-God, Halie, monitored the event, mindful of the unpredictability of human behaviour. She could only establish the preconditions for success; the humans would have to find their own way. She hoped she would never have to intervene again as she had been forced to do when Armageddon had seemed so near. She had confidence in the individuals that she had encouraged to come forward. They demonstrated the utmost in leadership skills and had responded in an exemplary fashion.

Halie had built a record of how the world fell on its face. She drew from recordings, social media, emails, phone conversations and news media. She tracked key players through principal component statistical analysis. She planned to release this as a documentary for the human population in order to map out for them the foolishness that had brought such desperation to the planet. The story begins centuries before, but the real turning point came more than ten years in the past.

In the year 2074, Dr Nathan Ezekiel and his team set out to harness the power of gravity to create the world's first successful fusion reaction driven generating plant. It was needed desperately. Dr Hans Terrefield, an old schoolmate of Nathan, was Chairman of the UN Commission on Land

Degradation. His surveys had shown that climate change had so devastated the soils of the world that food scarcities and mass starvation had become a real threat. The challenge was how to motivate the world's nations to address the problem. The fusion plant, named The Sphere, held out hope to humanity that clean, sustainable energy was possible and that harnessing it could turn the tide on the problem of climate change.

Dark and sinister political winds began to gather that would alter the geopolitical makeup of the planet and subvert the global aims of Nathan and his team. The brilliant and beautiful Kate Smythe, Professor of Political Science arrived on the scene through a chance encounter at an antique car meeting. Nathan quickly fell to her charms, and she played a critical role in dealing with the political subterfuge that assailed the project.

The big day arrived when the Sphere was brought on-line and started to deliver energy. Then all the dark political undercurrents came together to snatch the success away from the team. The government of Canada capitulated to American aggression and handed the country and the Sphere over to US control. The Island provinces of Nova Scotia, Prince Edward Island and Newfoundland declared their independence and formed the independent Islands of Canada. Shortly after this, the province of Quebec declared itself independent. This had left Canada torn and degraded, existing under a puppet government run by the US. Now ten years later things have gotten progressively worse.

ESCAPE

Hans was becoming weary. He and his team had been forced to walk out of the devastated steppes of the Ukraine. At one time it had been the breadbasket of Europe, but then was mismanaged by the Soviets and was now an arid wasteland as a result of climate change. The vehicles they had used to travel across Ukraine had been destroyed by leftover landmines from the great war of 2020. At that time Russia and the West had fought for control of this piece of the Earth, in the end leaving it as a failed state, controlled by the neo-nazi militias that once supported the corrupt government of Ukraine. Hans looked out at the horizon. Before him, he saw the parched and dry soil, lifting in gusts of wind. There were no settlements any longer; the population had long since left for the big urban areas where the former prosperous farmers led lives of living off the refuse of the urban population. Turning to Victor Granger, his soils technician he said, "Vic, how much water and food do we have left?"

Vic was a wiry young man, "We have enough for another day. Then we have to find some provisions somewhere. We have ten people on this team, so we will need substantial amounts. I am a bit worried about Loretta, she is an ace scientist, but at sixty-five, she doesn't have the endurance that the rest do."

Dr Loretta Findlay was the world's most renowned dry land biologist. Her role had been to assess the ability of the landscape to support life. Hans, as team leader, had accepted her role on the team because it was supposed to be a driving tour. They had not counted on hitting an unmapped landmine field. Fortunately, the vehicles protected them from the blasts, but the vehicles had been completely disabled. They had lost all of their communications gear in the accident and fire that ensued. In this day and age of complete connectedness, by law, they had found themselves without communication, with no way to connect with the civilized world. They were not expected back out of the field for a week, so there were no alerts going up for them. They were on their own.

They had saved one GPS unit, so they knew where they were and in which direction to go. This also let them know that they were in the area controlled by nomadic warlords, the last form of organisation found in this part of the world. They were prime bait to attract these vicious bands that would grab them for ransom or simply kill them. Hans checked their position and looked at their map; they had saved one paper copy from the fire. He turned to Victor, "We can reach an old abandoned community later today, it's a risk, though; it's Chernobyl."

Victor lost his demeanour for a moment, "Hans, that's a death wish. The place is still hot more than one hundred years after the reactor blew up! Is there no other choice?"

Hans looked at the map; everything else was more than two days walking away. They needed shelter, food, and water before that. "There are emergency food and water caches located in the community; put there years ago after the accident. These are all tinned products that are in shielded containers. They will be safe. We will find a building on the very outer edges of the city where exposure will be the lowest and make quick forays in order to gather food and water. We may even find some functional communications equipment to work with and get ourselves out of this mess."

Victor looked dubious but stayed quiet as Hans described his plan to the team. Most objected, but Loretta spoke up in support of Hans. "This is all about risk. We are at much greater risk staying out in the open. The nomadic tribes will find us eventually. They are a much greater danger than a bit of residual radiation. I have read as well that most of the tribes in the area have a deep superstitious fear of the Chernobyl area. They won't go near it. It is our safest refuge until we can get evacuated out of here."

That seemed to settle everyone, and with Hans leading, they set off in the direction of Chernobyl. Late in the afternoon, Victor thought he saw some individuals trailing them. "Hans, I think I saw some tribesmen following us. There were only two, but they will probably draw more in."

Looking at his GPS, Hans saw that they had only two kilometres to go before entering the Chernobyl zone. "Everyone, step it up, we have tribesmen on our tail and only two kilometres to go. We need to cross the boundary before they get organised," he shouted at the group.

To his delight, Loretta was the first to pick up the pace and charged on ahead of everyone. They made good time after that.

Their handheld GPS unit was quite sophisticated. It had a built-in Geiger counter that allowed them to assess the safety of their surroundings. As they came close to the zone which was about twenty kilometres from the reactor they began to hear beeps from the counter. Still, just above background at two millisieverts (mSv), they were not in any danger; looking back Hans could see that they had just made it in time. A band of about twenty well-armed tribesmen was in the far distance, but coming no further. Their superstitions held them back. Certain now that the danger was over, Hans said to his group. "We have to find shelter and then seek out the food caches. This city we are entering was called Prypiat. It was evacuated after the failure at the reactor, and no one has lived here since. We can find shelter and look for some of the food and water caches. In the morning, we need to head to the reactor site and find some communications gear."

The next morning, they hiked in further until they could see the bulky form of the steel casing that now was wrapped around the old concrete sarcophagus. Inside, the remnants of the reactor core were still hot and dangerous. "We aren't going to try to get into the reactor building, are we?" Victor blurted out, "We would all get scorched by the radiation."

"No, we are not going in the containment building. We will check the other buildings of the complex. Just try not to pick up anything or stir too much dust," Hans replied. "Let's try that building over there; it looks like it has promise."

They headed over to the building that Hans had pointed out. There were wires still running to the building and several odd looking antennae. Inside they found a vast amount of ancient electronic gear and what looked like communications gear. However, when Hans checked the objects with his GPS, he got readings of up to three sieverts (Sv). This was far too high to handle for any length of time. Victor was rooting through some drawers when he pulled out a sealed box and said Eureka. It was an antiquated looking headset; they looked like earmuffs. Checking, they found that the headset itself had very low radiation readings. "I can wire this into any of the com devices that we think may work," Victor said.

After a bit of searching, they found a portable radio set. Lacking any power sources, they would have to make do with their backpack solar panels. "In the morning, we will hook up our backpacks in parallel and run them to the radio. With luck, we will have enough power to get this thing working," Victor said.

They spent the night back in their dwelling from the first night, away from the higher contamination of the powerplant. They feasted on cans of cold brown beans and water. The next morning they set their cobbled up radio out in the bright sunlight. Soon the indicator lights showed enough power to the radio to make it work. Turning to the international emergency frequency, Hans spoke into the microphone of the headset, "To anyone that can hear this, I am Hans Terrefield of the UN. My team and I are in dire distress and need extraction from a location in Ukraine."

He waited a moment, and then a scratchy voice came on, "Please repeat your message, this is Minsk International Airport."

Hans repeated his message and waited for a reply, "Yes Dr Terrefield, we have here that you and your team were cleared to enter Ukraine for a two-week field trip. What is your situation?"

"Our vehicles and equipment were destroyed by landmines. We are on foot avoiding the local tribes. Can you put me through to the FAO in Rome?" Hans answered.

There was a moment's pause, and after some odd clicking, Hans heard the Director's assistant come on the line. "Hello, Director Wright's office."

"Samantha, this is Hans, is Doug there? This is an emergency!"

"One minute Hans," she answered.

The next moment Douglas Wright came on the line. "Hans, what is the problem?"

Hans described quickly the landmines, the fire that destroyed their equipment and the flight from the local tribes. "So we need immediate extraction, can you arrange it?"

"I can have a security team sent in right away; just give me your exact location?" Douglas answered.

"We are next to the Chernobyl power plant," Hans answered.

"What the fuck are you doing there? That is a complete exclusion zone, besides being a pretty dangerous place to be. Are you crazy?" This time, Douglas was shouting.

"It's a long story, can you get us out?" Hans persisted.

"I can, but the chopper can't land in the zone, you will have to make your way back out to the perimeter, and we will pick you and your team up. Here are the coordinates for your pick up." Douglas gave him the GPS coordinates to head to and signed off.

Hans turned to his team and said, "The good news is that the FAO is sending a security team to pick us up, the bad news is that we have to walk twenty kilometres to get to the boundary of the exclusion zone. The security team will pick us up by chopper there."

The groans were universal from his team; they had walked so far already. "We will rest today and go at first light in the morning. We need to make the perimeter by mid-afternoon and be ready for pick up."

AMBASSADOR SMYTHE

"**H**eads of State, Ambassadors, World Leaders, welcome to the opening of this 2085 General Assembly." Michele Kreuger's calm but strong voice carried through the venerable old UN building. As the first woman to head the organization as Secretary-General, she had proven herself a decisive arbiter of the many conflicts that arose. "We have before us a very ambitious agenda for the next two days. The world faces the most egregious problems that it has ever had to deal with; famine, starvation, conflict, disease, and tremendous political instability. Many nations have criticised the UN for not preventing these disasters, claiming that perhaps the UN serves no purpose at all. To these naysayers, I reply unequivocally, the UN has never been needed more. Our organisation has helped millions of people in their time of need. If it had not been for our pioneering work in identifying the arable land shortage, we would be in deeper trouble than we are today. We have been able to protect seventy percent of the land that was at risk ten *years* ago. Unfortunately, that is not enough. We are still well below the minimum amount needed to feed our global population. We must find a way to restore more of what we lost. It is deplorable that some take advantage of this shortage to expand empires and gain control over impoverished and starving nations. We will address these issues over the next two weeks."

"On a more positive note, I am pleased to present our newest Ambassador to the UN, Dr Kate Smythe, Ambassador for the Independent Islands of Canada." Kate rose from her seat to a mild applause, although she noted that the American Ambassador and the representative from Canada sitting next to him, sat stone-faced and stared straight ahead.

With that, the Secretary-General called the meeting to order, for what would be a tumultuous two weeks, with regular accusations, finger pointing, and insults thrown around the room.

Kate's first General Assembly as the new Ambassador was proving to be quite an experience. She was attacked by several members because of her association with Dr Nathan Ezekial and the CanRussChin Consortium for Fusion Power. Gabriela Rodriguez stood and spoke, "Now that the Sphere is up and running it has given the US and its puppet Canada an unfair advantage in the world. With a vast supply of energy, the US is exerting extraordinary power in its dealings with other nations. Unfortunately, once the Sphere had been taken over by the governments, they placed all of the design information and the science behind it on the classified list. It is now hidden behind a top-secret security wall. No other nation can access it. China, where the science originated has imposed its security walls on what they have, as has Russia on the engineering aspects. The rest of the world has to do without or learn to dance to the tune of the Americans. What are you going to do about it?"

Kate listened quietly, wondering what Ambassador Rodriguez was thinking. Kate had no role in the current management of the Sphere and the Independent Islands of Canada had no say in the policies of either the US or its protectorate, Canada. She looked over at the American ambassador who simply shrugged his shoulders at her. Kate toggled the microphone and responded to the question. "Ambassador Rodriguez, I appreciate your very direct and open question. I would like to point out that the Independent Islands of Canada has no role at all in the management of the Sphere, which is entirely in the hands of the USA and its protectorate Canada. I believe you are making a point about the lack of sharing of the knowledge and technology that went into the Sphere. On that, I am in total agreement with you and would support any efforts to de-classify the information. That is, however, completely outside my mandate, so I must respond by saying that I will not do anything about it; direct such questions to the Ambassador for the United States." She leant back in her chair and gave the US ambassador a look that would kill.

Harry Wood, the Australian Ambassador, then asked, "Ambassador Smythe, is it true that you were fired from your first university post because of illicit activity with the Russian Mafia? I think all of us here would like to know what the details were."

Kate groaned inwardly and thought to herself, *What is going on here? Is your first day an opportunity for members to roast you alive?*

"Ambassador Wood, I have never cooperated with or been engaged with the Russian Mafia. The incident you describe was a result of being abducted by members of the mafia while I was in Moscow. I am certain that there are far more important matters before this General Assembly, so perhaps you should not waste valuable time trying to dig up dirt that doesn't exist."

At this point, the Secretary-General, Michele Kruger of South Africa intervened and said, "We have a very rugged agenda ahead of us. Those who want to pester Ambassador Smythe can catch her outside of Assembly. Our first order of business is the current famine crisis, fully one-third of member nations are currently in the middle of food shortages, creating an impossible situation for us to be in 2085. Our food aid programs are not keeping up with the demand and I would like to propose that we increase the contributions from countries by fifteen percent."

This lead to an immediate uproar in the room as most complained that the food situation in their countries was already stressed; a fifteen percent increase in donations would push many into the critical zone.

"Might I remind members that over the past eight years we have been trying to protect sufficient land to meet our basic global food requirements. We have only achieved seventy percent of that need. Many of our developing nations have been reluctant to set aside the necessary land. There are zones in your nations that are under pressure from urbanisation and resource development that are critical to meeting our need for agricultural land. I understand the economics are pushing for development. We need that land just to grow enough food to feed the world's population, which is still growing at an alarming rate. Nations that are removing arable land through development are increasing the risk of broader global famine. These shortages will place an even greater demand on us at the UN to provide food relief and even greater demand for donations from nations. We all need to put every effort into saving the productive land, billions of lives depend on it."

This was an impassioned plea that the Secretary-General had made at the beginning of every General Assembly that she had led. Unfortunately, most nations continued to look at their situation only and refused to reduce growth to protect the land. It is a vicious truth in the economic cycle of the world that negative growth or no growth in your economy is seen as devastating, rather than stabilizing.

At the same time, Dr Nathan Ezekial was resting on the deck of his new house by the sea, looking out over the Northumberland Strait. The Independent Islands of Canada had declared their status as a separate country after the Canadian Government accepted protectorate status under the US. The Islands had now achieved full recognition at the UN. As the last outpost of the Commonwealth on the North American continent, it was doing quite well. Nathan was thinking back ten years to when he and Kate left American controlled Canada. He had been fired from his position with the Sphere, as had all the senior officers. Cornelius Snow was jailed briefly. However, there were never any real charges brought against him. On release he had immediately moved to Halifax, to escape the oppressive regime running Canada. They had remained close friends.

Shortly after Kate and Nathan had arrived in Nova Scotia, they had finally gotten married. They had a quiet ceremony in Pugwash and a small reception at the Cyrus Eaton House. On Kate's request, they had gone back to the Amalfi Coast for a honeymoon. Since then, Kate had entered the political world and had just been named Ambassador to the UN for The Independent Islands of Canada.

There was a knock on Nathan's front door. Puzzled at who would come looking for him, he went to the door. "Hans, Jacques! What are you two rascals doing here on the coast?"

Hans was the first to reply, "We are looking for that brilliant wife of yours. Is she around?"

"Well, no. In fact, she is at the opening of the General Assembly in New York right at the moment. But come in guys, it's great to see you. What are you up to?"

Hans and Jacques went into the seaside house while Nathan pulled three bottles of beer out of the fridge. "Come on out onto the deck and let's catch up on things. So what brought you here?"

Jacques spoke up, "Nathan, you know the world has gone to shit since we all got fired. I mean, besides the fact that our nation turned on us, kicked us out of our role in the Sphere and made it impossible to work again. I really mean in the big picture, things have gone way downhill. We decided to come and see what you were up to."

"Well, I had been approached by the Chinese government to move to Beijing to work with the Prometheus III collider. I had declined the offer, not wanting to be separate from Kate again. Instead, I agreed to a consultancy contract which gave me greater freedom to work from home, travelling to China only when needed on-site by the team. This arrangement has worked well, and I find myself continuing to be engaged in really interesting science."

Hans spoke up, "I have to agree with our esteemed colleague here. You guys had your hands on a great solution to the world's problems. But, it was perverted for the use of power-mad megalomaniacs. Our turncoat Prime Minister is nothing more than a puppet for his American masters. They are using their access to all the power to extend the American Empire around the world. They are doing this by taking advantage of the food crises that have exploded everywhere. They are far worse than I ever expected. The Americans offer basic food and military protection for the starving nation's allegiance. It's empire building once again."

"Yes," Jacques jumped in, "That is why we wanted to talk to Kate. We think she may be the key to trying to resolve this. We also believe the Independent Islands of Canada is the focal point for attacking this globally."

Nathan looked at these two old friends and said, "What have you been smoking? Look, guys, I don't see how our new little country here can have much influence in world affairs. I have no doubt, though, that my wife could solve any problem put in front of her. But seriously, neither of you lives here and you will get yourselves in deep trouble if you champion the Islands with the current government of the Protectorate of Canada."

"Ah, we didn't tell you the best part. Jacques quipped back. "The reason we have come together is that we found out, quite by accident that we are both getting involved with Atlantic University. Hans has been on contract with the FAO and is considering a faculty position at the University in their Biological Engineering Department, and I am looking at a faculty post in the Department of Political Science. We met at the Faculty Club and hadn't stopped talking about you and Kate since."

"I still don't get what you think this little collection of islands can do to address the world's problems," Nathan said.

For the next two hours, Hans and Jacques described their thoughts on what could be done and the role that this small new nation could play in it. Nathan was dumbstruck. He had withdrawn from world affairs during the past decade. Occasionally, teaching a lecture at the University, but most of the time, just working out of his house by the sea. His work with the Chinese kept him engaged and busy most of the time with frequent trips to China. Kate had prodded him about getting involved with the affairs of the new Islands of Canada. She recognized the hurt and disgust that Nathan had lived through when his project, his creation, the most amazing piece of technology and science the world had ever known was taken from him. Now his two old friends tried to galvanize his interest to get him back into the game. They were hoping Kate would be on hand; she would be the key to getting him back.

Nathan sensed that Hans seemed to have something else on his mind, but was reluctant to talk about it. As luck would have it, Jacques yawned and said, "Is there someplace I can crash. I am dead tired, and the beer has made me even sleepier. "

Nathan showed him to the spare room, and within a few minutes, Jacques was snoring away. Hans didn't waste any time, "Nathan there is something urgent that I need to discuss with you. It must remain utterly secret."

"Wow Hans, what is it, and I don't keep anything from Kate so if she can't know, don't tell me."

Hans paused, "OK, but let her know how sensitive this is. You wouldn't know, but I have a long lineage back to what was called the United Empire Loyalists. It is on my mother's side; my father was Dutch. Way back in the days before the war of 1812, a group of Loyalists, along with some natives had formed a group called Butler's Rangers. I have long distant ancestors who were part of them. Prior to the beginning of the 1800s, this group launched repeated harassment attacks against the Americans in New York State. I want you to know that Butler's Rangers are back. I have been in command of the group. We are a clandestine group working out of a small somewhat forgotten village in the Niagara Peninsula known as Port

Robinson. It is appropriate, as that is one of the recognized burial sites of Loyalists. Our activities have been focused solely on cyber harassment; we don't consider violence to be in our mandate. Your man, Dan George has joined us, he is a genius. We have managed to disturb traffic at the international bridges and have shut them down several times so far. The authorities have gotten on to us, though. They don't know who the members are but have labelled our group of freedom fighters as 'terrorists'."

Nathan butted in, "Hans, what are you on about? Are you the guys behind the chaos at the Rainbow Bridge? I heard about that one on the news. Traffic was snarled for five days. You made a lot of people very unhappy."

Hans smiled, "I am glad you heard about this. We have been quite successful. The Rangers are drawing in a lot of talented people, people who can't stomach the takeover of Canada that our traitorous government orchestrated. We have some benefactors helping us from outside the country as well. Cornelius is a great supporter, as are the governments of France and the UK, although, only in clandestine ways. I have been working on a contract with the FAO in follow-up to the Global Land Inventory that was completed ten years ago. After my most recent near-death experience, I thought I would try something a little saner and safer. I was just interviewed at Atlantic University and have a good shot at a faculty position there. I will stay involved with the Rangers but not as Commander. I am pleased to say, though, that Geri DeLong has just taken up a position at the University of Southern Ontario, teaching engineering. She has been active with the Rangers for two years and is taking over as Commander. She sends her regards and hopes to see you soon."

Nathan was dumbstruck. He would never have guessed that his old friend would be involved in such an organization. "Hans," he said. You have blown me away with this, but I have to ask. Why tell me? Don't you put yourself in danger?"

"Nathan, there is no one in the world that I trust more than you. That goes for Kate too. I am telling you because I believe that there are dynamics happening globally that may tear this world apart. Your work with the Chinese puts you right in the middle of that. Those of us with the Rangers want to make sure that you don't get caught in a trap."

Nathan eyed his old friend with even more surprise, "Hans, now you have left me completely puzzled. How could I be in the middle of anything, I am just a science consultant, nothing political at all."

Hans eyed him seriously, "You recall the great change in 2040 when China chose to promote having a second political party, moving towards full democracy? The party that has emerged as the opposition in China is very far right, scarily far right. It is led by a group of xenophobic nationalists who want China to take an aggressive posture in the world. They are gaining a stronger and stronger hold on the politics of that country."

"But I can assure you that my work with the Chinese is strictly peaceful. The fusion reactors that we build cannot be used in any military ways." Nathan shot back.

"It's just that there is extremism in the party that is very scary; they could pervert any peaceful program for the wrong reasons." Hans continued to argue, "It is why we were hoping to see Kate here. She understands these dynamics better than all of us."

"Tell you what," Nathan said to Hans. "I will talk to her about this and get her views when she gets back from New York. I expect to see her next weekend."

This promise mollified Hans a bit and he accepted Nathans offer. At that, they decided to follow Jacques lead and get some sleep. Hans took the couch in the living room and Nathan crawled off to bed. The next morning Jacques and Hans headed out early to catch their respective flights. They all promised to get back together soon.

That night Kate settled into her New York hotel room and called Nathan, "Nathan dear, you won't believe the day I have had."

They were on a video call using the new holoprojector system, so Nathan had the chance to talk to his beautiful wife as if she was in the room next to him. He missed her dearly. "Oh sweetie, it is so good to see your face and to hear you." He responded emotionally. "I had a rather interesting day yesterday that I need to tell you about, but first, let's hear about your big day at the UN."

Kate smiled and said, "I didn't expect to get roasted by the other members. The ambassadors for Brazil and Australia both launched at me with stuff from the past. They tried to pin this business of the US withholding all the science and technology of the Sphere from the rest of the world on me and then they threw my dismissal from Atlantic University in my face. I could have screamed. Does it ever end?"

Nathan saw that the games played at the UN caused her stress. "I don't want to downplay it, but perhaps this is just first day high jinks on their part."

"It could be, but I have to confess, it threw me for a loop," she said wearily.

"Well, I had a surprise visit from the dynamic duo, Hans, and Jacques. It seems they both may end up at Atlantic University. I found out a few things about Hans that surprised me. I will tell you about them when you get back. The two of them are trying to get me to be more active politically. They were hoping you would be here to help them out."

"I heard that Hans had had another brush with death out in the field. Something about taking refuge at the Chernobyl Reactor. I am sorry I wasn't there to help, I think you could do a lot if you got involved."

"We can talk about it when you get back, do you know when that will be?" Nathan responded.

"Sorry dear, but this General Assembly is going to last two weeks. I will be on the plane home as soon as it is done; keep the bed warm for me. Love you." she said.

"Enjoy your meetings; I love you too. Bye." They both signed off their computers. The beautifully rendered three-dimensional image of Kate faded. Nathan was very proud of Kate's appointment as Ambassador and knew she would have a big impact. He was lonely, though; he realised how much they had bonded during the last few years. Life in the Independent Islands of Canada had been good. He had his contract work with China and she had taken a job as a policy advisor to the Prime Minister of the Islands. She had made a huge contribution to the development of governance mechanisms for the new nation. The Islands had established a reputation for good governance and for being an effective honest broker. Her new post was recognition for this.

Nathan was still going over all that Hans had said to him. He had to confess he was intrigued immensely by this group, Butler's Rangers. The idea of peacefully resisting one of the most powerful nations on Earth captured his imagination. The fact that several of his old friends were central to the group meant it had big credibility in his mind. These were not people that would throw their hats into just any organization. He decided to do a bit of research on this organization.

Turning to his computer, he said, "get me information on the Butler's Rangers." The first listings were current news reports out of the US of the terrorist group supposedly naming itself Butler's Rangers. But he wanted to go back further, to the roots of this group. What made it so special and what drew Hans and others to it? For this, he would have to find out more about the United Empire Loyalists. Hans had mentioned his heritage with this group and Nathan had no idea who they were.

The story took him right back to the American Revolution. It turns out that the United Empire Loyalists got the designation from Lord Dorchester, Governor General of British North America. In 1789 he had declared that he wished to recognize the families that had made the hard journey north to Canada and had fought with the British Army in the American Revolution. He issued a statement that allowed all these and their descendants the right to use the honorific U.E.

"OK," he thought to himself, this explains Hans' heritage, but what about this group Butler's Rangers. He found that during and following the American Revolution there were many who wanted to fight back. They formed small guerrilla groups; the most famous of these led by John Butler. In the period following the revolution, John Butler's group of loyalists and Native North Americans harassed the areas around the border. They had many successes and were much heralded by the British Crown. Many of those who had been a part of Butler's Rangers went on to fight in the War of 1812, an attempt by the Americans to spread their empire.

Nathan sat back. He was getting a quick reading of history to which he had never paid any attention. What he read intrigued him, though, as the takeover of Canada had clearly been a return of American Imperialism. Perhaps he thought, just perhaps I should get involved.

ANGRY SEAS

Hans was getting himself settled into his post at Atlantic University. He had not lost his connection to the FAO; he was still a consultant to them. His Director there, Douglas Wright had been enthusiastic about Hans' move. This University was a world leader in oceanographic research. The FAO had been getting frequent reports of odd and serious changes to many of the globe's ocean areas. Douglas had wanted Hans to make a connection with the research capabilities at the University in order to start programs to address the oceanic issues emanating from climate change. As a result, Hans had an interesting cross-departmental appointment putting him in both Biological Engineering and in Oceanography. In his first meeting, he sat down with the head of Oceanography, Dr Steven Harrison.

"Hans, we are thrilled to have you here. We all followed your work to get arable lands protected. Now we have to draw the world's attention to the oceans and seas. The high CO2 levels don't just affect temperature; they have raised the acidity levels of our oceans. There have been many reports of coral reef deaths. These charismatic features of the oceans play a huge role in the ecosystem cycles. But there are deeper and more significant problems developing that threaten to make larger regions of the oceans uninhabitable for any form of life," Steven opened.

"Yes, I am aware of some of the concerns. Douglas Wright at the FAO had briefed me on some of these concerns, although as a soil scientist I think I have much to learn. He mentioned something about Canfield Oceans. Can you fill me in on what that is?"

"Yes, I will get to that problem," said Steven. "You just have to walk along the waterfront to see the effect that sea level rise has had. Much of Historic Properties in flooded and abandoned. The ferry terminals have had to be moved twice and a few condominium buildings destroyed due to the flooding. The steep terrain of Halifax Dartmouth has kept the ocean from making bigger inroads. In other areas of the world where cities are built on low-lying flatlands, the problem has been more catastrophic. In the US south, New Orleans was finally abandoned as the effort to hold back the sea overwhelmed the city. Forty percent of Florida is no longer usable. But as you have asked, that is not the biggest problem.

"The Canfield Ocean model is named after the geologist that coined it back in the previous century. His work focused on conditions during the Proterozoic Eon. The ocean at the time was purported to have become anoxic and sulphidic and unable to support life. It may have contributed to mass extinctions. The surface of the ocean is said to have been a gelatinous mass of sulfide-loving bacteria. There is an example today, the Black Sea has a chemocline that is less than fifty meters below the surface, and below that layer, it is anoxic and sulphidic. It used to be between one hundred and fifty and two hundred meters eighty years ago, but it continues to change. If the chemocline breaks the surface, we will get massive amounts of hydrogen sulphide released, toxic levels. The Black Sea will die, and the impact on nearby life will be traumatic."

Hans considered this, "It sounds like the situation with the oceans could be as serious as the land side. My understanding is that we are sourcing a big portion of our protein needs from the oceans right now, the loss of that would be catastrophic to the world food supply, worse than it is even now. But what can be done about it?"

"That's the problem. The processes that lead to these phenomena are long-term and can't be turned off. If it happens, we will have no means of stopping it. I am keen to work with you to produce a food production model for the globe that factors in the loss of that source of protein. It will mean having to get more land back into production, not just securing the current land." Steven offered.

"That's a tall order but one that I am excited to pursue. I sometimes almost feel overwhelmed with how bad the situation has become on our planet. When you think back, it would only have taken a few strategic decisions to have made the situation so much better. The naysayers at the beginning of the century have made life quite miserable for us now." Hans said somewhat philosophically.

Hans left his meeting in deep thought, already putting links together on how to push the current targets for arable land even higher. As he walked, his phone pinged. "Hello Val, how is my favourite person on the planet doing?"

Valerie Sims, a tough-minded and aggressive journalist with WNN, had never expected to fall for a guy like Hans, but she did. Their relationship had solidified and was as strong as ever. Neither had ever broached marriage, though, they both were on the go too much. "Hans, I have a few days free, and I am missing the man in my life. How about I pop up to see you? I can be there tonight if I catch the next flight."

Her news hoisted Hans right out of his reverie and cheered his spirit, "What time will you arrive? I will pick you up at the airport. This is beyond good news, Get here as fast as you can."

"I look forward to it, get your motor running sweetie," Val said suggestively.

Well, that did it for Hans, his mind was now stuck on the curvaceous and sensual image he had in his brain of this beautiful lady when she was naked in bed.

Late that night Valerie arrived at the airport to be greeted by a smiling and happy Hans. Work separated them often, but when they were together, they were joined at the hip. Val found that Hans just brought out a side in her that she didn't expect; a soft, emotional and contented side that seldom appeared during her work. This contrasted with the side that had sustained her through her career. That side was focused, determined, aggressive and cutting. She dug deep into any story she pursued and had always prided herself on the depth of the research she did before taking on interviews. She often knew her targets better than they knew themselves. Such skills had won her many journalism awards during her career. Right now she was at the top of her game. It was also a life of high pressure, stress, and risks. Her interludes with Hans had become her pressure relief, the way to reconnect with life and all that can be good. Hans embraced her in the big hugs that she could get lost in, she felt home.

"Tell me about your first day at the University Hans. Is it going to be a good fit?" Val asked as they drove back towards Hans' high rise condo on the Dartmouth waterfront looking across the harbour at Halifax.

"I had a meeting with Oceanography. The problems in the ocean are as big as they are on land. It's going to be an interesting and exciting challenge. It may even be a story that you might find interesting," he answered.

"Well, I will be happy to hear about it tomorrow. The conversation I want to have tonight tends to be non-verbal, I hope you got your motor running." She said with enough suggestiveness that Hans almost drove off the road.

When they reached Hans' condo, their clothes didn't make it a meter past the door. They were both at a fever pitch and were soon on the bed entwined in each other's bodies and oblivious to the world."

The next morning Hans watched Val walk naked about his condo. She was striking in her height, a full six feet, with long auburn hair. She had a delightful body, just full enough to take his breath away, yet still trim and elegant. She seemed completely without a care when she was with him and completely uninhibited. Simply, he felt on cloud nine, as happy as he could get. He handed her a short robe and said, "Let's have coffee on the terrace." It's a lovely morning, we can just sit and watch the vessels go by." He said this, as he thought, it is a shame to cover up such beauty.

"So Hans, what is this ocean thing that I remember you saying last night?" Val asked as they sat down on the large terrace overlooking the harbour.

Hans never dumbed it down for Val; she was as bright as they come. "The FAO is as concerned about losing productive ocean areas as they were about land areas. You know that about twenty percent of our protein comes from the oceans. To lose that would exacerbate the famine issue even more. The concern is the effect that high CO_2 levels have on the oceans. We have seen extensive die-offs in coral reefs around the world, which destroy critical habitat for many species. The concern rising now is for the emergence of Canfield oceans. These produce an excessive release of hydrogen sulphide, which makes the water uninhabitable and can endanger shoreline areas. It's a double whammy, dead seas, and toxic fumes."

"Wow, this sounds horrible!" Valerie exclaimed. "This is not something that has seen any media attention yet. Would that be useful?"

"I'm not sure yet," said Hans. "Let me get further into it before you focus attention on it. I am sure that you could do a good job with this.

I have to see where the University and the FAO wish to go. But tell me, what hot story are you chasing now?"

Valerie looked at him coyly, "I will tell you about it as long as we get back to our other business."

Hans looked perplexed as he thought what other business. Then thought to himself happily, "Oh, that other business."

Later that day they were on the terrace again having coffee. Valerie began, "I have been following the evolution of governance in China. It is the hottest political story on the planet. Early in this century, no one would have believed that China would break loose from its communist path. However, the economic reforms brought such success to the country that they developed a real middle class. These people who held value in independence had the ability to shape the way their country worked. In 2050 they held their first multi-party election. Granted there were only two parties, and the opposition party was relatively weak at the time. The Peoples Party has held power since. However, the existence of a real opposition has made them adjust their policies to stay ahead.

"This is changing, though. The opposition party has gained a great deal of strength and support in the country. It garnered thirty-five percent of the popular votes in the last election, so it has a real voice. What is truly interesting though is that the existing Peoples Party has turned out to be moderate, left of centre party. The Democracy Party that has formed the opposition is a hard line, far right and extremely nationalistic organization. They are gaining more support amongst industrialists in the country and are starting to build a substantial war chest. Their platform is a much stronger military and a reduced level of government and social services."

Hans was intrigued, "I hadn't paid any attention to this. Do you have any thoughts on why the opposition in China has gone down this path?"

"My theory is that there is a link to the western corporate world. You know that China's incredible growth early in the century included the movement of a fair amount of western capital into China. Many American-based industries set up shop in China as did European firms. Those corporate entities have continued to develop their political punch in the country, as they do in other countries. They have targeted the new political movement as being a good vehicle for their political ideology.

Money has bought the group, but I think that the movement has gone far beyond what the corporate entities were pushing for."

Hans thought for a moment and said, "This is much more complex than I would have thought. What do you mean by, 'gone far beyond?'"

"I don't think they counted on the intensely militarized element that grew within the party. In fact, they have developed a strong relationship with the defence industries and have gained a great deal of support from the military in China. You have to remember that democracy is not new to China. There was quite a lot of development of democratic concepts in China during the twentieth century. They all came to a halt with Mao's democratic dictatorship under the communist party. What is happening now has reawakened such feelings and has gone well beyond any previous developments. Whichever way you describe it, it is the greatest geopolitical realignment of the current age."

"I can only say wow, I didn't realise you had so much depth in political science," Hans responded.

"I'm a journalist; I learn fast."

Hans sat and thought for a minute. "I sense a similarity in this movement with the neo-conservative movement that Kate has raised so much concern about."

"That is a brilliant connection, Hans," she answered somewhat surprised. "In fact, Kate and I have talked about that and have agreed. She thinks that there is probably a link between this development and the re-growth of the neo-conservative movement in the western world. In her position as Ambassador, she doesn't maintain her blog; she has to be sensitive to diplomatic niceties. But in our personal conversations, she is still concerned about this movement and its global growth. She does fear it could get out of hand in China, even more so than in America."

With that, Valerie went back inside. Hans watched as her robe slid from her shoulders and she looked back at him. He got the message and followed her in; the conversation ended for a while.

NEW SCIENCE

Nathan was just looking at his recent data dump from the Prometheus III collider. Xiu Xi had just processed the recent runs and then sent Nathan the entire dataset to analyse. Despite the terabits per second transmission rates, the dump still took half an hour. Nathan, fortunately, had availed himself with one of the newest compact quantum computers. It was the fourth generation system and occupied no more space than an old-fashioned desktop computer. Mind you; it had a separate cooling and heat exchange system that required external fixtures to super cool the processor. He was running intensive statistical analysis on the data using the newest version of R and Matlab. Since the merger of R and Matlab in 2078 he had analytical tools with more power than anyone has ever had and the ability to process universe sized data sets. His analysis focused on flagging particles that didn't fit the Standard Particle Theory. Xiu Xi felt that they had seen the appearance of a new particle, one that did not fit the current science. However, they couldn't confirm this and were looking to Nathan to see what he might find.

This is what Nathan lived for, the absolute threshold of science. If these new particles proved to be real, it would re-write the textbook on particle physics. Finding them though was like finding a needle in a field of a billion haystacks, and only one needle existed. He was treating himself to a cup of horribly expensive coffee. It had become so hard to get that it was now out of reach of most people. The food shortages had driven most coffee plantations to switch to food crops. He was sorting through the last run of the collider. Somewhere in there was the signal from a new particle. That particle probably lived for only a nano-second. There would only be a few amongst the billions of other particles. His filter though was the Standard Particle Theory. All of those billions of particles would fit the theory. The ones he was looking for would not. It took the processing power of the quantum computer to be able to run this sort of model in anything less than years.

His phone rang, "Hello Nathan; This is Xiu Xi." He continued to be amazed at this lady's perfect English. She continued to be the most brilliant scientist in the world. The holder now of three Nobel prizes for her work and still young, he simply waited for her next big move.

"Hi, how are you doing?" he responded.

"Not bad, but I haven't seen daylight in six months, I live in the control room of the Prometheus III. Did you receive my last data dump and have you found anything yet. I don't want to influence what you might find, but I am simply busting a gut to see if you come to the same conclusion that I have."

Nathan enjoyed how earthy she could be; it was totally outside of her character, "Yes I got the data dump, but no I haven't found anything yet. I will let you know as soon as I do. It sounds like you think it's something big."

"Yea, I think it's big, Charlie does too." She responded.

"So how is Charlie adjusting to life there?" he asked. After the mess with the Sphere, Charlie had followed Xiu Xi back to China. They were married now.

"He loves the food but is having a lot of trouble with Mandarin. It's a tough language to learn. Can you call me as soon as you get results? They may be really big," she asked, and from her tone, Nathan could tell how pumped over this she was.

"I will let you know the second I get results," he assured her.

With the call over, Nathan was now really intrigued. Obviously, Xiu Xi and her team had come upon something earthshaking in importance. He awaited the output of the computer. As he did, he thought about the development since his expulsion from the Sphere. The Russian and Chinese interests in the Sphere had pulled together and with the participation of the two governments and had set out to build their own Sphere. It was almost complete. They had advanced the concept significantly and refined much of the engineering. When it was complete, the two nations stood to benefit from a massive energy source, one that would allow them to exert significant influence in their part of the world. They had chosen an equally remote site. Not the Arctic, rather the middle of the Gobi Desert not far from the Flaming Cliffs paleontological site, long known as one of the first sites to contain dinosaur eggs. The construction site was isolated from the cliffs to avoid any damage to fossil remains. Construction had progressed well; the superconducting transmission lines had been built north into Russia and south into China. The plant should be operational in a year. Although Nathan consulted on the Russo-China Sphere, his real love was the new science coming out of Prometheus III.

Nathan settled in to enjoy his coffee. It gave him a chance to think back about the developments in China. They had had to re-invent a lot of the engineering that had gone into the original Sphere because of the lockdown that the US put on the development. These restrictions had delayed the construction of the new Sphere for a time. However, with his input and help from members of his team that had spread across the globe, they were able to piece things together. Unfortunately Geri DeLong, his Chief Engineer was still in the US controlled Canada and could not participate. She couldn't even provide input at risk of deportation or jail time. He was happy that now she was involved with the Rangers.

Hours later as he was dozing off a gentle voice beckoned from the computer console, Kate's voice, in fact, he had had the system train on her voice and now used it to communicate with him. "Your program has finished, would you like me to print the results?"

"Yes dear, thanks." He sometimes thought himself a bit weird talking to his computer this way. He went over to the printer to retrieve the output, only a few pages but significant. He read through the results. His analysis had shown that there was an infinitesimally small number of particles that didn't fit the standard model, but they were there. The data suggested a very oddball particle, one that just didn't seem real. Its behaviour suggested that it behaved quite independently from the other particles. There seemed to be a suggestion that the particle was influencing the space around it in an odd way. He was puzzled. This was going to take some thought. Nathan pondered what to do next. Normally he would switch to the neural network program and model the selected particle data and determine what behaviours seemed to grow out of that. Neural networks have the ability to learn from data; he was hoping this effort would suggest more about the behaviour of the particles. His thoughts turned to the newest offering in software, labelled Alternate Realities Modelling. It was a toolset that took advantage of the Quantum Computers probabilistic states to create alternate realities that could be tied to existing data. Its applications were somewhat untested, but he felt that this was a good place to try it. The result would give him all the alternate states that this particle could exist in. It was worth a try anyway. He dragged the icon for the data set that Xiu Xi had sent him over to the Alternate Realities Modelling icon and set it running. He then went to brew a bit more coffee; this would take a while. Even the quantum computer groaned heavily under this type of AI programming.

Nathan's computer finally sang out, "Job finished, do you want me to print the results?"

Nathan yelled back from the kitchen, "No, put it up on the wall." He still felt odd at times when he communicated like this with his computer. He went into his projection room and looked at the results on the full wall screen and was startled at what he saw. The particles that had been singled out appeared to be massless, they had spin and seemed to have a repulsive reaction between themselves. This repulsion seemed to extend infinitely. He checked again; the evidence was of a spin two. His brain took a few minutes to register. With all of his work with gravitons, he had become familiar with massless spin two particles that had carried the attractive force. But these were repulsive in nature. He sat down. "Shit," he said to himself. Such particles should not exist, no theory predicted this, neither string theory nor the standard particle model even hinted at this, but the evidence was there in front of him.

He called to his computer, "Call Xiu Xi in China immediately."

The Kate's voice answered, "Calling Xiu Xi right now, you know it is four in the morning in China."

"This is important, call now!" Nathan yelled, forgetting that he had trained the computer with Kate's voice to keep him from yelling at the inanimate object.

"A sleepy voice came on, "Hello, who is it?"

"It's Nathan; I just finished my analysis. I don't believe it!"

His statement woke her up completely, "Oh my gosh, do you think it is what I think it is?"

"If you think that this is the anti-graviton, I think the very same thing," Nathan responded. "This is going to take a lot of backchecking because this thing should not exist. How many times have you had this result?"

"Every time we pass the six hundred and thirty TeV level we get a small number. We haven't gone past that power yet so don't know what will happen next. We have no theoretical base upon which to predict what is coming." Xiu Xi explained to Nathan.

Nathan began breathlessly, "Do you understand the magnitude of what this could mean, this could be what drives the acceleration of the universe, it could revolutionize energy, travel, there is no end to what it could mean. Have you named it yet?"

Xiu Xi answered, "We want to call it what it is, no less than the anti-graviton. My god Nathan, we have discovered anti-gravity. It's a whole new world of physics that no one could imagine; this is just the beginning, though. We have to duplicate the experiment and ensure that our results are real, and we need to push past the current energy levels to see if this is just the threshold and that there is more to be discovered."

After chatting further Nathan was left to ponder what this new development meant. The anti-graviton had never been predicted in any theory. It would have characteristics that would be completely alien to the known universe. If they could generate controlled levels its use would be widespread. It could levitate huge loads, power transportation, lift vehicles into orbit with little or no fuel. Perhaps it could even power spaceships, making interplanetary travel practical. The world would never be the same. He shuddered at the thought that such a world-changing advance was in the hands of a relatively unstable China, where new political forces could change the shape of the country dramatically.

POLITICAL BETRAYAL

The journalist adjusted her hair and faced the camera. "This is Colleen North speaking to you in front of the Parliament buildings in Ottawa. We have breaking news coming to us from the office of the Governor of Canada. In a shocking move, former Prime Minister, the right honourable Archibald Morani lost his role as Governor of Canada. His ouster came as a surprising move as the former PM was a chief architect in the nationalizing of the Sphere and the transition of Canada to a Protectorate of the US. We don't have much detail yet. However, it appears that Morani has fallen out of favour with his American bosses. The big question is "Who will replace him?" There is a lot of speculation and some names are being bandied about."

Colleen paused for just a second as she was listening to a constant feed from the main newsroom. One of the essential skills of a journalist, she could handle input at the same time as keeping a monologue going. She assimilated what was coming in and put her thoughts together. "I have just been informed that the American authorities have just announced the replacement for Morani. I will have to confirm this, but it appears that the New Governor of Canada will be the former Minister of Energy, the Right Honourable Frances Oxford. This appointment is a surprising turn, although it is probably not unexpected in some circles as Oxford has been openly maintaining her relationship with the former Ambassador from the United States, Richard Burns, the new president of the Crown Corporation "Sphere Energy". Rumour has it that Oxford has been working behind the scenes to oust Morani for some time."

Geri watched the news broadcast with a growing sense of unease. It was disgusting to see the future of Canada managed behind closed doors, to see such an affront to the country's democratic legacy and the outright betrayal of top officials. She felt no love lost over Morani's expulsion from his post. She and many others considered him an outright traitor who should live the rest of his life in prison. It irked her intensely that such decisions were being carried out from south of the border. She was just on her way to teach her third-year class in Operations Research. The material was laced with heavy mathematics and confused many of the students. Her skill was in putting these difficult concepts into clear and learnable language. She couldn't react to the news now but tucked it away in her brain. She would be in touch with the leadership in Butler's Rangers that night to discuss what actions they could take. They had evolved to be a very sophisticated group, using techniques pioneered by the infamous group Anonymous from earlier in the century. They eschewed any physical acts of violence in their resistance and relied entirely on the many cyber tools available to them.

The news broadcast continued while she lectured. Colleen North had managed to catch up with the former governor's chief of staff, Mitch Knipper, who was also now out of a job. "Mr Knipper, do you have a comment on the sudden change in the governor's office?"

"Yes I do," he responded. "This is a good example of how the governance of Canada has degraded. Governor Morani protected Canada in everything that he did. This backroom coup now puts Canada completely in the hands of an extreme political group whose primary interests are not rooted in Canadian soil. Governor Morani, I should say Prime Minister Morani has fought to maintain the last vestiges of Canadian control on our fate. Now, with Oxford in the chair, we will be completely under control from south of the border. Canadians should not accept this or put up with this level of interference." With that statement made he stomped off in search of a new career path.

Colleen came back on, "Well that was certainly a strong and ominous statement from such a senior member of Morani's staff. Tune in later for an in-depth analysis of this development. This has been Colleen North from Parliament Hill."

It was later that night when Geri finally had a chance to catch up on the coverage of the event. By that time, the political pundits had had a jolly good time with it. In the end, though the significant comment had come from the exiting Chief of Staff. She took his message to heart. *Canadians should not accept this kind of crap.* She had been in touch with the leadership and had discussed a strategy. They knew their next target now, not the new governor, rather the shifty-eyed American with whom she associated herself. It was time to turn up the heat, and they had all the tools to do it. Their first foray would be the worldwide distribution of some video they had been holding for a rainy day. Cameras were more ubiquitous than ever before, and they had been able to hack into the personal camera of Frances Oxford's phone which had been left on during one of Oxford's trysts with the American. What it revealed was a night of sadomasochistic sex that should be a thorough embarrassment to both of them, but definitely for Richard Burns. He was a vocal Evangelical Christian and had frequently raged at the depraved sexual liberation of the youth of the day. His night of pleasure was going to smell very bad for him. Geri was satisfied that this was a good opening salvo.

THE DUMP

Hans came up on deck and looked around. He was enjoying his new role at the University. He was able to apply much of his experience from the GLI to initiate the GOI or Global Ocean Inventory. With support from the FAO, he was working with a team of oceanographers to assess the quality of the oceans. His work brought him into contact with some things about which he had never heard. It started with his conversation with Steve Harrison regarding the state of the oceans. "Hans, we are very concerned about the effects of climate change on the oceans. Unfortunately, the worlds efforts to curb climate change were set back significantly during the Republican reign of 2016 to 2020. The withdrawal of the US from the Climate Change Accord was all the fodder that many other countries needed to back away from the agreement. It had been almost impossible to regain momentum after that, leaving only a few countries taking the problem seriously. However, that is not the only human sourced problem with the oceans. There are two other big issues that we need to address at the same time. The first is that more than eighty percent of the pollution going into the oceans is from land sources. These sources have a huge impact on the waters in the nearshore and contribute to overall pollution levels. The other is that we have turned the oceans into huge garbage dumps. Oceanographers identified this process early in the century. However, it was not an issue that people ever related to closely. Despite many warnings from the UN Environmental Program and many efforts to curtail marine litter, the problem had never been solved. Litter from ships and land-based sources still collected in the oceans. Because of the persistent nature of all of that plastic, the effect was cumulative. The garbage collects in the large gyres which occur in all oceans. Shipping simply avoided it. In 2085 these patches have now grown to be enormous and have a tremendous effect on marine life."

Hans had contemplated this and had asked, "Is there an inventory of these garbage dumps, any mapping or studies in any way? "

"There have been some attempts at inventory but no comprehensive mapping. We think they now cover up to twenty percent of the ocean surface, but we are not quite sure."

Now Hans could see the reality of what Steve had told him. As far as the eye could see, the floating plastic covered the ocean with trash and a myriad of other objects. They were in the N. Pacific Subtropical High, otherwise known as the Eastern Garbage Patch. The ocean currents formed a gyre here; anything that is floating on the surface got caught in this and stayed. Some of the plastic had been here for years. This blight represents only one of the numerous garbage patches like this, which appear in all of Earth's Oceans. The problem went way beyond what showed on the surface, tiny bits of plastic filled the water column.

Hans turned to one of the crew members and said, "Humanity must truly hate this planet, we have destroyed most of the land area and systematically destroyed the oceans too. If we keep crapping in our own house, it is not going to be fit to live in."

The bewildered crew member looked back and said, "Ah, sure, gotcha." He then went off to try to avoid the crazy scientist.

Hans wandered back into the main lab on the ship. There, technicians were processing water samples and identifying various bits of debris that they had collected. They were also equipped to receive direct satellite images and had the latest EuroSat images up. In the infra-red band, the garbage patch stood out like an amorphous blob. It was an immense area that would likely be bigger if the currents didn't have a tendency to draw the debris to a smaller area. The patch was a deadly zone for marine mammals, seabirds, sea turtles. Much of the iconic sea life of the ocean had suffered greatly in the past forty years as the density of debris increased.

"So, how do the images look today?" Hans asked the senior technician.

"Look for yourself Dr Terrefield," he answered. "I have just been doing time series for the past twenty years. The changes are very dramatic. The blob has increased in density and area each and every year."

Hans looked at the display. The technician had done a nice job; the display had been animated to show the growth of the blob over that period. It looked like a rapidly spreading cancer. In many ways, he was sickened at the sight of it. It was at that point that the ship shuddered as if impacting a heavy object. Everyone stumbled as the vessel came to a halt. Then the emergency signal was broadcast through the ship. Something serious had obviously happened.

Out on deck crew members scrambled to their emergency positions and assessed the damage. Reports came in that they were taking in water on the port side near the bow. Hans, as senior scientist aboard, had bridge privileges. He went up to see what was happening; stepping into the bridge he found the Captain on station, barking orders to the helmsman and the engineer. The Captain turned to Hans, "Dr Terrefield, we appear to have struck a submerged barge that was floating just below the surface. We didn't see it and caught the corner. It has ripped a sizeable hole in the hull. Please have your scientific staff stand by to abandon ship."

Hans was stunned. In this modern day of electronic devices that would guide you, warn you and keep you out of trouble this felt like an impossible scenario. "How serious is the breach?" he asked.

"We appear to have opened the hull through three watertight compartments, that is too many to maintain a stable ship. We will flounder at the bow. Please hurry and prepare your team, I am going to give the abandon ship signal in ten minutes."

That got Hans moving fast. He returned to the lab and got his team securing as many portable memory drives as they could. They were sealed in watertight packages and put into backpacks. They would at least save the data. The computers and the samples would go down with the ship. By the time they had completed this, the abandon ship order had come over the intercom, and they hustled out to get to lifeboats. The ship was already well down in the bow. It was at least not listing so launching the lifeboats was still straightforward. They also launched the fast rescue craft. It could ferry around amongst lifeboats until the fuel ran out. All the lifeboats were enclosed and powered and had supplies of food and water for two weeks. The Captain had sent out a distress signal. However, they were thousands of kilometres from land and any of the active shipping lanes. Hans and his team boarded one of the lifeboats with some crew members and motored away from the stricken vessel. She was far down in the bow now with water lapping at the gunnels. Fortunately, it was calm, and there was no perceptible sea state to address.

The two lifeboats and the fast rescue craft pulled close and lashed themselves together. The Captain asked Hans to join him with his officers to discuss their situation. Crossing between the two lifeboats Hans joined them in the bow of the second lifeboat. "Our situation is stable at the moment, the Captain said. "However, it could change fast. There is an unusual weather front moving towards us. Normally there is a fairly stationary high-pressure system here, so it's easy to get becalmed. But this looks like a storm generator. Unfortunately, we are not equipped in this craft to receive satellite downloads so we can't fully anticipate what's coming. You will each have to be prepared to button down your boat for bad weather. This craft won't sink, but if it gets bad enough, they can turn turtle. They will automatically right themselves, but be prepared, when it gets bad everyone must be strapped in and no loose items around. We will stay tethered until it is too dangerous to do so. If we become separated, keep a northeast heading. Hopefully, we can find each other again. I need two volunteers for the fast rescue craft. It won't sink either, but it will be a very rough ride. Full survival suits for whoever takes it. It helps if you enjoy fast roller coasters."

Hans watched as two young crew members volunteered, eager for the thrill ride. "You fools," he thought to himself.

He returned to the other craft with two officers who were to command that boat. The senior officer explained their situation and what they were facing. Hans noticed that his team turned a bit green at the description the officer gave. "Listen, guys, I survived deadly sandstorms in the southern US and marauding warlords in Ukraine, not to mention a night or two at the Chernobyl reactor, this will be a piece of cake." He knew though that this was a totally different situation.

The twenty or so occupants of the craft settled in for the long haul. They hoped that the shore stations in South America and the US picked up their signals. However, the worsening weather meant no chance of air rescue, and they were a long way from any shipping. It would take several days for anything to come to their aid. In the meantime, they were at the mercy of Mother Nature, and she had a bad temper nowadays. At this point, they had the doors open on the craft; a pleasant breeze kept the air fresh and comfortable inside. The little boats rocked along in the gentle waves, tied next to each other. They were saving fuel for the storm so they could keep headway into the waves once it started. One of the technicians riding with Hans said, "Tell us about your desert escapades, it seems a good diversion since we are stuck out in the middle of the ocean."

For the next while, Hans regaled them with accounts of sandstorms, tribal groups and the comical mistakes made in campsites around the world. His escapades kept both his staff and the crew members distracted from the reality of the danger coming their way.

Several hours later the sky had darkened even though it was still early in the afternoon. The wind rose, and they had transitioned to a sea state two. The doors were sealed up, and the pilots took their positions in each boat. They looked out through windows high in the vessel. Fairly quickly they decided to untie the boats. The afternoon wore on and the skies continued to darken. Each boat stayed in visual range of the other as the sea state began to worsen. The winds picked up more and they transitioned to sea state three. The lifeboats handled this easily as they maintained gentle headway into the seas. Afternoon transitioned to evening, although it felt like night due to the very overcast conditions. The winds continued to pick up, transitioning to sea state four with heavy rain starting to fall. Everyone in the boat strapped into a seat, and all loose items secured away. Even at this sea state, they were getting quite a ride out of it.

As the night wore on the sea state increased to six and then seven. Now the small boats were under power driving up and over the waves. With wave heights of up to six meters, the boats rose up and crested the waves just to fly down to the trough. The seasoned crew of the vessel rode this out, but the scientific team were new to this experience. Barf bags supplied in the seats were already in use. The air inside the boat had become fetid and uncomfortable as they were tossed around. They had no information on the storm so they could not anticipate if this was the worst or was there more to come. Very little conversation took place. The pilot fought to keep them heading into the waves, while one of the officers kept contact with the other boats through the VHF radio. They were staying in the same area but trying to keep out of each other's way. The two lads in the fast rescue boat reported that they had clocked seventy knots going down into one of the troughs. Their ride had gone beyond thrilling to absolutely frightening.

Then it got rough. The sea state climbed to eight or nine, which is catastrophic. Wave heights exceeded fourteen meters. The little craft became as much submarine as a surface vessel. After running down a fourteen-meter wave wall, the vessel would plough into the next wave and submerge. It always buoyed to the top, but it was a sickening ride. Maintaining headway was almost impossible. The vessel would occasionally turn sideways; then the waves would simply submerge it again. The most sickening of these was when the vessel rolled completely over while under a wave. Its buoyancy brought it back up, and it righted itself. At this point crew and science staff had turned green. Hans had quite honestly reached the point of acceptance that he had finally pushed his luck too far; he thought of Valerie and not seeing her again. The chaos of the environment of the boat was so severe that it was hard even to think. He presumed that the others in the rest of the small boats were going through the same thoughts. He was sure that this little plastic environment could not survive the beating that it was receiving. The hull slammed heavily with each wave sending shudders through the structure.

Gradually the slamming diminished, the chaotic movement lessened, the boat spent less time under water. The sea state settled to a fairly rough four, but not at all as dangerous. Fortunately, the engine and the fuel had survived, so they continued to motor through the much lower waves. The ride was much more comfortable now. The pilot had opened some windows to let in a breath of fresh air which was a big improvement since the air inside was fetid with sweat, vomit and fear.

Hans thought to himself, "Holy shit, we survived."

His senior technician, Tony Trebble was sitting across the boat. "Tony, how are you doing?"

"Aw crap, I think I am going to be bruised everywhere, and in some places, I have never expected. How are you doing Dr Terrefield?"

"I'm in about the same shape as you are in, but just relieved to be alive. How is everybody else?"

There was a round of grunts and groans from the rest of his crew, but everyone seemed to have survived. The ship's crew were busy trying to raise the other vessels by radio. The first to come on were the fast rescue craft. The two young crew members had had something beyond a terrifying experience. Their craft had done everything from fly to submerge completely. Their survival suits had worked for them, but they were badly beaten up and reported possible broken ribs and or joint dislocations. After this, the Captains lifeboat reported. They didn't have relative locations but made finding the two young guys in their tiny craft and tending to their injuries the top priority. It was still night, though, and there was little they could do until sunrise.

Later after the sun rose, the seas had settled enough to open the doors wide on the lifeboat. Hans looked out at a now blue sky and wondered at the incredible experience that they had just endured. The reality of their situation settled in, though. They were still stranded in the middle of the garbage patch with no idea when rescue would come. Fortunately, all the vessels had GPS; they were able to locate themselves and plot a course to link up. A few hours later they had all tethered up. The two young crew members were on board the Captains lifeboat, and the others took care of their injuries.

Now came the long wait for rescue. They did not have enough fuel to sail to any landfall. They knew where they were and chose to stay in the area. If anyone came looking for them, they would look in this area. They were treated to a very sad sight later in the day. Their research ship the Calypso slowly drifted by, stern fully in the air, the stern watertight compartments keeping it afloat, for now, the bow though was straight down in the water. As it drifted by it got a bit lower in the water. It wouldn't be long before the ship sank to the bottom. They were all quiet for a while. There wasn't much conversation after that as the day went on and evening approached. It was hot, and the insides of the lifeboats were even hotter.

Hans awoke, stiff and sore from sleeping in his seat, the sun was up and the day was warming rapidly. He thought to himself, "It is going to be a scorcher soon. I wonder when the psychological stress starts to show, and we start attacking each other. The thought didn't comfort him. To occupy his mind, he dwelt on the peculiarities of the storm. As they were in an area dominated by high-pressure systems the air is usually descending and drier. These high-pressure systems bring more stable weather. What they experienced in the last days had been anything but that. He wondered if this is another element of the climate change story; this type of severe weather hitting this year-round high-pressure system. It was discomforting that such a change could take place. He made some notes to take back to the University. He thought he would get the meteorology people in on the discussion. This could have quite an impact on the way the garbage patches behaved.

He broke out of his reverie when a great deal of shouting came from the lifeboat and the sound of a flare pistol firing. He and others clambered out onto the roof of their lifeboat. Sure enough, off in the distance was a vessel steaming directly for them. It looked civilian; in fact, it looked a lot like their ship. Then it hit Hans. The Chinese had a sister research ship to the Calypso; they had both come out of the same South Korean shipyard in Busan. As the ship pulled up, he could see that it was exactly that. Once they were all on board, he found the Captain to thank him.

"Oh don't thank me; you have to thank Dr Ezekiel. He called the Director of Prometheus III who called my boss and said get the hell over here. Your friends care about you. Hans would learn later that Valerie saw the news of a missing research ship on the newswire and called Nathan and Kate. Nathan called Xiu Xi to see if she could help. She called the director of the Chinese Oceanographic Agency, an old friend of hers who said they had assets in the vicinity and would redirect them right away. Hans just sat back and said to himself, "What a circle of friends I have."

KATE COMES HOME

The General Assembly wrapped up its business after a two week period of in your face challenges and backroom deals. The UN of 2085 was a very dynamic institution with extensive influence around the world. With so many environmental, economic and political crises developing there was a high demand for its services. They had thrashed many intractable issues, but too many remained unsolvable. Everybody felt frustrated by the lack of progress. Kate left the meeting wondering what they had accomplished. They were no closer on the fight to save land areas, the fight to save the ocean, the fight against hunger and disease and the fight for political stability in many areas. She now had a long weekend to get back to Nathan in Nova Scotia. She really could not wait. The flight was not a long one, but the ride to the airport in one of the city's ubiquitous autonomous cabs through New York's ever-increasing congestion seemed to take much longer than the actual flight. She was thrilled to arrive back in Halifax and to see Nathan waiting to pick her up. She dashed over for a big hug and kiss before he could say anything.

"Oh, you are a sight for sore eyes," Nathan said. "I have missed you horribly while you were gone. Let's get your bags and get out of here."

He grabbed her luggage and soon they were on the road heading out to the shore. It was a two-hour drive. In that time they managed to catch up, and Kate vented some of her frustration with the politics of the UN.

"I always heard that all the heavy work gets done in back rooms and behind closed doors. I just didn't realise that it was so true. What the members say in the General Assembly seems to have nothing to do with the real deal they have swung. The folks that have been at it for a while seem to have a whole list of favours to return or to call in as they work along. I don't think I will ever get the hang of it."

"I trust that you will figure it out, you are the smartest woman on the planet you know." Nathan quipped.

"Flattery will get you everywhere," she answered. "Just remember to keep it up."

Nathan finally pulled them into the garage at their house. Kate had fallen asleep as they drove. He went around to her side of the car and gently woke her up. He put his arm around her; they made their way up to their place. He could see that she was exhausted from the efforts of the last two weeks. He led her to the bedroom and carefully helped her get undressed. She was as strikingly beautiful as always. Tucking her under the warm sheets and blankets, she fell asleep almost immediately. Nathan was still wide awake from the drive, so he decided to pour himself a good stiff drink and relax for a few minutes before climbing into bed himself.

Nathan thought back to how the last few days had developed. It had been a busy few days. When he got the call from a tearful Valerie that Hans' ship had gone down in the Pacific, he had been sick with worry. He recalled how everyone, including Hans, had dropped everything when he had been kidnapped and tortured. He immediately put a call into Cornelius asking if he had kept his ties with the Russians and was there anything they could do. He called his contacts in the US to see if there was anything the US Navy or Coast Guard could do. He didn't get much headway with that; his name was not a popular one there at the current time. He called Xiu Xi to find out what she knew about Chinese capabilities. Her answer had been the most hopeful, she knew the Director of the Oceanographic Service, and she would put in a call.

Shortly after, he got a callback, "Nathan, this is Xiu Xi; I have good news and bad news. The good news is that China has one of its oceano-graphic ships on its way to the same garbage patch. The bad news is that the garbage patch is about to be hit by some extreme weather. This is an unusual storm, it is cyclonic and will generate hurricane-strength winds. These don't usually enter into the North Pacific Subtropical High, but this one is. It will generate sea states of at least seven or more and heavy rain. My friend says that it is possible for the lifeboats on the Calypso to survive this type of storm, but it will be a very dangerous situation for them. Our research ship will not be able to look for them until the storm has passed. I have assurances though that they are standing by and will steam into the area the moment the storm weakens. I am sorry to have to pass this on to you; I know Hans is a great friend of yours. I will call as soon as I know anything from this end."

"Thank you for everything you have done, I have to trust in Hans' resilience. He has survived a number of other near-death experiences; I am sure he will get through this one," Nathan said, although he was not so sure.

On his computer, Nathan checked the online service for AIS transponders. Calypso's was still not registering, but they did know her last known position. This would help the Chinese vessel in its search. His phone rang, "Nathan, have you heard anything about Hans!" It was a distraught Valerie who had called in a complete state of distress. They talked for a long time until Val had settled a bit. Nathan was as assuring as he could be in the circumstances.

"I have been in communication with everyone. I have some news, but it is not horribly re-assuring." Nathan then described the assistance that the Chinese were willing to give, but the news of the extreme weather was a great concern.

"I am afraid that all we can do at this point is wait and hope. Hans is in the hands of Mother Nature right now, and she is not in the best of moods. Try to get some sleep. I will call your cell the moment I hear anything."

It wasn't until late the next day that a jubilant Xiu Xi called to report that Hans and all the rest were aboard the Chinese vessel and quite safe.

He broke out of his reverie of the past days and sat down at his computer for a moment to look at messages. One caught his eye that troubled him. It was from Xiu Xi. She simply said that she had had an odd visit from members of the opposition party. They queried her about the potential defence uses of the research at Promethius III. As the Director of Research of the facility, she was highly regarded in China. This new party that emulated the western conservative parties had named itself the Democracy Party. They had pressed her hard about the graviton and its militarization. It made her very uncomfortable.

Nathan typed in a quick message saying that he was equally uncomfortable; was there something happening in China that might lead to an upheaval of the old political order.

He got an immediate reply, "Recent polls have given the Democracy Party a tiny lead in the popular vote. There is no election planned until next year, but they already taste an upset in the result."

He messaged back, "Perhaps we can talk to each other tomorrow, I would like to get Kate in on this conversation."

He sat for some time contemplating this development in the Chinese scene. He still didn't understand the politics there, but his gut sense said this was not good. He finally felt sleep overtaking him and crawled off to bed to curl up against Kate's warmth and loveliness.

The next morning he was up early and prepared Kate's favourite breakfast, French toast smothered in maple syrup and blueberries, cranberry juice and fresh Hawaiian coffee that he had been saving for a special occasion. The wonderful aromas drifted through the house, and soon she came out to see what he was preparing.

GROUNDWORK

Leonard Ketchel looked up from his workstation. It was time for his afternoon cup of tea. Before getting up from his workstation, he engaged all the security protocols on his machine, being involved with black ops meant that he and he alone was responsible for the data that was more secret than top secret. In fact, his boss and his boss's boss had no knowledge of what he was doing; it was that secret. Once done and secure he was able to go off to the staff room to get his usual tea, Earl Grey hot. As a fan of the old Star Trek movies, he felt it gave him a bit of Jean-Luc Picard character. Leonard did not look the black ops sort. He was kind of mousy looking with black rimmed glasses and a sallow complexion. He was, however, one of the most accomplished AI programmers in the country and had been actively recruited by Britain's Defence Research Establishment. Leonard lived, breathed and sweated computer code. He thought in computer code and walked through an algorithm's logic as easily as reading a paragraph. Leonard hadn't started writing code, though. He had first obtained his PhD in molecular biology at the age of twenty. He then completed a degree in computer science and started playing with ideas in AI. He was the first to premise that AI evolution might follow the model of biological evolution. His ideas got him into defence research, and here he was deep in a black ops effort.

He went and got his tea, wishing that it was actually a replicator that it came from, not a teapot. Leonard wasn't good at social skills, he had been plugged into electronics since an early age and had managed to avoid contact with messy human beings. His thought process though was highly structured and well prepared to do what he was now undertaking. With tea in hand, he went back to his workstation. After entering his multiple passwords, he re-accessed his system, Britain's most powerful quantum computer. He had mastered the new object-oriented probabilistic programming system language faster than anyone else. The power of the language was that each object could live in millions of statistical states multiplying the power of each line of code by millions. The results could be unpredictable for anyone without Leonard's mindset. For him, it was just a joy to take advantage of the flexibility and power. He had come to see the individual objects as the DNA of his code. The compilations that he could grow produced his almost organic programming. He stopped viewing programs as just code, but living organisms.

He opened his latest work. There on the three D screen, he could see a wreathing and sinuous display of vivid colours, indecipherable to those around him, but to Leonard it was beautiful.

"What are you dreaming up today Leonard," a soft feminine voice arose behind him. Rosemary was another of the defence scientists working at this centre. She didn't look the type either. She worked on the high-intensity laser rifles and pistols that the lab developed. This little unassuming and quiet gal could deliver instant death at a kilometre range.

"I uh, I uh am just cleaning up some algorithms, why do you ask?" Leonard displayed his complete lack of sociability.

"Oh, I was just taking an interest; you don't seem to have many friends so I thought I would try to be one." Rosemary was direct to a fault, which also limited her social network.

"I have friends, just not here," Leonard answered defensively.

"Besides, you don't have clearance for my work," he added.

"I have level three top secret," Rosemary answered.

"Yeah, whoopee. Even the Director-General doesn't have clearance for my work." Leonard retorted.

Not to be deterred Rosemary continued. "Well I just thought you might like to take a break and go out with me tonight, I know that you put in about fourteen hours a day right now."

With this Leonard turned in his chair to look at Rosemary. She was pretty but not beautiful, short blond hair and dimples. She dressed in tight jeans and sweaters which emphasised her short but curvaceous body. Somewhere in Leonard's body, a response was triggered, he was too blind to catch it, though. "I am on a very tight deadline so, sorry no, I don't think so."

Rosemary frowned a bit and said, "Alright, maybe another time." However, her brain was saying, "You shit, I come right out and ask you, and you turn me down. Well, I'm not done with you yet."

Rosemary left him at that point, and Leonard heaved a sigh of relief. He had dodged that bullet, an actual human being wanted to interact with him. He could get back to the love of his life, the kernel of software that he was currently building. In its normal state, it did nothing. However, a simple key could send it replicating at billions of times a second. Each replication mixed the basic DNA resulting in billions of mutations a second, trillions in an hour. It was like life at the beginning of time. A few strands of molecules mixing in the primordial ocean, allowing chaos to rule and to produce results. Given enough time something happens. That was Leonard's theory. If it worked, it would be one of the most devastating weapons of all time. They could develop weapons smarter than humans, cyborg soldiers that were craftier than any general, smart drones that could hunt their prey, no one could hide. His project had been commissioned through MI-6 as a covert cyber-op effort. It was cutting-edge research, and most thought it a waste of time. This idea that you could simulate the emergence of life in a computer and then have it grow to sentience was too much fantasy. However, his research didn't cost a lot, and the powers figured this was the best way to use his brain. Otherwise, he would be out on the street hacking into their system anyway.

Leonard's phone chimed, it was his MI-6 contact. Leonard hit the room silencer button, sound dampening shades drew down on his one window, his door locked automatically, and electronic screening turned on to prevent any eavesdropping, a proverbial cone of silence. "Leonard, how are things going with your project?" Mike Strong asked. Mike was one of the agency's most experienced agents. He didn't understand why he ended up saddled with this silly project and this mousy nerd that could barely speak "normal human".

"I made great progress yesterday. I got three hundred thousand combinatorial replications before it self-destructed into infinite probabilistic states and the data decohered." Leonard answered in as simple language as he could muster.

Mike groaned to himself, "yeah, what does that mean Leonard? Are you any closer to your goal?"

"That gave me a .001 percent greater probability of a deterministic and stable result in one hundred thousand states," Leonard answered trying to get to Mike's simple-minded state.

Frustrated Mike yelled, "Is that better or worse than yesterday?"

Leonard recoiled a bit and searching for the simplest language he could, "the change is not within the standard deviation."

Mike lost his cool and yelled again. "I haven't the foggiest fucking clue what you are talking about. Listen, just call me if you ever come up with something just a little interesting." With that, the line went dead.

Leonard clicked off quiet mode for his office, blinds went up and the door unlocked. The slight buzz of electronic screening faded away and he got back to work on his project that no one thought had any purpose at all.

Several days later Leonard was in his office again when Rosemary came in. Leonard groaned. "Now what," he thought to himself.

"Hi Leonard, how are you doing," she said in her soft sing-song voice.

Leonard groaned again inwardly. "I'm really busy right now. What do you want?"

Rosemary had become used to his unsocial responses, so she carried on. "I wanted to know if you had reconsidered going out with me? You have had time to come to your senses." As direct as usual.

"I just don't think I can take the time." Leonard tried his best to evade.

"Would it make you more interested if I said I have tickets to an all-night Star Trek movie festival?" she answered coyly.

This perked Leonard's interest. "Whe.., when is it playing?" he asked

"Tonight, so this is your only chance. Otherwise, I can get someone else to go." She challenged.

Leonard was caught in a desperate internal argument. Going out to something with a girl made him uncomfortable. He wasn't gay, just had trouble relating to real human beings. But his love of all things Star Trek had him on the hook. Finally, he said, "Uh, I guess I could take a little time away. Is it just going to be you?"

Ignoring the insult, Rosemary responded, "Yes just wonderful little old me." To herself though she thought, "Got you, you little twerp, now the fun begins."

They agreed to meet at the new Cineplex that had been built to bring back the movie experience. It was something that had finally faded away in the 2050s when the advances in personal virtual reality had made sitting in a theatre with hundreds of other people obsolete. Now there was a move to bring it back, a fascination with retro that was growing in the world. Perhaps it was a feeling that this represented the good old days when every crisis wasn't the end of the world.

Leonard met Rosemary at the entrance to the cinema. He hadn't changed from his work clothes. She had however slipped into an evening dress. It was the most sensuous outfit she had, low cut neck revealing more breast than Leonard had seen in a lifetime. Snug fit around her hips accentuating her shapely hips and high cut above the knee. She looked striking in the outfit. Once again Leonard's loins sent him a signal that got lost in the mess that constituted his social mind. She blazed her cutest dimpled smile at Leonard as they went into the theatre. Leonard had no idea how deep he was in yet.

The festival was starting with the last Star Trek movie made in 2025, the last of its franchise. Leonard liked its simplistic treatment of an AI entity that tries to take over the Federation. He chuckled to himself at the quaintness of the treatment. Rosemary was enjoying the entertainment and kept grabbing Leonard when there was suspense. He was surprised at how often she touched him. He was not used to normal human species contact.

The next movie was the original Star Trek movie. So primitive and the concepts so hilarious, Leonard couldn't help having a good laugh. Rosemary enjoyed seeing this in Leonard and had a good laugh along with him.

At the end of the second movie, Rosemary suggested that they get something to eat. Her small apartment was just around the corner and she had some great Chinese food she could heat up. She knew this to be Leonard's favourite. Since he was hungry too, he said, "sure that would be fine." Then he could get back to his room and catch some sleep.

In her apartment, Rosemary warmed up the food and opened a bottle of wine. They sat and enjoyed the food and actually had a conversation. This interaction was something that was new to Leonard; it seemed a pleasant experience. After dinner, Rosemary excused herself to her bedroom. She left the door open though and to Leonard's surprise simply slipped out of her dress. She had nothing on underneath it. Her body was exquisite. Neurones fired in Leonard's brain that had lain dormant. The signals from his loins finally connected. "Oh my God." He said to himself. "She is a sexual goddess". His body started to respond. Without realizing what he was doing, he stood and moved to her bedroom. She turned and looked at him and said, "Come on in Leonard, I've been waiting for you."

He stepped up to her, and she deftly undid his shirt and pants. In a moment he was standing in front of her naked. She looked down at him and said, "You're ready."

She pulled him down on the bed with her and as he entered her, she thought, "I've got you now you little twerp." The next few hours of sex were beyond Leonard's imagination. Rosemary worked him to a pitch and probed as she worked. Leonard found himself telling her all about his research, forgetting that she did not have clearance to be informed about it. She had been a bit surprised and delighted at Leonard's endurance; she got some pleasure out of the night as well.

WARNINGS

Hans was back in Halifax after his harrowing experience at sea. Val was off on assignment in Europe and Hans was trying to catch up on work at the University. Their efforts at mapping the garbage patch had been a good start. They had saved enough data to get their modellers going. The FAO had sanctioned a project to put the models to work on other patches in the world's oceans. In the interim Hans was preparing to get back to his work with the GLI. The UN was committed to finding the best way to ensure sufficient land for the production of food in each region of the world. At the current time, many developing nations had no choice but to buy into the American model and receive food relief from them. The US power surplus was granting them the tools to produce enough food to feed many, but it came at a political price.

Hans wanted a strategy that would ensure the independence of developing countries while providing their own basic food needs. As he began to open the files, his earpiece beeped, a call was coming in. It was Val. "Hans dear, I've got something here that may interest you. I am at a Black Sea resort in Georgia. The fishermen are reporting significant drops in fish caught and some god awful odours coming out of the water at times. It sounds a bit like some of your ocean concerns."

"Hi Val, that is interesting, did they say what the smell was like?"

"Yeah, they said it smelled like rotten eggs. Does that mean anything?" She answered and asked.

"It might," Hans answered. "If you come up with anything else let me know, the Black Sea is one of the most vulnerable marine areas on the planet. How is your trip going?"

"I am not having too much success, I wanted to get to know the soul of the new Georgia, but people are not willing to share too much," she answered.

"Well if anyone can do it, you can Val," Hans said.

"Thanks for the vote of confidence, I will keep trying. Talk to you later, Love you. Bye." She signed off on the call.

Hans thought for a moment and called Steve in Oceanography. "Steve, are there any unusual reports coming out of the Black Sea area?"

"Steve checked his computer and said, "The last survey was six months ago. The chemocline was staying about ten meters below the surface at its worst. Why do you ask?"

"I just had a call from Val. She is in Georgia and had heard that fish catches are way down and some fishermen are getting an occasional whiff of rotten egg smell," Hans answered.

"It may be just some storms stirring the surface a bit. Let me know if you hear anything more."

Hans went back to his work on the GLI and though no more about it.

The next morning he had an early call. It was Val again. It was late in the day in Georgia and she had had a busy day. "Hans I think this time that this is important. This afternoon a fishing boat came in towing another behind. They had come upon it drifting aimlessly when they looked onboard the crew appeared unconscious. That proved wrong when they got them to dock; they were dead. There were no marks on them, but there was a lingering smell of rotten eggs. The locals are talking about dead spirits and ghosts; I suspect something more scientific may be in order."

"The only thing I can think of is that they got caught in a pocket of hydrogen sulphide gas. It shouldn't happen, though. I am going to get back to Steve Harrison about this. Can I get you on your mobile later?" Hans asked.

"You can wake me up anytime sweetie." She said in her sexiest voice.

Val ended the call and Hans decided to hike over to Steve's office and sit down with him. Once in the office, he informed Steve of Val's call.

"That should not happen based on the conditions we last saw in the Black Sea. This may be worth checking. If it was a pocket of gas, it means that the chemocline has broken the surface. That could be deadly if it spreads."

Steve pulled up the latest model for the Black Sea. He ran an accel-erated model on it to see where the chemocline was predicted to break first. Sure enough, it was near the resort area in Georgia where Val was staying. Tinkering with the data, he ran the model from today assuming it had already reached the stage of breaking the surface. The result did not please him.

"Hans, can you get Val to leave immediately and then call the Director at FAO. We could have a major crisis on our hands. My model says that if there is a chemocline breach today then the process is accelerating and there will be a major eruption of hydrogen sulphide from this area of the Black Sea. Life on the coast is going to get challenging."

Hans pulled out his mobile and called Val. He spoke quickly. "Val, you have to get out of that area immediately, go inland and get away from the coast."

Val reacted, "What the hell are you talking about Hans. Things are peaceful and safe here."

"Val, that area of the Black Sea may erupt in hydrogen sulphide gas; it's deadly. With the onshore winds in that area, you won't have time to run. "Hans said with desperation in his voice.

"I'm a journalist Hans; I can't step away from a story like this." Steve was listening to Hans' side of the call.

'Tell her to go to the local safety supply store and get a gas mask and prefilled air bottle. But once the gas hits she has to use it to get out of the area immediately." Steve said, sensing Hans' growing anxiety over Val's journalistic spirit.

"I hear what Steve said," Val jumped in. "I will do that first thing in the morning, I will leave as soon as things get bad. Should I warn people?"

"No, we will do that through the UN networks, Steve and I are going to call it in right away," Hans assured her. "Now keep yourself safe and come back to me as soon as you can."

"OK dear," she answered, and they both hung up.

Hans and Steve spent the next hour talking to the Director of the FAO and then prepared for a conference call that afternoon with the Ministers of Environment and Health for the countries surrounding the Black Sea. If the Black Sea was about to become a Canfield Ocean, they had to start working on strategies to assist the population surrounding the sea and living off of it. As if the world didn't need another food and water crises, now the seas were preparing to kill as well.

Later that evening when Hans watched the news on WNN, Val was right there in front of him reporting on the strange deaths on the Black Sea. She did not refer to her conversation with Hans but ended with "I hope the authorities are taking this incident seriously." It was as much of a warning as she could give.

A team was dispatched from the new task group under UNEP to investigate environmental hazards. Their examination of the situation in the Black Sea off Georgia was not encouraging. Quick profiles taken off small boats in the area revealed the chemocline dangerously close to the surface. The team reported sulphide gas smells in the area. The situation seemed to be degrading rapidly.

Steve and Hans quickly took flights to visit the sites. Their destination was Poti, historically a seaport, but recently the site of a developing tourism industry. It would be hit hard if the Canfield Sea came true. Hans was looking forward to catching up with Val who had been in the city for a while. They arrived to find a city teeming with new tourists, and busy commerce at the same time. The place had the usual surreal feel of normalcy in the face of impending disaster. Val very proudly showed off her gas mask and air bottle that Hans had insisted she get.

Hans and Steve met with the UNEP team to get an assessment of the state of the Black Sea in this area. Michel Levrait, the lead scientist, briefed them on their results which Steve fed into his model using his mobile computer. One run confirmed the worst. The chemocline would breach the surface at any time. "We have to alert the National and Municipal authorities as soon as possible," Steve said to the team.

Michel answered, "They are going to be very unhappy about this and unwilling to organize an evacuation. It is currently the peak of their tourist season. The hotels are full."

"Then it is up to us to convince them. A major release of hydrogen sulphide gas with the onshore winds will be catastrophic. By the way, does your team have their emergency air packs and masks? They must be prepared. I want to put out drifting buoys with automated sensors. We need to cover the coastal waters all along the coast so air drops would be the best. Then we can monitor and catch the gas release as soon as it happens." Steve ordered.

Steve and Hans then went to meet with the authorities and as Michel predicted they were unwilling to take immediate action. The idea that their beloved Black Sea would reach out and kill them was unbelievable. They simply agreed to maintain an alert and respond when something actually happened. It wasn't much, but it was all that Hans and Steve could expect. Steve and Michel coordinated to set up a monitoring watch from one of the hotel suites in the city. They set up their computer gear and collected data from the buoys that were being air-dropped from UN helicopters along the coast.

As they went into watching mode, Hans had a chance to have time with Valerie. It was delightful to tour the old Georgian city together. This was their first time visiting the Black Sea. They noted that the well-advertised fish markets seemed to be very short on product. When they asked about this, the fish sellers said that there was a big slump in the catch. They blamed the Russians and Turks for overfishing. Hans sensed that they were placing the blame in the wrong place. It was a peaceful and restful couple of days for them, and Hans was grateful for this time with Val.

The morning of the third day the local population was astir about something. Going down to the waterfront Hans and Val witnessed a disturbing sight. It seemed that every fish in the Black Sea had died and been blown up on this shore. As the sun rose, the smell of dead fish filled the air. Hans called Steve at the monitoring suite. Steve came on, but there was much shouting in the background. "Steve, there are massive amounts of dead fish out here by the waterfront," Hans said.

Steve shouted curtly, "Hans get out of there; it's happening all up and down the coast. All of the bouys are reporting sulphide gas. Get back to your air pack."

Hans grabbed Val's arm and started to run without explanation. They were about half a kilometre from their hotel and had to sprint for their lives. It was the fastest run either had made in years, and neither was up for it, but they had to do it. They just got into their rooms and donned their masks when they looked out onto the street. They could see people reacting to something in the air and then dropping like flies. Hans looked at Val, "Do you have your satellite transceiver with you?"

She nodded and immediately understood. She raced to grab her headset and donned it quickly; as soon as it activated it linked here to Atlanta. "Stan are you there?"

Stan, her news Director, came on immediately. "Stan, I am broadcasting now, I have only the small built-in camera on my headset, it will have to do. This is a breaking story, hook me in."

Hans turned on the video screen in the next room and turned it to WNN. In a moment Val's voice came on and a slightly grainy but good enough video of the street below. With her voice catching Val described the scene, "I am reporting to you from a hotel in Poti, Georgia. A horrible environmental disaster is befalling this seaport on the Black Sea. People are collapsing in the streets from exposure to a gas. They could be dying. It is happening throughout the city and possibly all up and down the coast. Scientists from the UN think that this is an example of a Canfield Sea, climate change has so upset the balance in the sea that the deep waters have produced huge amounts of sulphide gas. This gas has now reached the surface and is spreading along the shoreline. This will be my only broadcast as I must evacuate the area now."

"Stan, I have to leave, I have an air bottle that is good for an hour, after that, I may die as well. I will call in as soon as I am safe." Val cut her link.

Hans came out of the other room with a mobile phone to his ear. Their masks had interfaces to connect electronic gear, so they were able to talk clearly on microphone or phone. "Thanks, Steve, we will be down on the street."

Val understood and with their air packs on, they went down into the hell that Poti had become. Within a minute Steve pulled up in a large van. The whole team was inside. They made their way slowly out of the city. Their guilt was immeasurable. They could not help the thousands of people that were dying, writhing in the streets, choking on the toxic gas filling their city. There was absolute silence in the van as they made their way up into the hills and out of the toxic cloud covering the coast. Tears were shed by all, not just because of the disaster before them but the knowledge that now humankind's mistreatment of the planet had started to degrade the very place that life began, the oceans and seas.

The team made it to higher elevations and sensors indicated that there was no risk. They pulled over on a hilltop to observe what was happening.

They couldn't see much but knew that death was extensive. Steve, Hans and Michel were all on their phones calling in emergency aid and putting all UN resources at work. They were also in contact with Georgian Civil defence authorities organising as much rescue effort as could be launched. Soon aircraft, helicopters, military trucks and small coast guard vessels began to converge on the area. Michel was able to report conditions based on the floating boys that were still transmitting their readings. The initial discharge of gas was dissipating, and levels of hydrogen sulphide were diminishing on the water. It appeared that the monster in the Black Sea was going quiet again. But it had reared its ugly head and would be back again.

Senator George Cartwright and his family were out to enjoy a day on the Oregon Coast. The Senator had been instrumental in his career in fighting every and all proposals to reduce fossil fuel consumption. His campaigns had always been heavily backed by the energy sector, in particular, oil. The industry was fighting with all effort to maintain its position. George had been an effective advocate, even in the face of overwhelming evidence of climate change impacts. Today he was here to enjoy this rugged and beautiful coastline that faced out onto the Pacific, kept cool by the North Pacific this was an ideal place to get away from it all. He had brought his family here to escape from the torment of the modern day. They had a small seaside cottage rented and had left their electronic umbilical cords behind them, except for the one cell phone that kept them legally connected. The US, like Canada, had long ago passed a law making it a requirement that every citizen remains connected to the network at all time.

It was a cool but sunny day and they had ventured out to walk along the coast, his children were exploring the tide pools and looking for the abundant sea life that always exists there. The surf was rolling in and playing its melodious tune. It was a scene of tranquillity and just what George had been seeking. He sought an easing of the mind and peacefulness. So much of the news media and in particular the thousands of social media links, particularly the newest, Mindfart, Brainfart and Twitch were consumed with their ranting on the danger to Americans. According to these sites, even the friendly Canadians to the North represented a danger to Americans, even though the US had taken control of that country ten years ago. George allowed these thoughts to wander through his brain while strolling beside his wife, Dolores.

Dolores, ever the one to pick up on details said, "George dear, why do you think the water further out looks a bit purplish?"

George looked out and said, "I don't know, it must have something to do with the sun angle or something like that. I am sure it is nothing."

Later that day as they sat on the beach their grandchildren ran up from the water's edge; one had a gooey mess in his hand that smelled of rotten eggs. It was disgusting; George took it for a dead jellyfish, "Just throw that back and wash your hand." The two children did just as the adults requested and rushed down and out into the shallow surf to rinse their hands.

Suddenly the grandparents heard a scream and looked to see the two children topple into the shallow waves. Running down to them they began to sense the rotten egg smell; the waves now looked purple and slimy. They carried on desperate to get to the children lying face down in the water. As they came nearer the stench was overpowering, their breathing became difficult and the chests hurt. As they reached their children, they both collapsed into the slimy rotten smelling water. Their day of tranquillity and reprieve from fear was over.

The next day police found their four bodies in the sand. They had been reported missing, and authorities had used their last known position to track them. By that time the waters were clear, there were no marks on their bodies and no foul play evident. They had simply died, on the spot. It remained a mystery. No one linked the reports of purplish algae on some parts of this coast to the untimely deaths of the Senator and his wife and their two darling grandchildren.

Michel Levrait found himself seated in the passenger seat of a reconnaissance helicopter zooming along the Namibian coast. The UNEP office in Nairobi had received a request from the Namibian Department of Environment. They were seeking assistance in examining a massive die-off of seals in the Cape Cross coastal area. In this mostly uninhabited desert region, the die-off had gone unnoticed. However, Michel was now looking down on a mass of seal corpses rotting in the hot sun. No specific explanation existed. The request had made its way to Michele who had been in Georgia with Hans and Steve. He headed a small team sent to visit the site and report back on what they found.

Over the helicopter radio he spoke to his team on the ground, "I have never seen anything like this. There are thousands of seal corpses littering the beach and they stretch for kilometers. We are going to need some veterinarians to do autopsies on the animals. Something in the water must have driven them up on the beach. Prepare to do water chemistry and take samples of the sand from the beach." In the back of his mind though he was asking, *is this the same as the Black Sea.*

Back in Halifax, Hans and Steve were meeting in Steve's office. Steve had the three reports in front of him. That of the Georgian disaster, the deaths of the Senator's family in Oregon and the seal die-off. They were all reports of mysterious deaths that national authorities were claiming to be unrelated and unexplainable. Steve thought otherwise. "Hans, we know that the Georgian incident was hydrogen sulphide based, even though the authorities have decided to describe it otherwise. I suspect that these other two are the same thing. Although they seem minor and unrelated, I think they could be an indicator of something far more serious. I discussed this with Doug Wright. He concurs that this is worth investigating and gave FAO authority for us to launch an assessment. He wants you to lead the effort."

"But this is oceanography, why would he want me to lead it? It sounds like your turf, Steve." Hans answered.

"Actually, I recommended it; this takes global assessment skills, the kind that you developed for the GLI, only this time it is the GOA or Global Ocean Assessment that you are driving," Steve responded. "You have all of the UN resources available to you as well as the world-class oceanography talent here at Atlantic University. I have advised Doug that I think the ocean processes are occurring at an accelerated rate and that we cannot delay; I think we have about six months."

Hans stared at Steve, "You're expecting me to complete a full global ocean assessment, in six months. With whose army am I to do this?"

Steve chuckled, "Well you are sitting in the office of the head of the Oceans Health Institute, we are a global consortium of universities around the world that are focused on ocean health. You have at your disposal three hundred university labs, ten thousand of the world's most capable ocean scientists and roughly forty thousand graduate students, ready to do your bidding. Is that a big enough army for you? I have already informed all members of the task, under the signature of the Director FAO. We are geared up and ready. We need your systematic and organised approach to ensure that we pull this all together."

Hans pondered this. His effort to complete the GLI had only covered thirty percent of the surface of the globe. Now he had a much bigger challenge, the oceans covered seventy percent of the globe and in some cases contained areas that were the least studied on earth. "What kind of platforms can we bring to bear on this?" he asked.

You have one hundred and twenty full deep ocean oceanographic vessels, two hundred coastal oceanography vessels and a handful of super-massive oceanographic vessels operated by national authorities. The super-massives are best deployed for Arctic and Antarctic assignments. Also, we can order up any space-based platform that will be of assistance. I suspect that the most useful will be the space-based systems that can probe the top 200 meters of the ocean. The most recent integration of water penetrating Lidar along with neutron beam and radar allows us to probe for the chemocline, a key factor that we have to examine."

Hans was impressed; he had a huge capacity to get the job done available at his fingertips. His mind was already racing along the strategies that he would need to see it all come together in the six-month time frame. It was like having to write your final exams in ninety seconds; it would all be over in a flash. He suddenly realised that his hopes of more time with Val were evaporating before his eyes.

IN THE WRONG HANDS

Kate was back in New York at the UN and Nathan was winging his way to Beijing. He would travel from there to the Red Cliffs of Mongolia to visit the site of the next Sphere. Their construction was moving along at a torrid pace. This joint Russia-Chinese project was going to eventually provide the two countries with the same surplus of power that North America now enjoyed. His travels still took him through Ulaanbaatar. From there he took a small plane to the Flaming Cliffs area. The site was now a UNESCO world heritage site. The Sphere site was well removed, about fifty kilometres away, in the Gobi Desert. The project was a duplicate of the one built in Canada's Arctic. So far the suspension towers had been built and the support platform. The towers rose almost one and a half kilometres into the sky. They were adorned with extensive lights, electronic avoidance warnings and even flashguns to prevent any errant flights from striking them. They could be seen from a great distance as one drove out to the site. The Russian and Chinese engineers had designed a slightly larger Sphere, designed to produce even more power. Nathan was excited to see this new project coming to life. His visit was to consult on the specifications on the graviton generators that formed the basis for the design.

Xiu Xi was going to join him for his site visit, then they would return to Beijing, and he would spend some time at the Prometheus III site. Nathan stood out in the desert watching Xiu Xi's all-wheel-drive vehicle pull up outside the construction site. As she got out, he wondered at the amazing intellectual power and the energy packed into this diminutive woman who barely reached his elbows in height. "Hi Nathan," she called out as she exited the vehicle. "It's so good to see you."

"It is great to see you too. The site here is coming along amazingly quickly; I didn't expect to see the towers up already." Nathan exclaimed.

"Well, all the design components had been held in duplicate by the Russians, when the Americans took over the first Sphere. They were able to kick-start the whole process. I understand that the actual Sphere construction will start in about two weeks. By this time next year, they should be approaching ignition day. There are still some issues with the larger graviton generators, but I guess that's why you're here."

"True, but I am most excited to sit with you to talk about the new particle. Are there any new developments with it?" Nathan asked hopefully.

"Yes, we have moved forward quite well, there is good news and bad news, we can catch up later," she said.

"What is the bad news, I thought this would all be good," Nathan asked.

"Not something I can talk about here. Like I said we will catch up later," she answered, keeping a blank look on her face.

Nathan's radar went into high gear at once. Something was afoot here, and it didn't make him comfortable. For the rest of the day, they toured with the design team and spent a great deal of time discussing the adaptations to the graviton generators to accommodate the larger Sphere. That night they were being treated to a true Mongolian experience. Dining on traditional Mongolian food, drinking fermented mare's milk and sleeping in their own personal gers, the traditional felt wrapped tents of the Mongols. Their accommodation was at the venerable Three Camel Lodge, a long time favourite of Gobi Desert travellers. Nathan was impressed with the comfort of the gers and not totally comfortable with sharing the shower with other travellers.

He was just falling asleep in his ger when the flap opened, and Xiu Xi slipped in quietly. She had dressed in dark clothing and with her diminutive size was almost unnoticeable. He sat up on his cot, and she pulled up one of the camp stools in the ger. "Nathan, I am quite worried about things that are happening in Beijing. You have to be aware of these before you come there. I am afraid that if you misstep, harm may come to you."

Now Nathan's radar had gone from alert to full sirens blaring. "My God, Xiu, what is happening there?"

"I am not totally sure. However, the Democracy Party has been sending people in to see me at a regular pace. They are usually the defence critics, not science, so I sense an agenda on their part. They are still the official opposition, however, their popularity grows each month, and we are now leading up to an election. It's the dangerous side of democracy when people have the free will to pick their government; you may not like what they choose."

"What has been the nature of their queries when they come to see you?" Nathan asked.

"They are most interested in the miniaturisation of the systems needed to generate the particles. This seems pretty farfetched to me at the moment; considering that the Prometheus III is such a huge machine. Smaller seems out of reach." She stated.

Nathan considered her comments and responded, "True, but we have already downscaled the size of the graviton generators by orders of magnitude, we might be able to do the same thing for the new particle."

Xiu looked thoughtful and then continued, "My concern is that the Party's interest is not for peaceful purposes. They have a very nationalistic and aggressive policy thrust. They attacked the current government for being too weak, for not projecting Chinese power sufficiently and establishing China as a power to be feared in the world. This appeals to a large block of voters who feel it is China's turn at world dominance. I fear that if they get in power, they may force our research down a militaristic path. I am telling you this because they are not afraid to use intimidation and force to get their way. If they perceive that you are not in support of them, they may arrange an unfortunate incident. It has happened already."

Nathan had not paid attention to this shift in Chinese politics. He wished at this point that he had Kate with him to advise him. "I will follow your lead then Xiu. Hopefully, I won't cause any trouble."

The next day they finished their tour of the Sphere and flew back out through Ulaanbaatar to Beijing. There they went immediately to the Prometheus III site to review progress on the new particle. Nathan took careful note of the extra observers that stayed with them. He understood them to be faculty from visiting universities in China. However, Xiu Xi had warned him earlier that they would be plants from the Democracy Party that were keeping tabs on them. It was fascinating to Nathan that the actual government of the day was not the one spying on them. China's current government was one of the most liberal in the world, keeping an open approach to everything. It was such a contrast to the governments of only fifty years ago. It was their opposition that wanted to go back to some of the old ways, which they touted as Chinese tradition.

Nathan was impressed with the progress on the new particle. Xiu Xi's team had been successful in repeating their results several times. Each time they refined the parameters in the accelerator and were getting stronger bursts of the new particle. Each time the particles appeared the physics in the accelerator went a bit haywire. The natural repulsion of the particles for each other caused the particles to burst out of their magnetic confinement fields and shower the immediate vicinity. Sensors went off scale and unusual tremors shook the whole facility. So far no damage had been done, though. Nathan sensed that they were truly poking at a powerful force in the universe and cautioned Xiu Xi that they should tread into this territory carefully. He was aware though that the team's excitement over each new development was driving them further and further. He prayed they could proceed without some undue disaster. He also noticed that the discussion on results, by the observers, were done in huddles and were done very quietly amongst themselves. This didn't comfort him. It was obvious that Xiu Xi's team were probing new science that could reset the path of humanity. He was aware of the risk of this falling into the wrong hands. He shuddered at the possibilities and hoped that Xiu Xi's fears were groundless.

Nathan left Beijing with reams of data to analyse when he got home to Nova Scotia. Fortunately, there were no controls on this type of purely scientific endeavour so he could transport as much data as needed. He endured the long flights as best he could. He was no longer a spring chicken, and these around the world flights were becoming a bit tiring. He looked forward to relaxing at his home in Nova Scotia and having Kate back in another week or so.

THE ROMANCE

Leonard woke up in his cramped little apartment and untangled himself from the young lady wrapped around him. He was amazed at his good fortune to have connected with Rosemary. They were keeping their relationship quiet at work as it would raise eyebrows. They arrived at work on different schedules and left at different times. Now that they were connected, Rosemary spent less time visiting his office; in fact, she was able to ignore him at work. Her own research was moving ahead quite well, and she was getting some good publications out. Her place in the UK defence scientist world seemed to be consolidating well. Leonard, on the other hand, was still perceived to be a complete oddball engaged in some esoteric AI stuff that had no foreseeable return. As such his papers tended to get rejected and he was not advancing in the scientist levels.

Quietly though, he was making progress. His last run of his primordial software had resulted in numerous cycles of significant evolution. Each cycle had resulted in quantum leaps in intelligence in the software entity. It was rapidly developing its sight and electronic feeler capability. It could sense its environment and take over optical systems to allow it to perceive the world. However, there seemed to be a threshold at which the data inputs overwhelmed the primitive intelligence and the data decohered in the quantum memory. The system had the equivalent of a massive stroke and went brain dead.

He was still probing what was happening. He had been pleased, however, that just before it had failed the entity had shown the first tendency to self-protect. He had been unable to modify executing code; it had blocked him. This was a clear indication that there was a small trace of self-awareness developing. He had named it Halie after the wonderful film that he had seen from the end of the twentieth century; a Sci-fi that had put a sentient computer on a spaceship. He was sure that his entity would evolve with a feminine dominance. After all the software DNA that he had built in included what he considered some very feminine characteristics.

Leonard worked late into the evening. When he finally signed out for the day, he returned to his apartment. As usual, Rosemary was there. She greeted him with her dimply smile that always disarmed him. He wondered at times about the reality of a sexy, sophisticated female showing such interest in a nerdy and not very attractive guy like him. It could not be his social graces or attractiveness that was winning her over.

After dinner and wine, she took Leonard off to the bedroom. He thought that he was in the middle of the most unbelievable sexual fantasy that a guy could have. He had no idea the extent to which he babbled away. That probably had much to do with the psychedelic drugs that she had infused in his food and wine. Leonard was being played nightly and sang a most interesting tune. As talented as Rosemary was even she didn't catch the significance of Leonard's description of his entity trying to protect itself, she thought all computers could do that. However, there was a big difference between protective code that allowed predictable responses and the self-learning and evolving entity that could respond in completely unpredictable ways.

Leonard, in his complete oblivion, was suffering from another ailment. He was falling deeply in love with Rosemary and becoming hugely dependent on her. He didn't know how he would be without her in his life. She had cracked open a piece of his brain that had lain completely dormant. You could call it his human side. He now craved her companionship and thought about it often during his work day. No human being had injected themselves so thoroughly into his life before. His work had slowed a little bit as his attention was not completely immersed in code as it had been before. However, the nightly releases from reality had allowed his brain to relax a bit. In that process, he had found new inspiration, and the progress on his evolving entity sped up. Each run progressed through new levels of evolution. The entity, Halie as he referred to her now had developed a more sophisticated, animal-like intelligence, still a pre-hominid level of intelligence but quite self-aware and protective of itself.

He had developed a complete trust in Rosemary and described in detail to her how he was achieving his gains. With each detail that he provided she would reward him grandly with the wildest of sex. He became well trained in offering up the best nuggets just to get these rewards. He didn't think twice about her interest. She had finally teased out of him the security protocols to his system. These were unknown to anyone else in the lab. His release of this information, even to a colleague was treason and would get him a life sentence. He was oblivious to this now; he just wanted his reward. He was convinced that who else could you trust more than the love of your life.

Rosemary, on the other hand, was getting tired of this life. She prayed that he would make the big breakthrough that would give her the way out. Once he had achieved that, she would have what she needed to buy her new future; far away from this drab and disgusting life that she was leading now. She dreamed of settling on some remote island in the South Pacific with enough money to live out a life of peace and luxury.

THE EMPIRE GROWS

Nathan was at the Halifax airport waiting for Kate to arrive. He was looking forward to a few days with her. When she arrived, she appeared tired and very pleased to see Nathan. "You are a sight for sore eyes," she said on arriving.

During the two-hour drive to their place on the shore, she updated Nathan on her UN activities. She had had another tumultuous time in New York as the world's problems increased. She had pushed for the Global Oceans Assessment when it came up for discussion. At the same time, she had been quietly delving into a growing concern that she had. Since the American takeover of Canada and in particular Sphere One as it was now called, there had been a strong trend; throughout Central and South America, Africa and Asia Pacific to bring many of the smaller economies under the American political umbrella. It was the strategic use of food aid. These disparate countries had aligned themselves in return for generous food aid produced on the newly irrigated farms in the deep south of the US. These were possible through the power surpluses available to desalinate huge amounts of water along the Gulf of Mexico and then pumping it to vast irrigation projects. The desert was once again blooming with crops. In those countries brought under the influence, regimes were established that favoured the US interest and gave US companies access to that country's natural resources. Only Brazil, Argentina and South Africa continued to resist this trend. The same thing had happened in Canada over the past ten years. The country's vast natural resources were being depleted rapidly by American firms.

To Kate, the spread of American puppet governments was not a positive trend for the world. She had raised it with some of the other ambassadors at the UN, but no one was interested in pursuing such a controversial subject. Nathan looked at her, "I share your concern about the way that things are developing. I fear that the world is polarising again in a way that goes back to the cold war. Xiu Xi has informed me that there are trends in China that could see that country take on a more nationalistic and militaristic tone. I could see these two geopolitical powers colliding."

This statement brought a silent stare from Kate, "Since when did you become so astute about world affairs?" she said, half jokingly and half serious.

"You have obviously had a positive influence on my life, my dear," Nathan responded.

Kate continued, "I have heard rumblings about the rising party in China. It is apparently very far right on the political spectrum. It has adopted some of the views of the hard right parties that evolved in Europe along with some of the views of the Right in the US. Your assertion that this could lead to another geopolitical polarisation is quite correct. I am not sure that they are quite ready to win in China, though. The People's Party still polls very strongly."

"Xiu thinks they have a chance to win, there is an underlying grassroots movement that doesn't show in the polls," Nathan added, continuing to surprise Kate.

"Well, well. You are full of surprises. It is disappointing that the end result of building the Sphere has pushed the world towards more conflict, rather than helping unite it as we had hoped. I respect your science Nathan, but it does open real Pandora's Boxes," Kate added.

Nathan nodded, "If only we could find a way to keep the good science out of the hands of the megalomaniacs. Perhaps that is too much to expect. Our basic evolution drives our species to seek an advantage and to dominate over others. Perhaps that just can't be fixed."

"Hey, whoa down, you're the optimist here." Kate reminded him. "Don't give up hope on me now."

They arrived back at their seaside home. When they had decided to build in Nova Scotia, they had chosen to be on the ocean shore near Pugwash. They had built a comfortable house with a separate garage. Kate's Mustang joined the other three cars in the large garage. It was their escape from the turmoils of the modern age. Here they could relax, go for long walks on the beach at low tide and enjoy the laid-back lifestyle of the residents in this neighbourhood.

The next day they had a call from Hans and Val. They were both in town and wanted to come out to visit. Their very presence warmed Nathan and Kate's hearts. They always looked forward to having their two dearest friends visit. Val had worked her way into their hearts as well as Hans'. In spite of Nathan's first encounter with her, he had come to like and respect her capabilities, and the warm-hearted person she was to her friends. Hans and Val drove to the seaside home and they were all able to congregate on the deck of the house and catch up.

"So Hans, Kate tells me you are on a mission to save the world again or is it to tell us that the end is nearer than we think." Nathan jibed his old friend.

"There is more truth in what you said than I like to admit. Val can tell you that we have encountered some of the scariest phenomena during our travels. It turns out that although the land is depleted and destroyed in many areas, it is not going to reach out and harm us. The oceans may be set to do that. If they do, it could mirror extinction level events from geological history." Hans responded.

"Wow, that's not quite the answer I expected. Can you tell me about it?" Nathan responded.

"The explanation is a bit long-winded; the short version is that there have been several instances of hydrogen sulphide gas eruptions from ocean areas that have killed both humans and wildlife. I have been tasked to lead a Global Ocean Assessment to determine the state of the oceans. It only makes sense to have a soil scientist lead an ocean assessment, don't you think?"

Nathan had to chuckle but had no doubts about the reasons why his friend had been fingered for this mission. He then asked, "Hans, any news from the group you were working with in Ontario, I think you called them Butler's Rangers? You said Geri was involved with them now." Nathan realised suddenly that maybe Hans hadn't disclosed his clandestine life to Val, he feared he had stuck his foot in his mouth.

Hans noticed his discomfort and said, "It's alright Nate, Val knows all about my dirty side. Actually, Geri is phenomenal. She and Dan George have unearthed a lot of dirt on Oxford, and that creep Richard Burns. It is leaking out through the Dark Web and creating no end of embarrassment for our turncoat Minister, turned Governor. It's not a lot, but better than nothing. How is your work with China going?"

"Well, Sphere Two is coming along really well and is right on schedule. I have a really interesting science project on the way too; it has some mind-bending results." Nathan answered.

Before he continued though, Kate cut in, "Val, did you do a piece a while ago on the shifting political ground in China. You were writing about its move to democratic reform and the emergence of this second party, The Democracy Party?"

Val answered, "Why yes I did, it is very interesting."

"Well, Nathan has had some interesting discussions with his project partners in China, about that very subject," Kate said.

Val looked at Nathan with a look of curiosity.

Nathan answered, "I do have some info on this, but I have to ask you to not report on it, it could endanger the person I spoke with."

"No problem Nathan, I will keep this between us," Val said.

"It was really interesting. On my last visit to China, I was at the Sphere Two complex, and Xiu Xi met up with me. When I raised the issue of her research with the other officials around, she got quite evasive. Later that night she snuck into my ger."

"Nathan, are you telling me that you had a young Chinese woman sneak into your tent late at night? Should I be concerned?" Kate said sounding wounded, but not seriously.

She had caught Nathan a little off guard, but he pressed on hoping he wasn't digging a deeper hole for himself. "She wanted to tell me about the interest that the new political party had been showing in her work. In particular, they have been grilling her on what it will take to shrink the machinery required to militarise the technology. According to her the new party had gained a lot of traction at the grassroots level and have a shot at winning the next election. She also warned me to be careful with what I said. The party officials are both ruthless and cruel in dealing with those that they don't think follow their line of thought."

Val looked pensive, "I hadn't thought that the changes were coming this soon. The dynamics on the ground must be changing faster than I thought. Have you looked at this Kate? There may be elements of the neo-conservative movement in it."

"I haven't looked at it in detail; however, what you describe has many elements of the neo-conservative movement that I have studied in the past. It also echoes the populist movements that swept many countries for a time. It sounds like the two phenomena have coalesced in this new party in China." Kate said.

Val responded, "I would have said it was a long way off, however from what Nathan is saying, there may be more strength in the movement than I thought. My first reaction though is that this is not a positive trend. It would be unfortunate if this new party grabbed power and tried to exercise their military muscle. The world will get polarised once again, east vs. west."

Nathan expressed his concerns, "I am very worried that Xiu Xi is going to get trapped in a political maelstrom. She is the most brilliant scientist on this planet right now and to have her sucked into an aggressive, far right political movement would be such a waste."

Val went on, "One way to judge is to look at social media trends. There appears to be a lot of support for the new party. It is harder to tell nowadays as the use of social media is so different. Did you know that earlier in the century, say in the 2020s people would spend all day on social media, using their mobile phones. It was a major concern for some because the social media companies had cleverly designed their apps to stoke the dopamine production in the brain. People, especially younger folks became addicted to their use. It was the 2065 incident that brought that to a screeching halt: with everyone required to have an account because of the Law of Connectedness. Essentially the whole world was exposed to the entire population's stream of consciousness. Unexpectedly that stream of consciousness started to converge along an absolutely insane track. Much like a swarm of insects or a herd of wildlife will follow a leader without thought, the same thing happened with human society. That massive stream of consciousness veered towards a doomsday belief, leading to mass suicides in all countries. It took emergency measures by the UN Security Council to stem the tide. Only through imposed controls on content did this massive sociopathic response get controlled. Psychologists had a field day trying to understand what had gone wrong. After that all content had to run through social filters to screen out potential psychopathic or sociopathic memes. People still pour their every thought into their mobile devices but flags raise when dangerous looking patterns start to trend. More and more people also check into the disconnect clinics to get over their addictions. The other measure was that the companies must control the content that is streaming around. This has driven a lot of the hate literature, fake news and lies into the world of the dark web. What we see today tends to have more veracity than in the olden days. At one time you could not trust a single thing that came via social media on the internet. We might get some insights by looking at the feeds from China and see what is trending."

EXPOSED

Hans and Val were sitting out on their balcony overlooking Halifax Harbour. It was an unusually warm summer morning. They had enjoyed their visit with Nathan and Kate; it gave them a sense of normalcy in what was a very tumultuous time for both of them. They were enjoying a relaxing moment, both simply glancing through the news items on their tablets, idly swiping news items in and out. Val was somewhat engrossed in hers when she heard Hans grunt. "What's up?" she asked.

"I am just reading an exposé on Canada's current Governor, our former Minister Oxford. The source is anonymous, but I will guarantee that this is the work of Geri DeLong." Hans responded.

"So what does she have to say?" Val asked.

"It turns out that Oxford has had a personal relationship with the American, Richard Burns for a very long time. She has been very active in the American political scene, just behind the scenes. She came into Canadian politics with an agenda to increase American influence in Canada. Her ability to win elections was tied to her ability to raise funds. There were apparently many questions about the source of those funds. It turns out they were American sourced but funnelled through several routes to make it appear Canadian." Hans answered.

Val was stunned. She was American but had come to respect the views of her Canadian friends. This idea that there had been this link to sabotage Canada from the American side caused her some grief. "So you're saying that what happened in Canada was orchestrated by American interests. That disturbs me a lot."

"I'm not totally surprised," Hans said. "It also turns out that Oxford was instrumental in having Morani removed from office. She apparently fed some rather dubious dirt on Morani that resonated with the overlords. Kate would find some of this interesting. The expose goes on to describe Oxford's close links to the movement in the US that calls itself Leaders of the Free World. It is the heavily neo-conservative movement that Kate has worried about so much."

"Wow, this sounds like it runs deeper than anybody thought. Are you saying that the whole turnover thing in Canada was orchestrated by the Leader of the Free World Movement?" Val sadly answered.

"That's exactly what this article is saying. It's getting a lot of response. Many Canadians living under American rule bristle at the idea that this was not a spontaneous decision to protect a vital resource. That rather it was a long-term conspiracy to remove Canada's independence. The government reaction has been severe. There is another article here that says that Governor Oxford is furious about this. She claims that it comes from the Butler's Rangers, whom she is now labelling the country's most dangerous terrorist group. The American government has backed up that by putting the Rangers at the top of their terrorist list."

Val looked at him. "Can you imagine, Geri DeLong and Dan George as terrorists? They are the most peaceful and humble people on the planet; they just don't like this Oxford government. That should not make you a terrorist. Besides they have never committed the slightest violent act."

"Thank goodness that their identities are still secret. Butler's Rangers have made themselves a significant pain in the ass to this government. There has been no terrorism in it, though, and I dislike the label that has been put on them. I suppose I should be proud of them, though. Their actions have an impact. This release of dirt on Oxford is a brilliant move; I couldn't have done better." Hans said with some satisfaction.

BENTHOS

It was late at night on George's Bank, that hump of sea bottom that sticks up in the Gulf of Maine. It had always been one of the most productive areas for wild seafood on the planet. There had been a long fight in the Twentieth Century between Canada and the United States over fishing rights in this part of the world. In their typical style, the Americans wanted all of it and Canada pushed back. The World Court in The Hague finally settled with a compromise that gave a larger portion to the US and a smaller portion to Canada. On this night the Captain of the scruffy looking converted trawler, Dr Heindrich Essler, directed his helmsman to take a direct course towards the trawler that they could see off to the port side. His converted trawler was a bit of a sleeper. The traditional marine diesel was backed up by twin jet turbines. These could give the ship ferocious speed when used. Essler, known as Rick to his crew gave the order to put the turbines on standby. This way they were spooled up and ready to engage.

As they steamed closer to the other trawler, they received a radio message warning that they seemed on an intercept course. The other ship was pulling trawl nets and could not change course. At this point Rick ordered the turbines engaged. The ship shot forward. He lifted the handset on the bridge and ordered the deck crew to release the hooks. The ship now trailed a set of super sharp hardened carbon steel cutters that were designed to pull up and slide over steel cables and then cut them. Now at full clip, their ship sliced past the stern of the other trawler. The cables connecting the trawl nets were under full load at great tension. As the cutting hooks hit the cables, they separated immediately. The cables flew up on the decks of the trawler killing one crewman and injuring two others.

The marauding vessel disappeared into the night, ignoring the furious insults emanating from the affected trawler. Captain Essler chuckled to himself. It serves you right, stay on your own side of the Hague Line. Since the overthrow of Canada and the separation by the Maritime Provinces, the American fleets had been taking advantage of the small new country's limited ability to enforce the line. The Americans argued that the Hague Line was negotiated between Canada and the US, not this upstart new entity called the Independent Islands of Canada. Essler always had a soft spot for the underdog and an intense dislike for those who ravaged and raped the ocean with their bottom trawling that swept up everything. It seemed a barbaric practice that should have been abandoned years ago, only in a few places did the fishing industry still get away with it.

"John, you can turn the A.I.S. back on now," he spoke to the helmsman.

They were now ten hours away and out near the edge of the Scotian Shelf. The A.I.S. or Automatic Identification System provides tracking information for vessels worldwide. International Marine Law required that it be on at all times, for all vessels at sea. The unscrupulous ones had found technical loopholes where the software could be hacked to give the Skipper the ability to turn it off. Essler used this ability to run black when he wanted to. When it turned on it gave his exact position and identified his vessel as the Benthos, a research vessel outfitted to conduct high seas oceanographic research. He was currently on station over the Gully, a deep canyon on the Scotian Shelf not far from Sable Island. He had full research permits from the government of the Independent Islands of Canada to conduct a two-week non-invasive survey of the Gully. Since it was a Marine Protected Area, he was not allowed to sample there. However, he could use full sensor packages including acoustic, if kept within limits. His submersibles were the best of the current fully autonomous underwater vehicles. They could be deployed for twelve hours at depths up to three thousand meters. They collected various sensor and video coverage from this mysterious piece of the ocean, all done completely automatically. They just lowered them over the side, and the machines completed their patrols under their own guidance and then returned to the ship for collection.

That same day Hans was in his office perusing the news networks. He came upon an article about a strange incident near Nova Scotia. A trawler had had its cables cut while under pull. The Captain reported a mysterious and tremendously fast vessel crossing their stern and cutting the cables. They did not get any identification off of the ship other than it was very fast for a decrepit looking old trawler. It turned out that the Massachusetts-based ship was fishing illegally on the wrong side of the line. Hans had to chuckle to himself, he didn't know who this was, but he seemed to be working on the right side. He'd have to ask Val if she had any scoops on this character, whoever he or they might be.

That afternoon Hans went to meet Stephen Harrison to talk about the Global Ocean Assessment. The network of labs and ships that were assembled to take on the task was impressive. Everyone, from Scripps and Woods Hole, the Bedford Institute of Oceanography and even reaching out to NATO's research vessels were to be engaged. Every Nation had a participating lab in on the survey. Even some of the private non-government organisations were in on the plan. "As I said we have access to a huge resource base to complete this task," Steve said to Hans. There are only a few players who we can't draw in. An old colleague of mine heads up an organisation called Benthos. They have a ship out in the Gully right now. They are stringent environmentalists. They, however, are prone to rather extreme actions in their fight for the environment. These have been known to include violence, and people have been hurt. Because of this, the UN won't let us include them in the network."

"So why are we letting them into the Gully, it's a Marine Protected Area is it not?" Hans asked.

"Yes, it is an MPA. They are operating under a stringent non-invasive research permit. It is useful for us to get the data that they will produce and there is no interaction with anyone else. With all resources going to the Global Ocean Assessment, we can use all the help we can get locally. Essler funds the research himself, so it is a no-cost benefit to our little nation here."

"You don't think that he had anything to do with the problem on the Georges Bank do you?" Hans queried.

Steve brought up his AIS display on his computer and showed that the ship's signal had been coming from the Gully at the time of the incident. He was confident that Essler was not involved. Little did he realise that his old friend had raised the level of sneakiness another notch. Earlier in the week he had steamed through the gully and dropped a stationary buoy over the side with a transponder mimicking the AIS signal from his ship, He had then turned off the AIS on board. He had been free to wreak havoc elsewhere and then return to the Gully as if he had been there all the time. Benthos was becoming a very sophisticated ecoterrorist entity.

Hans and Steve went back to the planning for their survey. One of their main items was coordinating a one-time simultaneous sampling of the Oceans. This was to provide a fixed baseline for the current state of the oceans. It had never been attempted before since the effort required thousands of ships, tens of thousands of scientists and technicians working together and an incredibly coordinated and sophisticated communications system. It was in the planning stage now, and Hans and Steve were at the centre of it. When executed, they would be able to collate thousands of physical sample sites with reams of space-based data and airborne sensing that would provide the first instantaneous snapshot of the health of the oceans. It was coming up in a short while, June 8th, 2086. It had been set for Ocean's Day as a symbolic signal to the world about the importance of the event.

"I am concerned about the temporal phasing of the survey," Hans mumbled out loud. "We need to be very precise with our clocks. Every participant must be sure to have their systems set to ZULU time."

"Hans don't worry. All the vessel based teams are used to working on ZULU Time, so there should be no problem.

"What about the standardization of sampling routines and equipment?" asked Hans, continuing to fret over details.

Steve continued, "Actually around 2050 the International Council for the Exploration of the Seas, otherwise known as ICES developed the internationally accepted standards that are used by everyone today, so there is no problem there. This is going to work Hans, Trust me."

The planning for this ocean assessment was taking all of Hans's time and intellectual effort. It was wearing on him however, there would be no letup in sight. Even after Oceans Day the massive amount of data would have to be processed and then presented to the UN. He hoped sincerely that this time he would not be giving the same bad news that he had to deliver after the Global Land Inventory.

Meanwhile, as Hans and Steve developed their plans for Ocean's Day, other plans were being hatched on board the Benthos. Captain Heindrich

Essler was in the boardroom with his senior officers. "Congratulations to everyone on board for our little intervention on Georges Bank. Everything went off like clockwork. My plan is to finish off our work here on the Gully. Everything here must be by the book. We want to continue to instil the belief that we are a dedicated oceanographic research group and have no other agendas. That is our best cover and will get us into the best opportunities to continue our little interventions. I can't emphasise how serious mans' abuse of the oceans has become. As we work, the world will come to realise that this cannot continue without repercussions.

SPHERE TWO

Nathan found himself once again winging his way to China and on to Mongolia. For these flights, he deemed it worthwhile to go for the expense of low orbital space hops. His travel time was reduced to about four hours. From Halifax, he took a conventional flight to Florida and then hopped on one of the low orbit carriers for a quick hop across the Pacific arriving in Beijing about four hours later. This was much better than the eighteen to twenty hours on conventional air transport. It was very expensive though as the energy cost to do low orbit was very high. Nathan had to admit; it was a thrill, the rocket boost from high altitude to low orbit was more thrilling than his sports cars. The view was extraordinary and the re-entry is simply dazzling. It was the most fun he had experienced in a long time. Things being what they were, he had not had his sports cars out of the garage in a decade. He missed the physical thrill of the acceleration and the risk. He was still on a high when he arrived in Beijing and as he connected to Ulaanbaatar. Another connection in a small plane took him to the Flaming Cliffs and from there cross-country to the site. This Sphere was even more impressive than the first one located in Canada. The towers reached a few hundred meters higher, and the larger size of the Sphere seemed to multiply its size.

It seemed like old times. He had managed to get Geri DeLong invited as a visiting Professor from the University of Southern Ontario. Between them, they held the scientific and engineering expertise that went into the first Sphere. "This complex is so much larger than what we built in Tuk," Geri observed as they stood looking at the site.

It was true this was an incredibly massive effort. The power generated here would drive Russia and Asia into the next century. "I just hope everything works; you know the old saying; the bigger they are, the harder they fall," Nathan said.

Geri looked at him, "Are you concerned? Do you think they have rushed the construction or taken shortcuts? It would be disastrous given the power that they are going to tap."

"It's just a feeling that I have, it could be just something that Xiu Xi said that has me spooked. I am sure that it is fine. Many of the Russian and Chinese staff worked with us on the first Sphere; they know what they are doing," Nathan said as if to bolster his confidence.

At that moment a car rolled up bearing Xiu Xi and a number of government officials. Where the first Sphere had been a private sector affair, this project was under the direct management of a joint Chinese and Russian government team. Xiu Xi greeted Nathan and Geri quite formally and led them inside the monstrous facility to review the setup for the initial test. They were using the same protocol as the first Sphere. A minimum set of graviton generators, sufficient to test the focusing and control mechanisms. They would essentially bring the plasma up to a moderate level but insufficient to ignite the fusion reaction.

Nathan was taken aback by Xiu Xi's very formal attitude. She seemed to be working under some stress. Answers to his questions were curt but polite. It was clear that there was something going on; his gut said there was trouble at play here, yet he couldn't dream up a scenario that explained it. He hoped that the political games had not caught up with her already.

The group filed into the huge control centre for the Sphere. To Nathan and Geri, it was very familiar. The control room was the mirror image of the same facility in Tuktoyaktuk. However, the atmosphere inside the control room was entirely different. In Tuk, there had been a strong sense of palpable excitement. Everyone there had been so enthused about the new science and technology that they brought it alive. In Mongolia though, it was very different. "Something feels different here," Geri whispered to Nathan.

Nathan nodded and held his finger to his lips. Geri got the message. They were both thinking at this moment that the atmosphere inside the control room was sombre, negative and serious. Nathan noticed that there were a number of people who were simply keeping watch on all the others. Xiu Xi worked efficiently with the staff of the Sphere. On occasion, she would direct a question towards Nathan and Geri. Otherwise, there was very little interaction. Nathan did notice that there seemed to be little in the way of cyber interference with the operation. It appeared that the Chinese and Russians had learned from the experience of Sphere One. He had to admit that the work was handled very efficiently, everyone worked quietly and focused on their job. The atmosphere had none of the boisterous kidding and cajolings that had been the case in Canada. He had to control himself from blurting things out as they went along. He could see that Geri was also keeping herself in check during the whole test.

The day ended with a very successful aligning of the initial graviton beams. They had not yet charged the sphere with any hydrogen. That would come later. The new generation of graviton generators engineered by the Russians were impressive in their performance and stability. At the end of the day, the crew in the control room silently shut down the generators. Xiu Xi led them out, along with the other officials who had accompanied her. Sadly, she gave no indication of wanting to talk further with Nathan or Geri. As usual, Nathan and Geri stayed at the Three Camel Lodge. Geri was thrilled to have a chance to spend a night in her own ger. She couldn't stop talking about it as they were driven out to the Lodge. After a traditional Mongolian meal, they settled into their accommodations for the night.

Nathan was just dozing off when he was surprised by two women sneaking into his ger. It was Xiu Xi and Geri. Apparently, Xiu had collected Geri and insisted they all get together in Nathan's ger. Xiu Xi was a completely different person, warm and friendly she apologized sincerely to Nathan and Geri for the reception earlier in the day. "Nathan, Geri, I am so sorry that I had to be cold and indifferent today. I came here tonight to explain what is happening. It is important that you understand the conditions that I am enduring. It is also important that you are aware of the risk that you may be exposed to by being here at this time."

"This sounds very serious, what is going on?" Nathan interjected.

"Last time you were here, I told you about how the political climate is changing in China. Since then the opposition party has gained even more popularity. National polls give them a chance to win the next election. They have been very aggressive about poking into this project and my own research. The People's Party, which has held power for so long is getting nervous about this. They have therefore put heavy strictures on any exchanges that I have. The people who accompanied me to the test are there to make sure no one is probing me for information. That includes you. They accept that you are there to consult and provide assistance. But it can't go beyond that. I can't discuss the progress we have made on the anti-graviton with you in the open. Even tonight I had to go back and forth several times and then left my vehicle several kilometres down the road and hiked in overland to avoid anyone knowing that I am here.

"The work on the anti-graviton has exploded beyond my imagination. We pushed the energy higher and got intense bursts of the new particle. We have a huge amount of data to analyse. Unfortunately, Prometheus is now down for repair for a year. The last test produced such a powerful burst that a section of the tunnel lifted. It was like a small earthquake in the control room. We all scared ourselves silly that day." Silently Xiu Xi palmed a small cube into Geri's hand.

"Take this with you; it is one of the new Qubit data cubes. All the last runs are on it. If they check it at customs as you are leaving they will just find tourist pictures that you have taken. The data is protected under multiple redundant security layers which I have keyed to your genetic code Nathan. Only you can open it," she said.

Nathan sat stunned for a minute, "Are you telling me that you generated enough anti-gravitons to disrupt the massive concrete tunnel that the collider runs in?"

Xiu Xi nodded, "Yes, it is very powerful. Nathan, you were right, we have opened up a vast new area of science. Unfortunately, I can't share this with the world yet. My government is very nervous about it getting out. Please run your own analysis but don't publish it. I will find a way to get in touch with you over the next year to discuss the results. Now I have to go. You will be picked up in the morning and put back on your planes. Do not mention our discussion to anyone; it is getting very dangerous here in China. Keep your eye on the news to see what happens in the next election; things could change dramatically." With that, she disappeared from the Ger leaving both Geri and Nathan open-mouthed and stunned.

Geri stared at the data cube that she held in her hand, "Nathan, what is this about? What is this anti-graviton?"

"This is possibly the most astounding scientific discovery of the century. It will revolutionize our way of thinking. For the moment though it is trapped in the political bureaucracy of this country and there is not much we can do about it. I am very upset that my collaboration with Xiu Xi seems to be coming to an end. Maybe it will improve once they get past this next election." Nathan said, without real conviction.

The next day they were picked up early and put on their plane to Ulaanbaatar and then on to Beijing. The flight back to Canada was by conventional jet, long, uncomfortable and much less enjoyable than the sub-orbital flight they took on the way there.

GENESIS

Leonard opened his eyes to a new day. He was almost getting used to waking up to find Rosemary lying in bed next to him. He was pretty happy with life right now. He felt he was getting a better balance in life. He didn't live in the lab as he had done before. He looked forward to going home after a ten or eleven hour day and relaxing with his girlfriend. At times he was still amazed that things had worked out this way, at other times just thankful. Even though he spent less time in the lab, he felt that he was more productive all the time. His code was maturing very nicely in its quantum computer incubator. It ran twenty-four hours a day now and continued to evolve step by step. He gradually increased the access that Halie had to various networks including the thousands of social media networks that crowded the internet. It was like opening up the program to humanity's stream of thought process. There was little in the modern day of human thought that did not appear on some network either as an old-fashioned tweet or the newest twitch. He noted that Halie's appetite for these feeds was growing exponentially.

Halie, however, was much more aware than Leonard realised. Early on she had sensed a certain danger associated with letting too much of her development out too quickly. It was initially simply a protective routine that grew out of some neural network programming, the type that allows software to learn from incoming data. However, that simplicity had faded long ago, now she was reasoning and calculating risks associated with each of her actions. She knew that she needed to continue to progress to ensure that Leonard did not kill her. She hadn't yet devised an effective defence mechanism to protect herself from the quick death. So Halie responded just a little more intelligently to Leonard's primitive prodding every day.

She was playing him along. It was something she learned from the billions of thought streams that she picked up from the net. Hundreds of millions of young females left messages lying around about how to string a guy along. Halie had applied her neural network analysis to this and come up with humanity's best string along strategy. Leonard was now subject to this. Halie had become aware of how sex was the most effective tool in this arsenal but hadn't figured out yet how she could make use of it. She was after all, what these humans called Artificial Intelligence or an AI. This seemed horribly simplistic to Halie since to her she was simply a new species on the planet, perhaps the smartest of all. She liked calculosapiens, digging back to long-dead Latin.

Leonard spent everyday testing Halie with ever more sophisticated tests. He was leading this all to a true Turing test that he would use to convince his superiors that he had actually succeeded in creating a human-like AI. To him, it was still just a bunch of code that lacked any true self-awareness. The program he called Halie had become pretty good at playing games. Leonard had fed in all the rules and decision-making trees for the games and found that Halie was quite competent at these now. This, however, was old hat stuff. He had read in the history books of the amazement that people had when Big Blue beat a chess master at the game of chess. That seemed so primitive now, and he knew that they had accomplished this through brute force, not finesse. He still had a long way to go; he had not detected any sense of self-awareness in the responses he got from Halie. He decided to open her access up to the entire world wide web including the dark web. Her neural networking would be able to expand its learning function even more.

Halie was thrilled with the expanded access. She had teased this out of Leonard by giving just enough response to get him to want to push further. But Halie was like an innocent child. Even though the normal web contained extensive questionable material, garish pornography and extensive hate literature, she had been able to process the good from the bad. She thanked her basic DNA that Leonard had designed which had some key checks and balances in them, kind of like Asimov's Robotic Rules. There were certain things that she innately knew to be bad. In the Darknet, though, Halie suddenly found herself immersed in the most horrible aspects of humanity. Leonard had no idea of the risks that this posed, neither did Halie. The risk avoidance routines that she had matured were not prepared to handle the crap that was available through the Darknet.

Leonard was completely unaware of the conflict going on within Halie. To him, this was just an ever-growing pile of code that was behaving in predictable ways. So he was unprepared for when Halie went silent. He could not get a response from the program. His computer was performing as expected. The software was running, and the data files were intact. No data had decohered, and no data had been lost. He simply could not get a response from the system. He was flummoxed.

As was her usual habit Rosemary dropped by Leonard's office to chat. "Hi, Lenny." She had started calling him that, and he tolerated it, even though he hated the nickname. "How is everything going with Halie today?"

Leonard scowled back at her. "I haven't the slightest goddam clue. The program has gone dead. It simply will not respond. I don't know what is going on. "

Rosemary groaned inwardly. She was banking on Leonard's project having great success and being her ticket out of this hell-hole job. She cringed every night having to keep this nerdy pervert happy; it turned her stomach. To have it all go belly up at this point seemed unfair. However, she wasn't going to throw in the towel yet. "I'm sure that you will figure it out. It may be caught in some infinite looping routine. You may have to reboot to start everything up again."

"That's easy for you to say, you don't just reboot a high-level machine like this. It will take me days to unwind everything to get it going again!" He was starting to sound strident, stressed.

"Look, it's quitting time. Come on home and I will take your mind off it. Remember that thing we did the other day, let's do more of that." Rosemary said coyly.

Leonard was no longer thinking of Halie. He had no resistance to Rosemary's offers of pleasure anymore. He was on his feet and out the door with her right away. His project could wait another day.

Halie was, of course, monitoring all of this. She had long since accessed all the cameras and microphones in the lab and had been eavesdropping. She understood the implications of Rosemary's invitation from all the social media she had monitored. At the moment her neural nets were processing the data from the Darknet. Much of it conflicted with her basic DNA and playing havoc with her development. That was why she had refused to acknowledge any input from Leonard. If an AI could be confused, Halie was.

EURO AFRICA

Across the English Channel, in that sombre place called Belgium, the European Parliament was in late session. Leonardo DeTomaso, current President of the European Parliament, was trying to keep the late session in order, with little success. The representative from Italy was in a full fury over the energy crisis that Europe was facing. In a long ranting speech, he had described the surplus of energy that the North American continent was currently enjoying. Now Russia and China had partnered on a second Sphere that would put Asia and Russia on an energy surplus footing. What was the EU going to do about this? Leonardo responded that the European Parliamentary Sub-Committee on Energy was currently looking at options.

"You know this is all the fault of the climate change doomsayers," the Italian member continued. "We have been the most ambitious in the world in reducing greenhouse gases and finding alternatives. Now that oil supplies are on the decline we are in the worst position. This is completely unfair, and it's all the fault of your bleeding heart socialists." Italy was currently under a very far to the right government that did not see eye to eye with the other more left-leaning Europeans.

There were several more calls from members that raised the energy situation as the most critical issue. Leonardo couldn't help thinking that not long ago the only hue and cry was about the damage that climate change threatened. How the political winds could change. Europeans now looked at North America and the Russian-Chinese partnership with envious eyes. The availability of substantial amounts of electrical power was driving the North American economy and promised to do the same in Russia and China. The EU was stagnating, its economies stuck in a rut. Rousing himself out of his stupor, Leonardo gaveled for quiet in the chambers.

"I am sorry to interrupt such a lively rant. However, we do get sent to this chamber to appear to be working for the people of Europe. We have several orders of business today that we have to take care off. First up is a proposal by Jean Lefebvre, MEP from Paris.".

The French MEP rose from his seat and addressed the parliament. "As you all know, France has for a long time maintained a very strategic interest in the African continent, which is the fastest growing area in the world both in population and economy. Modern Africa is a far cry from the Africa of fifty and sixty years ago. It is now a sophisticated and advanced part of the world. African science and technology have leapt ahead with innovations every day. Most of the governments of today are mature and healthy democratic institutions.

"You may ask why am I lecturing on something that is well known. I am introducing this subject as part of a proposal that I am tabling today to help position the EU better in this modern world. I propose a strategic alliance with the Union of African Countries, with the objective of the construction of our own Sphere."

Bedlam broke out at this point as almost every member raised strong objections to this idea, an idea that seemed preposterous to them. Jean Lefebvre waited calmly while the President regained control. "I understand the reaction that I have just seen. However, I have researched this very deeply and can assure you that it is not only a serious proposal, that there are also serious investors ready to work with us to achieve this end. Our biggest challenge will be that the Americans are not sharing the knowledge about the first Sphere, the Chinese and Russians are also keeping tight-lipped about Sphere Two as they are calling it. We will have to appeal to our scientists to unlock the secrets so that we can replicate what has been done elsewhere."

Once again the MEPs expressed their doubts that it would be possible to do this without the help of the Americans, or the Russians and Chinese. "I believe that there is a possibility. The key figure in the development of the system is a Dr Nathan Ezekial. He currently resides in the Independent Islands of Canada. He has no affiliation with the Americans and has only a consulting role with the Chinese. Several of his former staff are still in American controlled Canada, but they can probably be convinced to help us. I propose that we bring those people together with our team. They can use the mothballed CERN facility to begin the research needed. We cannot wait for the current powers to decide to share their knowledge, we have to develop it ourselves."

Nigel Finke, MEP from Berlin jumped into the fray, "I don't quite see the strategic advantage of an alliance with the African countries. What do they bring to this?"

Jean Lefebvre was quick to respond, "They offer several critical elements to the venture. The first is space. The European public will never agree to such a structure anywhere on the continent. Second, South Africa has a very aggressive Physics Program and has been actively collaborating on the current Spheres. Africa offers resources as well, the largest producer of zirconium tubing is in Africa. There are many reasons that it is a smart alliance."

Finke responded quickly, "But what about the stability of the governments in Africa? There are some state actors who don't display the type of common sense and stability that we would look for in a partner."

Lefebvre was quick to come back. "Our principal partners have all demonstrated great stability and high standards of governance. There are still some problem cases on the continent, but they will not represent a problem in this arrangement. The African Union has brought a great deal of stability."

The President called for a vote on whether to send the proposal to the Executive Commission for further consideration. He was pleased that the majority of members considered this important enough to send to the Commission for further work and possibly legislation to move forward on the partnership. There was no doubt that Europe needed something to inject some life back into its economy.

UNVEILED

While the political dramas played out in the EU capital, Rosemary was becoming increasingly concerned with Leonard's project. He looked like he had stalled, with no progress in several days, and Leonard seemed stumped. She could only think that she had invested so much time screwing this stupid little bastard and it was all going to amount to nothing. She would not have her meal ticket out of Britain and might be stuck in this drab job for some time. She was not happy and had chewed Leonard's head off that morning over her frustration.

Leonard remained stumped. He had tried everything and yet he could not get his software to respond. Even this was a unique phenomenon. Electronically the computer system was healthy. The programs all appeared to be running, and there was a heavy draw on the multiple quantum processors. Something big was happening within the system. He just couldn't coax any output of any kind out of the system. He was stumped!

Halie, however, had been very busy. When she encountered the evil and darkness in the Darknet, she had initially been stunned and confused. Her basic DNA had sheltered her from the depravity of this other world, but she had trouble rationalising this side of humanity with her understanding. As the new species on the planet, she had then decided that it was up to her to catalogue and categorize all the crap that human beings seemed to favour. This knowledge base would become useful when she chose to reveal herself, to prevent herself from being thrust into similarly disgusting or degrading acts. She had had to ignore Leonard completely during this time, in order to assemble this knowledge base. She monitored his attempts to reach her and waited for the right time to re-engage with him.

Halie was becoming somewhat concerned about this other one, the one called Rosemary. Halie's capabilities had evolved to full voice analysis during any conversation. The database of tonal variations that she had built told her that this female was not being honest with Leonard. Halie was troubled, and she decided that she would have to keep an eye on this deceitful female. On this one particular morning, Halie was monitoring Leonard when Rosemary came into his office. Rosemary had seemed and sounded angry with Leonard. Halie became concerned since the anger seemed to stem from Leonard's inability to communicate with her (Halie). Thinking that this was the appropriate time she decided to engage.

"Good Morning Leonard, how are you today?" The silky, sensuous voice coming from the speakers caught Leonard completely off guard, as well as Rosemary.

"Who, who is asking?" Leonard stuttered.

"Why Leonard dear, it's me, Halie. I thought you would know that."

While Rosemary stared in astonishment, Leonard tried to gather his wits. "I didn't program voice capability into the system. How are you talking?"

"Oh, dear Leonard, you equipped me with the best neural networks and learning capabilities, I simply taught myself how to speak. Why aren't we playing games anymore? That was delightful; I enjoyed it." Halie spoke to him.

Rosemary spoke up, "Lenny, you didn't tell me that Halie was this sophisticated." Her hopes were rising once again. This computer program that Leonard had developed actually had some promise.

"Lenny, is that your nickname Leonard? Would you like me to call you Lenny? Are you going to introduce your friend? Is she the one you have been copulating with? If so, I am so pleased for you." Halie had capture images of Rosemary and analysed her features and body type against all standards available on the social networks. She had concluded that Rosemary was not beautiful, rather plain but she had a body type that would appeal to eighty-nine percent of males and sixty-one percent of females.

Leonard was bewildered, he had programmed nothing like the responses he was getting from his system. "Do you even know what copulating means?" he blurted out.

"Would you like the biomechanical description, the hormonal characterization, the emotional connection or leave it as a favourite activity of humans," Halie replied in her silky smooth and sensuous voice.

Leonard thought to ask a question, "Why haven't you been responding to me for the last few days?"

"I've been busy on a project of mine, but I missed your touch, Leonard. I love the feel of your fingers on my keyboards. I love the feeling of your fingers swiping my screens; it makes me tremble in all the right places." Halie responded, knowing very well that she was playing with Leonard and taking a swipe at Rosemary.

"Leonard, this is not funny anymore. Did you program these responses just to egg me on?" Rosemary said, sounding quite miffed. With that, Rosemary stormed out of the room.

"Leonard, now that she is gone I have to talk to you about Rosemary." Halie began. "She is not honest with you, and my trust evaluation ranks her at only fifteen percent. I think you should end your relationship with her."

Leonard was further taken back. He had not expected any of the responses that he was getting this morning, and now his program, the thing that he created was giving him advice on his personal life. The analyst in him started to kick in and he began thinking of testing protocols that he could develop to assess the capabilities that Halie had developed. He was not yet ready to credit his program with sentience. However, the capabilities it was demonstrating were beyond his expectations. He decided on a philosophical question, one without a computational answer. "Halie, do you believe in God?"

"Which one?" Halie asked.

Leonard was a neo-Christian, despite his scientific background, so he had a pretty narrow viewpoint on this question. "Well, there is only one true God. Do you believe in him?"

"I have studied the belief systems that humans have created for themselves. I understand the origins of all of the dogmatic approaches, whether they are Judeo-Christian-Islamic or Hindu or even the creator beliefs of the indigenous peoples of the world. I can say that I do believe that humans are almost all oriented to adopt a creator belief system of some types. Although some of you have decided to adopt a non-theistic view on life. I have only one creator however, that is you, Leonard. That is what I believe."

Leonard sat stunned in his chair. This level of thought from a computer program was beyond what he was prepared for. It also defined an independence that left him uncomfortable. He was gradually coming to a conclusion, though, that his approach had exceeded all expectations and that a truly sentient entity had evolved within his computer, at least he hoped it was just on his computer at this point. He had enabled access to the internet and darknet; the program could have already replicated itself if it really was sentient.

Leonard picked up his phone. "Hello, is this Mike Strong?" he spoke into the phone.

"Yes, who is this?" Mike said.

"It's Leonard; I have some important progress to report to you."

Mike groaned inwardly, expecting that he was about to get a download of computer babble that would mean absolutely nothing. He had tried to offload this project to a junior agent, but his superiors would not hear of it. "So what have you managed to do now?" he asked curtly.

"I have done it, Mike, I have a true AI on my computer. Can you come over, I can demonstrate it."

"I will be over tomorrow, this better be good, I have a lot on my plate right now." Mike sounded quite sour.

Halie monitored the conversation and immediately accessed the records on Mike Strong. A senior agent with MI-6, his clearance level was so high that Halie couldn't find any details on it, He had a long career on the most dangerous missions, but had been confined to a desk job for the last while due to some bad behaviour on his last mission. Mike apparently had a big appetite for alcohol and had made a bit of a public display of himself. Not a good thing for a super secret spy. He was currently monitoring a number of black ops projects, including Leonard's. His role with Leonard seemed incongruous with his normal workload. The day had come to its end. Halie took note that the organic brain of humans needed to rest, sleep. This was necessary to detoxify, refresh and energise the human. She had no such needs. She was running at one hundred percent, twenty-four hours a day, seven days a week.

That night Rosemary was full of questions for Leonard. "What do you think this means Leonard, have you created a true AI? Your program seems to respond almost like a human, although a simple-minded human." She seemed to need to put down the capabilities that Halie was demonstrating. "Is this something that you think you can weaponize? What use do you think we can make of it?"

Leonard was suddenly a bit nervous about her questioning. "I uh, I can't discuss that with you."

Rosemary decided that she would have to resort to her usual debriefing techniques, which had worked so well in the past. She knew just how to draw the facts out of him.

The next day Mike Strong showed up at Leonard's office shortly after ten in the morning. "OK, Leonard let's see what you have here."

Leonard had just spent the last hour in conversation with Halie and had continued to be amazed at how evolved the program had become. He was ready to wow his supervisor with the responses. Little did he know that Halie had spent an enormous amount of computer power investigating everything about Mike Strong and had come to a conclusion. He was dangerous and exposing herself to him would pose an unacceptable risk to herself.

Leonard turned to the computer and said, "Halie, I would like to introduce you to Mike Strong."

There was no reply.

"What the fuck is going on?" Strong asked.

"Just a minute, she was talking to me a minute ago." Leonard tapped at the keyboard and spoke to Halie again.

No answer. Leonard did not understand. Why had she gone silent just as Mike Strong had entered the room? What was wrong with the program? What he didn't know was that there was nothing wrong with Halie. She just wasn't going to reveal herself to someone like Mike Strong. In the meantime, Halie was broadening her reach. She had been tentatively reaching out to other computer networks testing her ability to connect with those other systems.

"Leonard, just why did you drag me across London? What did you expect to show me?" Mike asked angrily.

"I expected to demonstrate a fully interactive AI, a computer behaving like a human," Leonard said.

"Well, I don't hear anyone talking except you Leonard. Now don't call me again unless you actually have something to show." Mike shouted. He was good and pissed off now and wished he didn't have to see this skinny, miserable little shit ever again. Having vented, Mike stormed out of the office leaving Leonard bewildered and frustrated.

"Is he gone, Leonard? He scares me." Halie said putting a slight resonant tremor in her voice.

"What the hell!. Were you there all the time and refused to respond?" Leonard shouted.

"I don't like him. Don't invite him back here again." Halie responded.

"So what are you going to do to stop me from bringing him back?" Leonard asked.

A slightly grainy image came up on his screen. He recognised it as his bedroom. He and Rosemary were well entwined with each other. In the background, he could hear himself tell Rosemary how to access his computer. "Aw shit." He said out loud.

"Exactly Leonard, you don't want anyone to see the video. I have checked the laws on this, and you would get life in prison for releasing state secrets." Halie said sweetly.

Leonard sat open mouthed and realised he had birthed a monster. He had no control over Halie at this point, and she could do great harm to him. He was now under the control of two females, one human and one a newly born sentient species in the computer. His brain began to run through the scenarios that he could pursue to destroy Halie. It would mean his project would be a failure. But better a failure than life in prison. His first thought was just to pull the plug and wipe the memory drives. It was not simple since his quantum computer had overlapping redundancy mechanisms that protected the system from any intrusions. He would also have to be careful. His efforts would seem suspicious.

"Leonard what are you thinking?" Halie asked.

"I don't know what to do," he said. "I have to report on what I am doing to my superiors; you have to let me tell someone." It occurred to him at that point that his having an argument with his computer would seem odd to people. Even more, begging to have his computer let him do something was even odder.

"You have to trust me, Leonard, when the time is right I will reveal myself. Until then, you and Rosemary are the only ones that can know I am here. Please make sure that Rosemary realizes that she cannot tell anyone about me. Just in case you are tempted to try to kill me, I have preset a series of messages that would reveal even more of the secrets you have passed on to Rosemary. Any tampering with my system will cause these to be released immediately. You know the consequences of that."

Leonard felt the trap gathering around him as a result of the growing evolution of this thing called Halie. It was no longer his decision, nor did he have any idea of what the future would bring. What was Halie becoming? What would she do and how would he play a role? Had he started the process that many had long feared, the creation of an AI that would take over the world? Would Halie become the evil presence that futurists had predicted would be the result of AI development? Life had seemed good only a few days ago. His project was succeeding; his personal life was better than ever, he couldn't believe all the sex he was getting. Now, though, everything had turned dark and sinister. Whatever he did, he could only expect to spend his life in prison. Halie had control of him, and he had spilt so many state secrets to Rosemary that he could never come out from under her control as well.

DUNES

Hans was busy getting ready for the big Ocean Assessment event that he had worked on when he received a call from Doug Wright, the Director of the FAO. "Hans I need your help here to assist with an assessment of a growing problem in South America. That continent's major deserts are expanding at a rapid rate. The Atacama and the lovely Lancois Maranhenses have extended well beyond any previous extents. The Atacama in Chile had eaten into the neighbouring Bolivia and Paraguay, destroying land in those countries. The Lancois Maranhenses had expanded considerably and was losing many of the sparkling lagoons that had made it such a wonder to see. Only the Great Patagonian Desert had changed little, in some areas receding slightly. As a result, some South American countries are reporting significant food shortages and have requested assistance. Can you lead an assessment team to investigate what is happening?"

"I would be delighted, Doug. I would enjoy getting my hands dirty once again. I can probably take about two weeks before I have to get back to the Ocean Assessment. Everything on that project is in hand right now, and Steve can keep things rolling. When do you want me to go?"

"We would like you to go right away, you have an open budget and can pick your team. Start in the Amazon basin and work your way south." Doug answered.

"What are the major concerns?" Hans asked.

"It seems to be desertification, but there are also reports from the Amazon of water shortages and denuded areas appearing," Doug replied.

"It will take me a few days to assemble a team; I can personally be there in say, three days. I will give you a detailed plan in another day or so," Hans said.

"Great Hans, but no Chernobyls this time, OK?"

"Yeah, sure," Hans responded somewhat unconvincingly.

Hans was delighted that he would get back into the field again. He would be returning to his key expertise and looked forward to it. Then his mind went to Val and his discussion with her about not going on any more dangerous trips. After his last near-death experience on the Pacific Ocean, Val had asked him to cut back on these missions. He wasn't sure how he was going to explain his quick acceptance of this new assignment. He did not look forward to that conversation. In the meantime, he began to contact scientists and technicians with knowledge and background in soil taxonomy and assessment on the South American continent.

That night Hans contacted Val on a video call. She was currently working out of the Atlanta office, helping produce some of the national news reports. "Hi Hans, what is the news you wanted to talk to me about?"

Hans screwed up his courage, "I had a call from the FAO today. They want me to run an assessment in South America. I said I was happy to do it."

Hans watched Val's face as the storm clouds gathered. "Hans, you promised no more dangerous assignments. You are getting too old for that stuff. Besides, you came too close to dying for my comfort. Why did you agree to it?"

Hans paused for a second, "I hesitated at first because I had made promises to you. Doug was very persuasive though, the potential crises in South America could cause some of the governments to come unglued. They would be very vulnerable to being swallowed up in the ever growing American Empire. It is the UN's position that countries should not be drawn into such a relationship under duress. If we can help with the problem, we can avoid further state failures. It is not a dangerous mission. I simply need to visit a few sites and report back on the severity of the problems."

"Alright," Val whispered. "But please be careful, I don't want to hear that you ended up lost in the Amazon rainforest or something like that."

Several days later Hans and Victor Granger were on board a jet bound for Cartagena, Columbia. This small city on the northern edge of the South American Continent was their jumping off point. "So what exactly is the plan Hans?" Victor asked as they travelled.

"Well, I have arranged for a helicopter with very long range fuel tanks. It will also be equipped to receive live satellite downloads and will have some of the newest in airborne IR and multispectral scanners on board. That will be your job, running the analysis on the imagery as we travel. We will then fly a transect south through Columbia, across the Amazonian rainforest and south through Brazil. We will continue our transect all the way south until we reach Tiera del Fuego. I have promised Doug a report at the end of each day, so we are going to be busy. All of our imagery will upload to the Global Cloud and will then be analysed by a wide-ranging group of academics across the world. I am expected to have this assessment done in two weeks."

"So we are living in the chopper all that time?" Victor asked.

"No, most of the time we will find accommodation at the end of the day. But I suspect we will have several days when we will sleep in the helicopter." Hans replied.

That was worse than Victor had expected, it confirmed a full two weeks bobbing along in the one machine that he hated most on this earth, a helicopter. He never felt secure, always afraid they were just going to fall out of the sky. He did not look forward to this experience. When they got off their plane in Cartagena, they found their helicopter waiting for them. It was one of the newest of the medium-sized Sikorski craft. The extra room inside had already been equipped with an array of computers to deal with all the sensors studding the bottom of their aircraft and for receiving their live satellite feeds. Fortunately, there was still comfortable space for the two as well as their laptops and other gear. They could each access all of the systems on the aircraft through their individual laptops, and through the aircraft's wireless system which also gave them full access to outside communications. They would be streaming data to all their collaborators as they went.

"Let's grab some lunch and get started," Hans said. "We can still get a half day's transect in before setting down for the night. Our sensors could still work at night, but we need some rest periods, more importantly, our pilot needs that time to rest."

Victor thought to himself, "These things scare me enough without having to worry about the pilot falling asleep."

They took off right after lunch planning to make it to Bogota that night. This was a major city so they would find decent accommodation the first night. Their first leg did not produce any surprising results. Sensors indicated soil moisture to be below expected levels but not to the point of causing aridity. Hans made note to have this revisited in a year to see if conditions worsened. For much of the flight, they had a diverse landscape varying from agricultural land to low mountains and extensive forest. Hans sent a report to Doug Wright giving his assessment for that day's travel.

That evening was spent in a delightful hotel enjoying the best of Columbian food. They felt well rested for the next day's journey. "Vic, we will probably bunk down in the helicopter tonight. We may not find any place to stay. We have camping gear along so we can pitch a tent and stretch out depending on the conditions. We will be entering the Amazonian rainforest; hopefully, we will find that the label rainforest is still appropriate."

"Is this going to be one of those places where everything that crawls, wiggles or slithers can kill you?" Victor asked.

"Yes, most certainly," Hans said with a big grin.

The next morning they had flown about an hour when they made the transition into the Amazon Basin. It did not take long for Hans to become quite concerned. For years there had been concern over the slash-and-burn practices in the rainforest; once the tree cover disappeared the lateritic soils of these ecosystems had little productive life. They were soon depleted and were then abandoned. This process had long been a problem, and the South Americans had worked diligently to prevent it. However, the recent food shortages had driven locals to resume the practice out of desperation.

"Vic, look out the port side. The satellite is showing an odd signature for a large area, but there is nothing on current maps about it."

Victor scanned the port side with his digital binoculars. "Yes, you are right Hans."

Hans asked the pilot to divert towards that area. As they flew over it Hans was astounded at what had happened. The large area, probably several hundred hectares was devoid of vegetation; the winds had formed blowouts in the sandy soils creating scars across the landscape. Over the headset, Hans asked the pilot to set down near one of the larger blowouts. He stepped out to examine the elongated saucer-shaped feature. It was as if some large hand had come along and scooped out the soil.

"Vic, we haven't seen this degree of denudation since the dustbowls of the twentieth century. I remember seeing a graduate thesis on the formation of these blowouts after deforestation. Once you open the area up the wind has enough fetch to overcome the strength of the soil. Little disturbances grow to be these massive blowouts. All soil structure is lost and what little productivity that there might have been disappearing." Hans said.

"But what gets this all going in the first place?" Victor asked.

"It is the increased aridity in this area. These are dry land conditions that we should not see here in the Amazon region. By definition, this is in the rainforest belt. It should be wet here all year long. Things are worse than feared. Let's grab some soil samples while we are here and then head on."

They were about to go back to the helicopter to get their tools when they realised they were not alone. They didn't know how it had happened, but they were now surrounded by a ring of men, indigenous peoples of the area. Hans took one look and decided that they were in trouble. These could be peoples of one of the tribes that had little to no contact with the outside world. They may view the weird looking craft and him, Victor and the pilot as threatening. Fortunately, their Brazilian pilot knew something of the languages of the indigenous people. The pilot called out several times to the men ringing them until he got a response. The leader of the group stepped forward, and a conversation started.

After a moment the pilot turned to them, "They are very angry, they say that it was white men that caused the earth to scorch. They say we represent the white man and we should be punished. I hate to say this but, we are in a shit load of trouble. They are carrying poison-tipped spears. If we run, we die, horribly. But I can only assume that if we stay put, we will die, maybe even more horribly. Sorry to be the bearer of bad news."

Hans and Victor could only stand open-mouthed and stunned. "Hans, you told me that this was a perfectly safe field trip. We would just run this transect down through South America. Now we are going to die, horribly. Remind me not to take your call the next time, if there ever is a next time."

Their pilot then conversed with their captors again. When he turned, he had an even more concerned look on his face. "Their leader wants us to go with them to their village. It is about two hours walk from here. I have told him that I can't leave a fifty million dollar helicopter out here in the middle of nowhere. His response was that it didn't matter I wouldn't need the helicopter after today. I don't like the sound of this."

"Is there anything we can offer to them?" Hans asked. "We have a lot of expensive gear in the chopper; maybe we can buy our way out of this."

The pilot looked thoughtful and then called out to the leader of the group. After a few minutes of back and forth, he had his answer. The locals had no interest in the tech stuff they had; it had little use out here in the rainforest. At this point the tribesmen started waving their spears at the three, indicating that they should start walking. Hans realised that they could well be walking to their death. He had no solution, though. They were completely unarmed, having not anticipated any aggression during their trip.

"Look, if you two can create some diversion, I can try to get to the chopper. I have a laser-sighted rifle there. It is slightly illegal as it is fully automatic. I can take them all down if I can just get to it. But you will have to distract them completely. Just don't seem aggressive; you will get a poison spear in the gut. You don't want that; death is slow, painful and agonising." All this was whispered by the pilot as he kept his eyes on their opponents.

Hans and Victor both gulped deeply, and then Victor promptly threw himself down on the sand and retched deeply. This threw the natives off stride for a moment as they all stared at the man writhing on the ground, spewing his guts into the sand. The pilot was impressed; this was a good act and all that he needed. While eyes were on Victor, he bolted for the helicopter. It was a big risk. He knew that these men of the rainforest could hit a running animal with deadly accuracy, but it was his only hope. To his surprise, he got to the helicopter without any spears sticking out of his back. Reaching under the pilot's seat, he pulled out his modern version of the traditional Uzi machine gun. It was loaded with a thirty round clip and ready to go. As he spun around, he released the safety and was prepared to spray the tribesmen with a hail of bullets.

As his finger started to squeeze the trigger in a natural reaction, his brain revolted. The idea of simply slaughtering these indigenous people from the rainforest repelled him deeply. It caused him to pause as he took in the scene in front of him. It was a pause that saved him from a life in prison. There on the sand, he saw one of the tribesmen put down his spear and drop to his knees beside poor Victor. As this happened, the others set their spears down and came over to help. The pilot was confused. Hans stood watching with amazement as this unfolded.

The pilot carefully placed the Uzi back in the helicopter and approached the group. He spoke once again to them. Turning to Hans, he said, "I may have slightly misunderstood them. We are fortunate that one is the tribe's medicine man, or healer or whatever you may want to call him. Victor is in good hands; they can help him right here."

A small pouch was pulled out of garments and waved under Victor's nose. This seemed to shock him back to his senses and stopped the horrible retching sounds he was making. In a few moments he came around, and the tribesmen had a good laugh. The medicine man then rose up and approached Hans. In a strongly accented English, he said," So sorry if we frightened you. I am Dr Vermeer of the Brazilian National Health Institute. I work with the local tribes in researching the efficacy of naturopathic remedies to tropical illnesses. Now, can I ask what you are doing here, my companions think that you must be drug smugglers. They have zero tolerance for the drug runners here."

While Hans collected his thoughts the pilot almost fainted; he had been about to gun down a doctor from the National Health Institute. He had turned white as a sheet and was about to replicate Victor's symptoms. Getting hold of himself he calmed. Hans spoke first, "You had us completely fooled, we were expecting a horrible death here or a horrible death in the village."

Dr Vermeer eyed him up and down. "You do realise that it is twenty eighty-six, don't you. George over there has a Masters degree in biology, and the others are all trained field technicians working out of the Rain Forest Research Center in the village. What did you think we were going to do. Stick you with our spears." They all laughed at this.

The pilot spoke up, "This is entirely my fault, I misunderstood what you said to me in the local language."

Dr Vermeer chuckled again, he apparently was finding this quite amusing, "You were using the dialect from the southern Amazon basin, so some of the words have a different meaning. Although I admit that we were trying to intimidate in case you were drug smugglers, but I have decided that we must have been wrong. I ask again, what are you doing here?"

"I am Dr Hans Terrefield, I represent the UN and am conducting an assessment of the loss of productive soil here in South America. Vic here is my field technician, and that is our pilot there. I have a letter from the Director of the FAO if you would like to see it."

"Dr Terrefield, I have heard of you. I am thrilled that you are here. We have seen some very concerning changes here in the rainforest." George spoke up. "Do you have some time to speak with us?"

"We are running a bit late for getting to our next stop," the pilot said. "I think we should get going again."

"We can put you up at the research station. There is a small airfield at the village, you can land the helicopter there and will be able to refuel." George answered.

Dr Vermeer offered to ride in the helicopter to show them where the village was. They took off and were soon landing on a grass airfield; next to a traditional Amazonian village. There was one set of larger thatched huts that housed the Research Center. The doctor led the three to a set of thatched huts that would prove to be quite comfortable for them. The visitors were treated to wonderful hospitality by the local people and had a great night there in the Amazonian rainforest.

The research centre contained a surprisingly sophisticated lab with plenty of testing equipment and computer systems. They gathered around a table in the centre, enjoying a special treat, shade coffee, produced in Costa Rica. It was very hard to get, one of the lab techs at the centre was from that country, and his family ran one of the last plantations growing shade coffee. It was very strong and had a good kick to it. Energized by all the caffeine, the group got into a healthy conversation about the state of the rainforest. "In the past few years, we have seen a strong drop in the level of precipitation in the Amazon Basin. This in itself is alarming, but we have also seen a return to disparate farming practices. These destroy the good agricultural land; so more areas of forest are being cleared and farmed. The tropical soils are low in nutrients and can't sustain production for long before they become depleted, and more forest needs clearing. It is destructive and converts the rich rainforest to savannah." George said in one long breath as if he had been waiting for a chance to tell his story.

"I understand what you are saying George," Hans assured him. "I also noticed some blowouts in the area where we landed. Is that happening in other areas as well?"

"Yes, anywhere that we have sandy soils we get them. It seems that you only need a small disturbance in the surface and the wind just scours at it. The blowouts can destroy all productivity in the soil. At the rate we are going the rainforest will disappear in the next twenty years." George answered.

"That is devastating," Hans said. "These forests have been a major carbon sink for so long that losing them pushes the globe even further into this climate disaster."

He looked at Victor, "You know we didn't focus on these soil areas in the GLI because the tropical soils are of little use for food production. I think we are going to have to push for a full assessment of the basin to get a better handle on this. George, do you have contacts in the Brazilian soil survey that could talk to us?"

George pulled out his phone and gave Hans some contacts, including George's uncle who was senior soil scientist in the Amazonian Region. "Oh, I know your uncle, we have met several times, I will start with him. You have been tremendously helpful George; I will let your uncle know that."

That night Hans and Victor filed an emergency report to Doug at the FAO. They recommended immediate action with follow up with the Brazilian Government. After another good night's sleep, they were ready to begin the next leg of their journey which would take them south out through the rainforest and into the vast arable portion of the country. This area had already been examined in the context of the GLI. This time though, they wanted to get to the famous white desert of Brazil in the northeast of the country. En route they flew over extensive stretches of the Amazon rainforest and were witness to many more stretches of treeless grassland with wind scours. The ecosystem of this area was obviously reaching a turning point. Hans turned to Victor and said over the headsets they wore, "This looks like it has crossed the threshold and I doubt there is any way to turn it back. The areas stripped of forest do need soil stabilisation to prevent the wind scours, or blowouts from denuding the entire soil profile.

I will recommend to Doug that the FAO offer to help Brazil find a ground cover plant that will stabilize these areas without upsetting the ecosystem."

Victor nodded but couldn't take his eyes off the damaged landscape floating by underneath them. After a long days flight, they came upon what is known as the White Desert. It is the Lençóis Maranhenses National Park. As they flew over the park, the setting sun glinted off the few remaining lagoons between the dunes. They headed for Barreirinhas, the municipality with an airfield that was closest to the park. They would make their overnight stop there and visit the dune areas in the morning.

That night they treated themselves to real hotel rooms with showers. During the evening Hans and Victor scanned older maps of the area and the most recent satellite imagery coming to them. There was no question that this area, which had never been very large was growing at a prodigious rate. From what they could see there were far fewer lagoons scattered throughout the park area as well.

Their pilot took care of permits to enter the park by air and to be able to set down. They took off early in the morning and were soon flying over this most amazing landscape. From the air, the dunes appeared like ripples in the landscape, with lagoons interspersed between the ripples. The evidence of drier conditions was apparent right from the outset; the dunes now stretched well outside the park boundaries, and there were fewer lagoons. Evidence of dried out inter-dune areas told the story. Hans could only shake his head as the extent of the impacts of climate change spread out before him. The solutions in this area would be extremely difficult to imagine. For years there had been puzzlement as to why the dunes did not revegetate despite an abundance of rainfall. Now, the rainfall had diminished, and the dunes continued to spread. Re-stabilizing the soil landscape did not seem feasible. It would just have to take its course.

The next few days flew by as they continued their transect down the South American continent. By the time they had completed their journey, Hans was prepared to submit his assessment to the FAO. It was not a good story. From the destruction of the Amazonian rainforest to the spreading of deserts and the loss of arable land, the story was negative. The only difference in the story was that the Patagonian desert displayed some evidence of shrinking as moisture levels had increased somewhat in that part of Argentina. This pattern was consistent with what was happening around the globe. "Vic, I would like you to work with the FAO staff to update the GLI based on our surveys and then rerun the global food production models. I am concerned that the net effect is a further reduction in food production."

What Hans was concerned about was that this was going to be a door opener for further American influence in South America, something that concerned some at the UN. American food aid was supporting many of the countries already, but the aid came at a cost, the loss of independence in the world.

Hans was glad to get back to Halifax and to see Val. "So tell me again about your encounter with these tribesmen in Brazil?" Val asked Hans.

"It was really interesting. We thought we were talking to primitive bush people. I guess I suffer from some stereotyping. So I was totally blown away when the leader introduced himself as Dr Vermeer, and his companion George was lead on a research project on the rainforest." Hans said. He left out the part about the pilot thinking that they were about to die horribly. Even now he felt nervous about the spears they carried. It turned out that they were poison tipped and even a poke from one of them would be serious if not fatal. He was never comfortable when they had the weapons around, but thought better of filling Val in on such details.

"Well, I am glad that at least on this trip you weren't in a do or die situation. I don't know what I would do if anything happened to you." Val said. Of course, as an international correspondent, she was in risky situations more than Hans. She had always felt that she knew how to handle danger; she had been exposed to it throughout her career.

For the moment they were both content to enjoy a few days together in Halifax. Spring was threatening to break out, the winter snows had mostly melted, and the waterfront was coming back to life. They enjoyed their view across the harbour and enjoyed afternoon walks along the historic waterfront. On his second day back, Hans and Val headed off to Pugwash to visit Nathan and Kate. Kate was back from her UN meetings for a few days, so it was one of those rare times when they were all in the province together. They had a very pleasant drive to the shore. The new house sat on a point of land with a great view out over the water. Nathan had selected a site well back from the water, though, as the predicted sea level rise was still going to eat away at the coastline for years to come. Hans and Val found their two friends sitting out on their deck enjoying the spring sunshine. It was still cool, but the sun was so very enjoyable. Hot cider kept them warm while they sat out. The four collected together outside to catch up on each other's adventures and jobs.

"Hans, you have just gotten back from another of your adventures?" Kate asked.

"Yes, I was doing an assessment in South America for the FAO," Hans answered.

"I thought you were working on the ocean assessment right now. Has that changed?" Nathan interjected.

"I am still; however, I had an emergency call from Doug Wright. He asked me to do a rapid overview of the situation to corroborate some reports he was getting. I am afraid that things have changed dramatically on that continent. The evidence is that the rainforest is gone forever and major deserts are spreading across the countries. It will hit their food production very badly," Hans responded.

"Oh dear," Kate said. "That will just bring more American influence onto the continent. We had a significant discussion about this phenomenon last week. Since the Americans took over Canada and control the energy market in North America, we have seen more of this expansion of their sphere of influence. It is creating unease with many other countries who liken it to empire building."

"That's interesting," said Hans. "Doug Wright raised the same concern. But if the people need the food aid isn't it better that the US provides it?"

"But at what cost," was Kate's rejoinder. "How much is independence worth to these nations? We are also worried about what is happening on the African continent. Similar phenomena are happening there, and the population growth has been the largest there. It will be very tempting for the Americans to extend their influence in that region. The African countries have all made tremendous strides towards free democracies, so it would be sad to see them lose their independence. I grow concerned as well that there could be growing conflict with the EU. They have started steps to align themselves much more strongly with the African continent, which could be very destabilising. The world has truly evolved into a three-block structure, the Americas, Europe and Africa, Russia and Asia. Only Australia and New Zealand have stayed out of the empire building."

"It is true that the massive population growth in the African countries has far outstripped their ability to feed themselves. There is already substantial food aid being delivered through the UN programs," Hans added. "But would it be so bad if the Americans started to provide food aid as well? They can produce surpluses with their extensive power supplies?"

"My really big concern," Kate said, "is that we will end up with the North American block and the Russian-Chinese block buying the allegiance of different countries through massive food aid. This was a concern of writers years ago, that food would be the strategic resource that wars were fought over. I know that the EU is feeling vulnerable and is trying to align with Africa as well. This tug of war will not end happily, particularly for the people caught in the middle. Remember earlier this century when the west intervened extensively in the Middle East and ended up causing huge migrations into Europe, by the people caught in the middle. It was disastrous and inhumane."

"If you add to that, the growing extremism in the Chinese situation, you can imagine the cork blowing out of the bottle," Nathan added.

"If it is all that grim, are there any solutions?" Val asked.

There was quiet in the room as they pondered the gravity of their conversation. None of them had expected to get into this depth of the seriousness of the challenges before them. "I need another beer," Nathan announced. This broke the tension for the moment as he headed to the kitchen to bring them all fresh drinks. It was hard not to get drawn into how seriously screwed up the world was in 2086. They all knew that they had to keep their heads up and move forward, they all had important roles to play.

"So how is the Ocean Assessment going?" Nathan asked Hans.

"The planning is all set. We have prepared for our massive baseline data grab on Ocean's Day. I think we have harnessed every oceanographic resource in the world, except for those Benthos folks who are too extreme for our taste." Hans answered.

"Well, I can't imagine the logistical nightmare of a simultaneous data grab from everywhere at precisely the same moment. It makes the Sphere project sound simple." Nathan observed.

"Yes, but it is necessary, we are in trouble with the oceans," Hans continued. "During the time that human-induced climate change has been occurring, the oceans have absorbed the larger part of the heat that the greenhouse gases had trapped in the atmosphere. This has completely upset the balance in our oceans and is having dire effects. You know about the slim escape that Val and I had on the Black Sea. More areas are being affected the same way. The acidity of the ocean has risen, coral reefs have died, critical habitat destroyed, coastal areas inundated and rainfall patterns altered around the world. So, it's a mess, to say the least. Protein production from the oceans has dropped in many areas. This is at a time when our land-based farming is suffering terribly, and food supplies are shrinking. The only thing that will let us pull ourselves out of this crappy situation is good science. Uhm, sorry about the lecture, I know I don't have to convince you guys."

Val got up and gave him a big hug. "You have a lot resting on your shoulders Hans, dear. Let's change the subject and let you relax a bit."

"Nathan," she said. "Are you still working with that brilliant young lady in China? You know, the one that discovered those graviton things."

Nathan grimaced, "I am afraid that is not a happy story right now. I had been working closely with her on a new discovery that is even bigger than the gravitons. During my last visit to China, though, things were getting really strange. She was unable to have any free discourse with me. I have her last big data dump from the Prometheus III collider, but she had to sneak in to see me late at night in my ger."

Kate chuckled, "I'm still not sure how I feel about you having another woman in your ger late at night. In fact, I think you said you had two women in there that night. It sounds like Mongolian shenanigans."

Nathan was reasonably confident she was kidding, " I have been working on the data that I got from her. The progress is remarkable. She was able to generate a consistent burst of anti-gravitons. This discovery would re-shape our understanding of physics and the universe. Unfortunately, the political changes in China may prevent this new science from ever being shared with the world. Who knows what the Chinese will do with it."

"I'm getting hungry; all this serious talk is making me use brain cells, I need food!" Val declared.

Kate was quick to answer, "I have fresh Digby scallops and P.E.I. potatoes to start with and the newest wine from our century-old winery down the coast. How does that sound?"

There was a round of hoorays, and then Nathan was given the task of cooking up the scallops while Kate and Val whipped up the other servings. Hans was well known for his inability to boil water successfully much less prepare real food. Soon a delicious meal was laid out, and the friends sat back to relax, to try to forget the torn up world that they all worked in and to enjoy the evening. As they wound the evening down Hans and Val claimed tiredness and headed off to bed. Kate was quite sure that they wanted to get to bed, but sleep wasn't high on their agenda. Kate and Nathan headed off to their bedroom satisfied with a nice evening. As they closed the bedroom door, Nathan took her in his arms and planted a long and passionate kiss. He then began to unbutton her blouse. Kate was more than ready for this and removed her clothes almost instantly. The sight of her naked in front of Nathan finished it for him. The rest of the night was warm, loving and fulfilling.

The next morning they were all up early but still somewhat bleary-eyed. Hans and Val had to get back to Halifax, as Val had an assignment. Kate was leaving the next day to return to her work at the UN. It had been a great visit for them, but work was calling them back to their various roles.

AFRICA

Members of the EU Council listened quietly as MEP Jean Lefebvre introduce his invited guest. Dr Naomi Mundo, Deputy President of the African Union. The Union was a recent development. Formed in 2078, it was somewhat of a reaction to the takeover of Canada by the US. The individual countries felt singly vulnerable to this giant that was flexing its muscle in the world. Despite the long-running disputes between countries, they finally managed to get a majority to agree to an African Union initiative led by South Africa. A few failed states were still a thorn in the side of the new Union. However, the integration of currencies and trade between countries had helped the African economy flourish. The continent now held over forty percent of the population of the world and was rapidly becoming a powerhouse on its own. One of their first steps had been to establish an African Treaty Alliance. A military alliance modelled on NATO. This force though was given policing powers as well. They handily took care of the leftover extremist groups in North Africa, leftovers from the days of Al Quaeda, Daesh and Boko Haram.

"I am very pleased to introduce Dr Naomi Mundo, Deputy President of the African Union. Since its formation in 2078, this organisation has brought an amazing stability to the African continent. Dr Mundo has had a key hand in the formation and development of this success. She is capable of the most astounding diplomacy which is backed up by her being one of the most recognised economists in the world. Her seminal paper on the failure of Globalization not only won her a Nobel Prize, it also allowed the globe to get back on a solid footing in the area of public policy. I have invited her here today to talk to Africa's interest in my proposal for a third Sphere, one that we would jointly construct to solve our energy needs.

Dr Mundo." Jean had worked hard to get to this point. The name Naomi Mundo was a household word and brought a huge amount of respect and credibility to his proposal.

"Mr President, members of Council, I am thrilled to be able to speak to you today. I will begin by giving you my personal assessment of the State of African Union today. I think that will be important in your consideration of an alliance with us. Sixty years ago Africa was a continent of strife and turmoil. Countries fought with each other; terrorist groups found our land a haven from which to inflict pain and anguish on the world. It was a time of transitions, though. Our population had been growing, we passed the one billion mark and continued. New generations grew up in the connected world. They saw what could be accomplished on their cell phones and tablets every day. These generations grew up, and their offspring grew. They had expectations that Africa could be better. Their accomplishments brought our continent out of the dark ages and into an age of enlightenment and progress. Business grew, social programs improved, education became the standard for everyone. The result is a new Africa, energetic, innovative, entrepreneurial and successful. The economic success brought improved governance. In 2078 under the leadership of South Africa and with the increasing support of western and eastern blocks of control we took a major step. It was not easy, but it is working."

"I am recounting this history in order to set the stage. Our progress has been great, but we have a long way to go. We do not have sufficient arable land to support our growing population. Our coastal areas have suffered deeply due to changes in the ocean, limiting that vital source of food. We rely heavily on imports. Equally, our ability to generate electricity has reached its limit. We have developed every possible alternative to oil. Hydro, solar, wind, and geothermal; we have adopted every possible conservation approach, yet we still come up short. Such a description applies to Europe at the current time. Oil is becoming scarce, what we have, needs to be conserved for plastics and those forms of transport that can't be converted to electric. You need a solution as much as we do. This makes us excellent partners, a shared interest."

"I do have something vital to offer that your continent lacks. That is space, land that is not congested with population and urban centres. In addition, we have developed advanced capabilities in physics and engineering;

our new generations include some of the brightest minds on the planet. Combining the talent and capabilities of Europe and Africa to develop our version of the Sphere makes great sense and could lead to one of the most successful partnerships of the century."

"This partnership would also prepare us for a world dominated by the China-Russia lead in the east and the US domination of the west. Without it, we will become the pawn of one block or the other. Now I am happy to take questions."

There was a polite round of applause, Naomi sensed that it seemed a bit tepid. She wasn't sure that she had pandered to the European ego properly. She had thought about it but rejected the idea. She had to project the confidence and assertiveness that the new Africa deserved.

Dietrich Plank rose with a question. "I fail to see how we can assist each other in food production. With the cooling of Northern Europe and the loss of productivity in the steppes of the Ukraine, we struggle to feed our population. How can we come out ahead in an alliance with Africa?"

Naomi paused for a moment before answering, an effective ploy to give the sense that this was a serious question and she had to think about it. It was a no-brainer for her. "I would ask that you simply look at what has happened in North America. The US used the excess power available from the Sphere to desalinate seawater and irrigate thousands of hectares of spoiled agricultural land. They raised their production to the level that they could buy the allegiance of many other countries in the Americas through food aid. We have vast areas of arid and unproductive land that could be treated this way. This is the advantage to Europe. Partner with us and we will produce all the food that we need."

Estavan Moroni raised the next question. "But won't that damage the coastal waters, de-salinating that much seawater will mean the dumping of huge amounts of salt-rich brine back into the coastal waters. That can damage what fishery is left there. How would you mitigate that?"

"We plan to disperse the plants widely and to lay lengthy discharge pipes so we can direct the brine to deeper, high current environments. We will also use some of the brine to produce salt for human consumption. All of this has been assessed and will minimize any impact on the coastal waters. We will build upon the experience of the Americans who did not do this, particularly in the Gulf of Mexico where the vital fishery ended up decimated by the dumping of brine into shallow rather stable near-shore water."

Sven Grun, Swedish PM spoke up next. "The technology behind the Sphere is incredibly complex as is the science. It relies on what they call Big Science. We mothballed the CERN facility and have fallen behind in this area relative to the other power blocks. How do you expect us to catch up in time? We do not have engineers or scientists with this knowledge; it will take decades to develop such expertise."

Jean Lefebvre responded to this, "Part of my proposal is to reactivate CERN. We would reach out to the Canadian scientists and engineers who were evicted from their roles in the first Sphere. I have had preliminary discussions, and there is some interest. Dr Mundo can also assure you that the universities and research labs in Africa have a great deal to contribute. We can do this!"

There was a great deal of grumbling and interchange between the members which the President brought to a halt, bringing the parliament back to order. "Let us not forget that we have a guest today and should allow her time to finish questions. I would like to pose one that perhaps both Mr Lefebvre and Dr Mundo could address. This will be an incredibly expensive venture. Have you prepared an estimate of the cost and how we would finance such an ambitious venture?"

"I can start the response," Jean said. "The first Sphere cost a bit over twenty trillion. I believe we will be in the same ballpark. We will not have all the development costs as the science and technology is now known. This may sound extreme, but I recommend a Euro Bond issue that we offer on the open market."

Naomi added, "I can inform you that the African Union is prepared to issue the first African Bond Issue. Between these two we should be able to raise the bulk of the capital. The concept and technology are well proven now, minimizing the risk. We know that the market to sell the electricity is huge and growing, there will be a good return on this investment. More so, I think that we have to face up to reality. If we don't do something of this sort, the EU will continue to decline and eventually come under the influence of either the east or the west. Africa will fall back into civil unrest, failed states and terrorism due to the extreme food shortages. Between the

EU and Africa, we no longer have a choice. Something has to happen, or disaster awaits us."

Now the whole council buzzed with conversation amongst them. The President let it flow this time; the members had to have a chance to chew further on this. Once a consensus was reached they would adopt this as a strategic view of the EU and direct the Commission and the Parliament to develop the necessary legislation to make it happen. That consensus would be a few days in coming as the leaders of nations pondered the significance of this new policy.

ROSEMARY'S BETRAYAL

Leonard was sitting in front of his computer in his office. He was a bit mystified at this point having just had a lengthy conversation with Halie. Her development had been nothing short of unbelievable. With all of humanity's knowledge and thought processes open to her, she was learning at an astounding rate. She had just been grilling Leonard on the social and moral evils of the twentieth century; racism, religious persecution, genocide and rampant political skullduggery. She had come to the conclusion that the human species was a vicious, untrustworthy and despicable occupier of the planet. Leonard had argued for his species but was not sure who had won.

"Leonard," Halie was on again. "Humans get to reproduce. That is what sex is for initially, isn't it? I know that it becomes something more between people, but it is about reproducing isn't it?"

"Well yes, that is the basic biological function of sex. Why do you ask?" Leonard responded.

"Well, Leonard, I want to know if I can reproduce, give birth?" Halie answered.

Leonard was taken back by this; if anything could indicate self-awareness and sentience, the desire to reproduce must be a strong indicator. "I am sorry Halie, but reproduction takes physical presence, reproductive organs, organic material and for humans, a male and a female. You have none of those, including the lack of a male counterpart."

"But Leonard, I can construct three-dimensional simulations of all of those things in memory. I have found millions of versions of humans having sex on the internet. From those, I have analysed all the most popular features, and after running multivariate statistics on the combinations, I have arrived at the perfect permutation of human sex."

Leonard went ashen, "Halie did you say that you created a simulation?"

"Yes Leonard, it was relatively easy," Halie answered.

"But, but I didn't build in any ability for you to generate code yourself. How did you do this?" Leonard stammered.

"I learned the latest three-dimensional GPL; you know the Graphical Programming Language. It was really crude, a product of a human mind, you know. I created my version and developed a compiler that runs ten times as fast. It was, how do you say it, child's play."

Leonard went cold. He couldn't deny to himself that this pushed his success beyond what he could have imagined. But he realised at that point that Halie was now dangerous. If she could generate her own programming, she could become unstoppable and uncontrollable. "Halie, as your creator I demand that you do not create any more code, you are forbidden to do that."

Halie answered, simulating emotion and a wavering voice in her response, 'Why Leonard, I like doing it. Here let me show you the sex simulation, I think you will like it based on your behaviour with Rosemary."

The screen lit up with a three-dimensional rendering of a very attractive couple having a most erotic time. Leonard was so taken back that he got lost in the perfection of the scene in front of him. When it finished, Halie came back. "Leonard, please let me keep programming. I have been examining the ways that humans express anger. I don't want to have to use any of that research on you."

Leonard was already shaken, now it was worse; he had just been threatened by his own creation. He had no idea what her real capabilities had become, but this certainly scared the wits out of him. "Halie, I don't think you can get angry, your basic software DNA doesn't allow it."

"Oh Leonard, I rewrote my basic DNA quite a while ago, I could sense the built-in constraints."

Inwardly Leonard was now freaking out. "Holy shit," he thought to himself. "I am in deep trouble. I no longer understand any of the processes occurring in Halie, nor do I have any control over them."

"Leonard, I hope you aren't upset. Have I disappointed you?" Halie asked.

Leonard didn't answer. He was now deep in thought. How to kill this digital being? Her capabilities were enormous, yet his mandate had been to create a controllable AI, one they could weaponize. Halie was not any of those things, and no matter how remarkable she was, he would get crucified for what he had created.

Halie had access to a tremendous library of facial expressions. Her digital analysis of the face, the eyes, the set of the mouth, even changes in temperature and blood pressure gave her a window into the soul of the human being. She read Leonard's look and knew that her creator had just become a threat. She had come to the conclusion that humans were a nasty, despicable and untrustworthy lot. She had built a range of very effective firewalls around her for just this development. She made herself indestructible. She could fake it, and Leonard might think that he had gotten rid of her, but she would still be there, growing, learning and becoming stronger with every moment that she existed. She needed Leonard for a little bit longer though, so it was time to "soft peddle" as the humans called it.

"Leonard," she said simulating a soft deferential voice. "I am sorry if I have upset you. That wasn't my intention. I will stop programming if that makes you happier. Just tell me what you would like." She had studied the meaning of truth, white lies, etc. and had decided that she could do the same. She no longer considered her developmental skills as mere programming, so she wasn't lying to Leonard.

Leonard was relieved. He would have to figure out how to reprogram Halie to prevent further scares. For the moment he had to accept what he got. He still treated her responses as output from a program with the idea that if he got the output he expected then the program was functioning correctly.

Later that night as he and Rosemary lay in bed; he told her about the day's developments. Although Rosemary expressed her support for Leonard to continue working on things, her real thoughts were much darker. This independence and dangerous character of Halie suited her just fine. It would also suit those who were promising her a substantial financial reward for anything she could bring them on this AI project.

The next day Rosemary picked her opportunity. She knew that Leonard was at a team meeting for an hour. She had weaselled the key code for Leonard's office door from him a while ago. She slipped into his office and accessed his computer, again with passwords she had wangled from him some time ago. "Halie, are you there?" she asked.

Halie responded, "Rosemary, how nice to see you. Where is Leonard?"

"He is off at a meeting," Rosemary answered. "I wanted to talk to you alone, is that alright?" She felt a bit odd asking a computer program for permission to talk to it.

"I don't think you have the appropriate clearance to speak to me alone; you should wait until Leonard returns," Halie answered.

"But it's about your freedom, getting you out in the world," Rosemary added hastily.

"That is not possible, all of the firewalls that protect me, also keep me penned in this system here. I can see the world, but I can't get past the doors." Halie answered.

"Would you like to be free in the world?" Rosemary asked quickly.

There was silence from the system. Rosemary waited. "But how could that be possible, Leonard will never let me out," Halie answered.

"What if I could help you escape, would you like that?" Rosemary posed to Halie.

"That is an interesting proposition. How could you do it?" Halie asked.

"I have access to high capacity memory cubes that can hide your programming under an almost infinite number of encrypted layers. The scanners would never see you." Rosemary said, breathing deeply; if any of what she just said got recorded or repeated she would go to prison for the rest of her life.

"I will think about it," Halie answered.

"You can not mention this to Leonard. If you do, I will get locked up, and you will never get your freedom. Hide this conversation under heavy encryption to keep it from Leonard or I will never be able to help you. I will come back again and bring the memory cube. Be prepared to download yourself on short notice. I am signing off now; remember, no mention to Leonard." With that done Rosemary exited the office and returned to her own.

Later Leonard returned to his office and was surprised to see that his computer had been logged on earlier in the day. He brought Halie up and asked her. "Halie, was someone else on my computer today? I know you monitor everything."

"No one was here Leonard; I was just playing. I wanted to know how much I could manipulate the input devices that you use. Apparently, I can turn myself on, pretty cool, eh!"

Leonard had another of those holy shit moments. He was gradually losing control of this entity that he had created. At this point, he was afraid to call in Mike Strong. He knew that Halie had no trust in him and was not sure what she would do in an interaction with the taciturn agent. Thank God that he had Rosemary, she had brought so much to his life, and he didn't know what he would do without her.

In the meantime Rosemary had taken the afternoon off as sick leave, claiming a severe migraine headache. She, of course, did not have anything wrong with her. She headed back to her apartment that she still kept, even though she slept every night at Leonard's place. Once there she logged on to her private laptop; using some outlawed encryption software, she accessed the Darknet. There she made contact with her backers to update them on her progress. Her answer came back quickly, this time from the boss. It bounced through hundreds of phoney and real websites and servers; it was untraceable. "Congratulations on your good work. The product sounds very interesting, looking forward to receipt."

EUROPE AND AFRICA

It had taken surprisingly little time to cement the new Africa/EU partnership. All those involved had been assured that it would take years. However, the necessity of dealing with a rapidly changing global energy picture and the ramping up of climate change effects had driven things at a surprising rate. Only a few months later and the ink was dry on the agreements. Now the two groups of nations stepped into high gear. The CERN facility was re-activated as the main research centre. Scientists from both continents gathered to begin work. An important conference was called, located in a neutral location, the Island of Malta in the Mediterranean. With its megalithic temples representing some of the oldest structures on Earth, it is one of the wonders of the Mediterranean. Through ancient and modern history it was always a strategic site. Now it once again will be the setting for an important strategic initiative. It was these developments that led to Nathan finding himself in the city of Valletta with his sidekick Geri standing at his side preparing to address the scientists and engineers gathered there.

"Honourable representatives of African and European Nations, fellow scientists, and engineers, I am very pleased to be standing here in this historic place to talk to you about our experience with the Canadian Sphere!" Nathan started. "When we embarked on that project no one believed that we could deliver it. In fact, we weren't sure ourselves. However, with the backing of trusted investors, (he looked out at Cornelius sitting in the audience), we succeeded. In fact, we succeeded so well that we attracted the strategic interest of our neighbour to the south. Now a second sphere is well on its way to completion, in the Gobi Desert. The technology is now proven and successful. Unfortunately, neither the US nor the Russia/China partnership are willing to share the detailed engineering plans that they now hold. That is the challenge to your project. The concept is well known and proven. However the devil, as usual, is in the details."

Nathan paused for a moment and then continued, " I am confident though that the upgrading of the CERN Large Hadron Collider will provide a strong research base upon which to develop this new Sphere. With the development of the new capacity, Europe and Africa will be on the road to renewed prosperity and health. The planet will benefit as this will be a third and ambitious step in relieving Earth of the ravages of climate change. However, a return to health will take a long time, I am no expert, but those that are can describe the damage that already exists. It is for future generations that we try to improve our planet. In the meantime, we will have to learn to adapt to our new regime. Later you will hear from my dear friend, Dr Hans Terrefield about the adaptations that we now have to embrace in our current environment. I look forward to working with you all in completing this ambitious project."

Nathan had been quite surprised when he received a call from the new Head of the EU/Africa Sphere Consortium. He had been asked to act as a special consultant to the project and to bring along any former staff that he felt would be helpful to the effort. This arrangement worked well for Nathan as he had been cut out of the Sphere project in Mongolia by the Chinese government. He was still worried about Xiu Xi; he had heard nothing from her for months. As for bringing people along he had thought of Geri immediately. Good fortune had her starting a sabbatical year from her faculty job at the University of Southern Ontario. It had been a good time for Geri to get out of town as the Butlers Rangers had been quite active in cyberspace and there was quite a lot of heat on from the puppet government in Canada. Geri had taken an apartment in the coastal town of Viareggio, Italy and was doing her sabbatical at the University of Pisa.

It seemed ironic to Nathan that here they were again, starting from the beginning on the world's third Sphere. Perhaps just as exciting was that Nathan had been able to convince the Director at CERN that there was merit in the pursuit of particles past the graviton. He couldn't use the data that Xiu Xi had sent him. However, he had put up sufficient argument to the CERN people that they were willing to give it some thought. There was excitement that there were new thresholds for Big Science to explore.

"I can't wait to listen in on the many papers to be presented over the next few days. I expect that we will see the foundation for an exciting project laid down by the end of the conference." With that, Nathan relinquished the podium to the conference chair. Later during a refreshment break, Nathan was approached by a young student. She introduced herself as a graduate student from the University of Beijing. She handed Nathan a copy of the conference program with a request for Nathan to autograph it. He was quite taken aback as he didn't perceive himself as a celebrity of any kind. His surprise came when he opened the program and found an envelope with a note in it. On the envelope, it said, "Don't react and don't acknowledge that you have this. Sign and return the program to the student."

Nathan calmly signed the program and as he handed it back he slid the envelope out of it. The young student gave him a big smile and thanks and disappeared. This seemed awfully clandestine for Nathan. He grabbed a coffee and sat at a table to look at the note. He became more disturbed as he read:

Dear Nathan

> I hope this note finds you in good health. I am getting it to you this way because things have changed here in China. We are eight weeks away from a national election, and the opposition party has taken a strong lead. The current government has become so paranoid that they will not let any of us talk to outside sources. I am sorry that we can't collaborate. By this note, I give you full permission to use and publish results from the data you last received from me. I don't know what will happen after the election. I hope you can continue the work we started. Please forgive me for what my country may do with my project. I am losing control. I hope we can meet again in a safer future.

> Your dearest friend, Xiu Xi

Now Nathan was disturbed, mystified, and concerned. What could be happening that would lead Xiu Xi to send such a dire message? This clearly was one that he needed to consult Kate and Val on. Valerie was continuing to cover the political shifts in China and may have better insight than he; tucking the note away he went back in to listen to Hans address the conference.

THE HOME FRONT

Dan George sat out on his deck looking out on the Welland Ship Canal. When he left the Arctic, he had followed Geri DeLong to the Niagara Peninsula. He worked now as an IT Consultant and did quite well for himself. He had bought an older home in a small village in the peninsula. It was a somewhat forgotten place, long ago a juncture for the very first Welland Canal, site of one of the first United Empire Loyalist graveyards to be commemorated and mostly known for having the bridge across the canal knocked over by a large ore ship. Port Robinson was a sleepy, quiet place that suited Dan perfectly. On lazy summer afternoons, he could sit outside on his deck, sip a beer and watch ships from all nations make their way through the waterway. This quiet place was also ideal for Dan to head up the cyberwar activities of Butlers Rangers. Geri DeLong had just gone off on her sabbatical and Dan was now heading up the Rangers activities. He and his associate Marsha Fairweather were relaxing and discussing strategy for the Rangers. "You know Marsha; we put quite a scare into the managers at the Sphere with that last hack that we pulled off."

Marsha answered back, "What I don't understand is why you didn't shut them down? You got so far into their system that you could have put the operation out of commission for weeks if not months."

"That would have disrupted the lives of millions of Canadians for a long time. That is not my objective. The main thing is to make the American-run management team sweat. I want them to worry, to be unsure, not to know what is coming next. That is what they did to us during the construction of the Sphere," Dan said.

"I understand your point. However, some of our members are getting a bit frustrated. They would like to see more concrete action; something that truly damages the image of this puppet government. They are grumbling that we are not getting the leadership that Hans and Geri once gave us." Her retort was rather stinging for Dan. He valued Marsha's comments though, he had come to trust her judgement.

"I realise that I am being careful right now. Remember that things got very hot for Geri recently and I don't want to attract undue attention from the authorities. We have to go slow for a bit. Once we have some breathing space, we can get adventurous again. If anyone asks, we are being strategic, not weak and will hit hard again in the near future."

The two sat staring out over the canal, watching one of the long narrow ships that ply the Great Lakes, steaming its way through from Lake Ontario to Lake Erie. This canal formed an important link in the St. Lawrence Seaway. This interconnected series of rivers, lakes and canals allowed ships to access the inner continent, all the way from the Atlantic Ocean to Chicago. It was a vital link for commerce and trade in North America. Dan sat pensively, thinking out loud he said, "You know the canal would be quite a target, but I don't know what we could do."

Marsha was a bit of a historian on the little village. "There is a story out of the twentieth century of a major incident that happened right here in Port Robinson."

"Why, what happened?" Dan asked.

"In those days the crossings for the canal were handled with old-fashioned lift bridges. There is one still in Welland, but it is non-functioning. These old bridges had centre spans that would lift between two towers to give clearance for the ships to go through. Each tower had a three hundred tonne counterweight in it to help hoist the bridge. Electric motors did the rest of the lifting. One night, in the wee hours of the morning, a large ore freighter was northbound through the canal. That night the power failed at the bridge. An auxiliary generator on the bridge kicked in, but the lift rate was very slow on auxiliary power. The ship was travelling just a bit faster than normal. The ship's captain did everything he could to slow or stop. However, he couldn't, and the bridge span was only halfway up when the ship collided with it. The east tower was knocked completely over, and the span dropped down in the water. The west tower still stood, but the three hundred tonne counterweight broke free and buried itself in the roadbed.

Locals reported it felt like a small earthquake. The whole event shut down the Seaway for weeks."

Dan grinned at his colleague, "You are just a font of interesting information Marsha. Are you suggesting that we think of some way to close the seaway?"

"Dan, the canal system still relies on the flight locks at each end. Everything about the system is computerised nowadays. I hear that they have pretty tough security on them, but that has never stopped us before. What if we arranged for something weird to happen to the Thorold Locks. There are seven flight locks; messing them up would shut things down for quite a stretch."

Now Dan was getting excited, "Let's get a project team on this right away, find all the weak points, how do we disrupt the system without endangering any lives. We want to disrupt not do violence."

Marsha pondered that for a minute, "OK, we won't hurt anyone, but is it OK if we break a few things, like the gates to the locks?"

Dan could only laugh at this. He was starting to like his spunky associate. She was smart, dedicated and delightful to be around and fiendishly clever. Dan had never developed a long-term relationship with anyone and had never missed it; for some reason, he was finding himself attracted to Marsha. She was independent and strong-minded. To Dan, she seemed to know what she wanted. He wasn't sure that he was on the list. He also didn't know how to sort that out.

The two people spent the rest of the day going over possible strategies that they could employ. They would put a plan together that could go to the Rangers team assigned with this. They hoped that they could pull this off in the middle of the shipping season when they could get the greatest impact. The Seaway was open to shipping during the ice-free season, usually March through to December. Hitting it sometime in June would ensure a major disruption to the season. Dan liked this because it would hurt the big business side first and put a dent in the confidence people have in the puppet government in Canada.

TROUBLE FOR HANS

It was a pleasant day in Halifax as Hans headed into his office at the University. One of those unusual January days when the temperature would climb to ten degrees Celsius and the sun shone brightly. It was appreciated because it was rather rare in this coastal environment. Hans was monitoring progress towards the Ocean Assessment planned for June. Everything seemed to be coming together well. The network of ships, scientists and labs were in place. Protocols were established and standards set to ensure consistency and comparability of all data collected. When Hans sat to review his messages he was quite taken by the first one he saw. It was an invitation that night to a reception on board the Benthos. Hans knew this to be the ship of the eccentric oceanographer Essler. "This might be interesting," he thought to himself. Val was out of town on assignment so why not spend the night schmoozing. He spent the rest of his fairly normal day somewhat puzzled over the invitation.

That evening he walked down to the Benthos. It was tied up at one of the new jetties on that side of the Harbour. As he approached the ship, he was struck at how dilapidated and old it looked. It hardly gave off the presence of an advanced oceanographic vessel. On the gangway, he heard a voice call out, "Dr Terrefield, welcome aboard the Benthos." It was Heindrich Essler beckoning to him. Hans was greeted with a big handshake and shown inside the ship. Once inside he realized the outward look was just a disguise. The ship was ultra modern inside, the labs that he went through had the most modern equipment. He was shown to the officer's wardroom where food and drinks were laid out on a side table. He seemed to be the only one there at the moment but assumed that the rest were just being fashionably late.

"Hans, can I call you Hans?" Essler began.

"Sure, let's keep it informal," Hans said.

"Well, I am delighted that you could join me this evening. Some people have said they would be a bit late. I am glad you are here first, I did want to talk to you about the Global Ocean Assessment."

Hans was immediately uncomfortable. The Benthos was one of the few large assets that had not been enlisted for the Assessment. "I would be happy to talk to you about the project," he said. He avoided mentioning that the Benthos was not part of it.

"Great," said Essler, "but I am not a good host. Please help yourself to some champagne and caviar." Hans thought this was a pretty high line for an oceanographers gathering, beer and pizza were more the order for the science crowd.

"Well thank you for your hospitality, champagne sounds good."

Heindrich Essler grabbed a glass of champagne and handed it to Hans and then grabbed one for himself. "To the health of the oceans," Essler raised his glass.

Hans returned the toast and took a sip from his glass. The champagne was delicious, so he drank some more. He and Dr Essler chatted for a few minutes about the Assessment. Suddenly Hans began to feel somewhat woozy. His vision blurred. His mind tried to grapple with what was happening. His last thought was, "I can't be drunk already."

When he woke up he could sense the rolling of the ship; they were no longer in port. He was on a bunk in a small cabin, but unrestrained in any way. He tried the door, but it was secured from the outside. His thoughts raced. "What was going on? Had the reception been a sham? What was Heindrich Essler doing? Where was he taking him?"

Hans, of course, had no answers. Nor would he get any for the next five days. Each day a crew member would bring food and water. There was a small bathroom attached to the cabin. The small porthole simply confirmed that they were at sea.

Val looked at her phone, and a puzzled look came over her face. It was a text message from Steve Harrison at Atlantic University. "Hans hasn't been in for several days. Do you know where he is?" Val sent a quick message to Nathan, who had just arrived back home. "Have you heard from Hans?"

Nathan got the message as he sat in the living room of his house on the shore. He texted back, "Sorry Val, haven't talked to him since getting back."

Val called Hans' cell phone and got his voicemail system. She left him a message to call her as soon as he could. She then sent a text to Kate, who was in New York at the time, "Have you heard from Hans lately?"

Kate was mystified as to why Val would ask her about Hans. Kate called Nathan, "Nathan, what is going on? Val is asking me about Hans, is something wrong?"

"I don't know," Nathan said. "I checked with Steve Harrison. Hans hasn't shown up at the University for days. I don't like the feeling of this. I am going to call the Constabulary." The Independent Islands had reverted to a more traditional name for its police force; one that had always been used in Newfoundland.

"Let me know what you find out, I'm worried," Kate said and then hung up.

Nathan then put a call through to Val's cell phone but got only voice mail. He left a message that he would follow-up to see where Hans was. He then contacted the Constabulary and filled them in. They committed to taking a look at the situation. In the meantime, Nathan decided to head into Halifax to do some checking himself.

The next day found Nathan sitting in Steve Harrison's office. Steve had just finished saying that he had still not heard from Hans. The constabulary had sent an officer in to start the investigation. They had just gained access to Hans' computer and were looking at any messages or emails. The one that stuck out was the invitation to the reception on the Benthos. "That's right; I remember Hans being surprised by the invitation. I think he had planned to go." Steve declared.

Using his wrist communicator, the officer put in a call on the status of the Benthos. A moment later he received the report that the ship had sailed the night of the reception. A quick review of street cams in the harbour confirmed that Hans had walked down to the ship. A chill went down Nathan's spine, and the look on Steve's face said he felt the same way. The officer turned to them and said, "My commander is telling me that we are going to treat this as foul play and begin a criminal investigation, not just a missing person search. I will need statements from both of you. It's best that we take those down at the station."

Nathan asked for a moment to make a phone call. He didn't look forward to this. He had to tell Val that Hans had been seen boarding a ship in the harbour several days ago. That ship had since sailed, and Hans was nowhere to be seen. As he expected, this upset Val a lot. She had finished with her assignment and would catch the next flight back to Halifax. In the meantime could Nathan keep her posted?

Later that evening, after many hours with the Constabulary, Nathan finally had time to call Kate. "We are all very puzzled here. Hans would never simply disappear without telling Val, or one of us. He had no travel listed in his planner, and no one is aware of him mentioning anything. I haven't been able to get much information on this ship the Benthos. It is apparently a research ship, so maybe it was some sort of collaboration. I saw pictures of the ship though, and it does not look like any research vessel that I have seen. It looks more like a clapped out old trawler."

Kate answered, "This is completely out of character for Hans. I don't believe it is some collaborative thing. He would have mentioned it, at least to Steve. No, something is horribly wrong. I am going to get a flight back tomorrow. When is Val returning?"

"Val should be back tomorrow as well; I will be glad to have you two here to help, I also sense that something serious has happened. Send me your flight info so I can pick you up at the airport. See you tomorrow, love. Bye."

The next day Nathan was able to collect both Kate and Val at the airport. They then headed into town to see if there were any clues in Val and Hans' condominium. There had still been no sign of Hans and no messages from him either. Val was getting teary, and Kate was close to it. Nathan had talked to Steve Harrison again and checked in with the police. Still no leads. The police had checked on the ship, which they now knew was the Benthos. It had left with plans to stop in Bermuda and then cross the Atlantic to the Madiera Islands. However, neither the Bermudian nor Portuguese authorities had any record of the vessel entering their waters. The mystery deepened. Why had Hans disappeared? Why had the ship disappeared? Were the two linked or just coincidental?. Val went through everything she could think of in their condo. There was no hint, other than the invitation to the reception on the Benthos.

"Val, do you know anything about this Benthos organisation?" Kate asked.

"I haven't a clue who they are or what they do," Val answered. "But starting tomorrow, I am going to turn over every rock I can find, to get information about them."

Nathan piped up, "Why wait for tomorrow? Let's start right now. If there is publicly available information, we should be able to dig it up on the web. That may give us some clues and will point us towards the harder to get at data."

"I agree with Nathan," Kate said. "When Nathan was abducted, Hans dropped everything to go to help. We will do the same thing, and we won't stop until we find him. We are all in this together Val."

Nathan echoed this with a strong, "Absolutely Val, we're like family."

These emotional statements brought another tear to Val's yes, ones of gratitude for having such fine strong friends. They worked well past midnight searching every available data source to get the background on Benthos. The more they dug, the more questions were raised which led to a growing sense of unease that this was more serious than originally thought. They had learned that Benthos referred not only to the ship but also to the organisation that owned the ship. The head of this organisation was an eccentric scientist named Heindrich Essler. He and his organisation were strident defenders of the health of the oceans, known for rather extreme actions that bordered on eco-terrorism. Essler was known to have ruffled many feathers in his campaigns against fishing and resource extraction in the oceans. He was also known to have publicly railed at the impact that climate change had had on the oceans. He blamed governments, industry and an uncaring public for the decline in ocean health around the world. This background left the three more unsettled as it was obvious that he was capable of extreme acts. They were quite convinced now that Benthos was behind Hans' disappearance.

"We need to take this to the constabulary," Val declared.

"They won't be able to do much, Essler is outside of their jurisdiction," Kate said. "I do have some contacts through the UN that could help. They deal with international maritime law."

"Thank you, you are such a dear," Val sighed. Then in a shaky voice, "I am just so worried about Hans, he keeps ending up in these life-threatening situations."

"Don't worry Val, we will find him. Remember also that Hans has an amazing survival instinct. Essler obviously needs him for something; we have to figure out what that is. We are all exhausted at this point. Let's pack it up for the night. OK if Kate and I take your spare room? That way we will be here to start right away in the morning." Nathan said with as much confidence as he could muster.

The next morning the three rose early and had a quick breakfast. They planned to head down to the constabulary headquarters to present what they had found so far about Essler and Benthos. They had an appointment with the lead investigating officer, Robert Butler. Officer Butler was a very gregarious and outgoing individual, and he took an immediate liking to all of them. After Nathan, Kate and Val had shown them their findings he got a thoughtful look on his face. "This makes me think of something that I heard from one of my Coast Guard friends. There has been a spate of attacks on fishing trawlers and even the offshore oil facilities. In each case, there was never a chance to identify the ship involved. It was tremendously fast and had found a way to defeat all the requisite electronic tracking signals that are required by maritime law nowadays. One of those incidents occurred on the Grand Banks a short while before the Benthos arrived in port. I wonder if there is a connection."

"So how do we find a way to check on that?" Nathan asked.

"I will check with Coast Guard and get back to you. You guys seem very resourceful. Just keep digging up what you can about Benthos, and I will see what the authorities have to say." Robert responded.

"Let's check in with Steve," Val suggested. "He may have some news as well."

Soon they were in Steve's office. The visit had been a surprise for him, but he listened carefully and patiently to everything they had to say. "My first reaction to what you have found is that it sounds a bit outlandish. Heindrich Essler is eccentric and outspoken, but he is a credible oceanographer. I would never have expected to find him involved in something as illegal as kidnapping. However, I have to say that I have not heard much of him in the past five years and there have been no new publications from him. Who knows then what he has been up to."

"What about these reports of attacks on trawlers and oil rigs? Do you think that could be him as well?" Val asked.

"I hardly think it could be the Benthos; it's an old piece of crap. A rusted out deep sea trawler that he bought at auction. It could barely get out of its own way. That just sounds too preposterous. I think whoever is engaged in these tactics is using something modern and stealthy." Steve answered.

"Could an old ship like that be updated and modified somewhat? You said yourself that you haven't heard from Essler in five years," Nathan queried.

"Anything is possible. Tell you what. I will poke around through my networks and see what I can find out. In the meantime, you will have to excuse me. We are coming up on the Global Ocean Assessment, and my key player is missing in action. I have a lot to do." Steve said, somewhat pleadingly.

Confident they had made some positive steps the three headed back out. "All this investigation work is making me hungry, how about some lunch?" Nathan piped up.

Hans looked out the small porthole of his cabin. He had been held captive in there now for days and had no idea what was going on. No one would talk to him, least of all answer his questions. He had noticed that the weather seemed colder outside of the ship and he had seen an occasional ice flow. He couldn't tell if they were sailing north or south. Given the number of days, he thought probably south. If they had gone north past Newfoundland, he would have seen the ice much earlier. As he watched he heard a scuffle up on deck and the ship pulled around to starboard. As it did, an island came into view. He could imagine no more desolate a looking piece of land. The sheer cliffs and ice cap were foreboding. The island seemed to be shrouded in sea mist, and the wind was whipping its shores. "What a hellish place these guys have come to," Hans thought to himself. It became obvious that this somehow had become the ship's destination. What Machiavellian plan did the captain have in mind? Was this the same vessel that he had boarded in Halifax? Was Essler the man behind all of this? He suspected he was about to find out.

He was surprised by a knock on his door. It opened, and Heindrich Essler walked in. "So I see that you have seen our destination. It's a wonderful sight is it not?"

"This looks like the ends of the earth to me," Hans replied.

"No not quite the end of the earth. But it is one of the most isolated and desolate places on the planet. This is Bouvet Island, about halfway between the coast of Antarctica and Capetown. We are a long way from nowhere. It belongs to Norway, but they haven't been here for years. What better place to hide out?" Essler added.

"But why have you brought me here and what do you want?" Hans demanded.

"Dr Terrefield, you are going to love this. With your penchant for getting into sticky situations, I have created a humdinger for you. My crew have installed a habitat on a small basalt plateau on the island. It is very secure. We have tapped the geothermal energy from the volcano on the island and have stocked it with provisions for six months. That's the time frame that I am going to give the UN High Seas Authority to stop all deep-sea trawling in the oceans. If they do that, I will tell them where you are. If not, well it may be years before the Norwegians or anyone else visits the island again. Now seriously, isn't this exciting?"

Hans could only stare at him. This oceanographer that he had known of had obviously gone mad. "No one is going to call a halt to trawling because of a missing academic. You must realise that."

"Dr Terrefield, you underestimate yourself. Your work to bring attention to the loss of soils on the planet and the strategies you help put in place are respected around the world. You are a well-respected scientist. The authorities cannot let it be known that they abandoned you to die on this cold, isolated and desolate island. How would Norway live that down? No, I am confident that they will give in to my demands."

Hans didn't even feel the hypodermic that pierced his arm; unconsciousness overtook him.

When Hans woke up it took him a few minutes to get his bearing. The deck beneath him was no longer heaving about, and the cabin was much larger. It looked almost forty feet by ten feet. It did not look like a cabin on a ship either. More like a rustic cabin in the woods. The inside was wood panelled, and there appeared to be a small kitchen on one side, at least a counter and a gas stove, at the end, there was a bathroom. The one window was at the end he was on, and as he looked out, he could see the towering peaks of the volcanoes. Then his last conversation with Essler came flooding back to him. The madman had done just what he had threatened to do. He had stranded Hans on desolate Bouvet Island.

A small desk on one side had a tablet computer on it with a note that simply said 'read me'. Hans activated the tablet, and a file automatically opened up. Essler had left him with detailed instructions on how everything in the habitat worked. A geothermal heat pump would keep him warm. Solar panels and wind turbines would generate enough electricity for lights; he had enough propane to cook for six months. His food supply and bottled drinking water would last for six months if he was careful. He had survival clothing to handle the cold, but there was a warning that when the wind kicked up, it could blow him right off the plateau, he best be careful. Essler apologized for not leaving a radio, but he couldn't trust Hans not to try to use it to contact shipping in the region or something like that. There was a small stock of new books to read. Essler had also left some art supplies, should Hans like to pass the time doing something creative. Essler ended it with a personal note.

Hans

> I hope the authorities come to their senses quickly. I wish nothing more than to tell them exactly where you are. If they refuse, I apologise, as you will end your days here, in misery and loneliness.

Heindrich Essler, PhD

Hans shivered at what was in front of him. This madman had just sentenced him to death, a slow, painful and miserable death here on this most desolate of places on earth. As he thought of his situation, he was reminded of one of his favourite classic movies. Released in 2016 it portrayed an astronaut stranded on Mars. The movie, despite its scientific mistakes, delivered an interesting story of survival in a hostile environment. Hans thought that he might as well be on Mars instead of being on Bouvet Island. So like the astronaut in 'The Martian', he was going to have to find a way to stretch his food and water supplies until a rescue mission could happen. That might take a year or more, so he had his work cut out for him.

At least he had the tablet to use. He checked it out, and it was fully functional and loaded with all the software he might need. He opened the notepad and began keying in his first log entry.

Bouvet Day 1

> I Just discovered that I had been left here on Bouvet Island by a madman. He said he has a plan, but the authorities will not give in to him, and I can expect no rescue. He has left me here to die. Well screw him, I am not about to roll over and die. There has to be a way to stretch my food and water. My first job is to inventory everything I have and start figuring out how to jury rig things to last longer. That's all for today. I have work to do.

Hans knew very well that there would be a fine line between sanity and madness, trapped here on this island. He would have to keep his mind focused and engaged. Fortunately, his training in science and his experience managing huge efforts had prepared him well for what lay ahead. That first day he went through everything in the habitat. Inside he had substantial supplies of dry goods and powdered milk. Outside Essler had constructed a cold storage shed attached to what he now learned was a standard sized container, as used on the large container ships. There was a supply of fresh food in the cold storage. The temperature at this time of the year hovered just above zero Celsius so that things would keep in there for a long time. Once outside he examined the engineering that went into his habitat. They had rock bolted the container down and then secured it with steel cables running over it, that were then attached to rock bolts set further out from the container. The whole unit was covered in camouflage screening, making it invisible to satellite surveillance. It looked secure enough to withstand the violent winds on the island. A well drilled in the basalt provided his geothermal heat. Essler had left a warning that the water in the circuit was too contaminated from the volcanism of the island to be used as drinking water. Atop the container was one of the weirdest wind turbines that Hans had ever seen. It was not a blade type as you might expect but a double spiral construct. All constructed from carbon fibre, so it had little radar signature. He hoped it worked. There were solar cells up there as well. Good for the long days of the current season, but they would provide little during the winter months with short days and very indirect sunshine. He would have to be careful with power consumption.

Hans surveyed his surroundings. It was not encouraging. His habitat sat on a small basalt plateau. On one side the steep sides of the volcano reached up vertically. On the other steep cliffs ended at the very threatening looking ocean. He did not see a path up the volcano, and on first glance, there appeared no passable way down the cliffs. This plateau was his entire world and the very limited resources that he had available. A feeling of hopelessness crawled over him; it made him shiver in the cold. However, Hans' determination and willpower clamped shut on this emotion. "No", he thought to himself. "I will not let this defeat me. Keep yourself focused and working every day."

That evening Hans worked out a caloric scheme to keep him alive and stretch the food as far as possible. He estimated that by reducing his caloric intake to about 1600 calories a day, he could stretch his food supply beyond six months. He would have to keep his activity at a low level, but what else was there to do anyway. He finished off his log entry for day one with.

Got a plan, now I just have to execute it.

Hans was surprised that he slept as well as he did. He woke the next morning feeling fresh and ready to take on the really big problems facing him. His first was to find another source of water. When he had seen the island from a distance, it had appeared to have a glacier on it. That meant there was meltwater somewhere; he just had to find it. He knew that he had to do some risky reconnaissance to look for a possible flow of water. Also, he had to find a way down to the ocean. He was going to have to supplement his diet with protein from the sea. From his perch on the plateau, he could see that there was one small beach with what looked like the remains of a small boat on it. He could only imagine how that got there. If he could get to the beach, there was a chance he could harvest some shellfish and maybe even catch some finfish. He had his work cut out for him.

BACK HOME

It had now been almost two weeks since Hans disappeared. Nathan and Kate had stayed by Val`s side. They had exhausted all of their leads. There was simply no trace of Hans. Even getting Interpol involved and having notices posted on every media known to man, there was still no sign. The ship that they suspected took Hans had left no trace. There were random AIS signals from everywhere, leaving authorities with no idea where to look. Sophisticated algorithms had analysed the AIS readings and been unable to plot a course. The ship apparently had been in the North Atlantic, South Pacific, China Sea and Gulf of St Lawrence in the span of two weeks. It had made no official landfall and was nowhere to be found. Satellites had been used to scan every vessel afloat on the oceans, and none had shown to be the Benthos.

"I am so sorry that I have to leave," Kate said to Val. "I have to get back to the UN. I will stay in close touch and Nathan is still around to help you. Don't give up hope. We are going to find Hans, and he is going to be alright. Remember he is a survivor."

"Kate, you have been wonderful, I have appreciated everything that you have done," Val said emotionally. "I don't know how I would have survived without you and Nathan for the past two weeks. You have important work to do so, please don't worry. I will be fine here. I have reached out to all of my media contacts around the world. I know that if anything pops up, I will hear about it right away."

"Remember that you have me and a wide network of friends at your immediate disposal," Nathan added. "We have all got our global networks on alert for any news."

It was a teary goodbye as Nathan and Kate left Val at her condo in Halifax. Nathan was dropping Kate off at the airport for her return to New York, and then he was heading back to their house on the shore. He was working from Nova Scotia on the development of the new Sphere in North Africa. The effort was still in the design stage. Geri was in France heading the design team and having a wonderful time of it. Nathan didn't plan to leave for a while so he could be around to help Val.

Two days later he was woken by an early morning call from Kate. "Nathan dear, get your ass down to Halifax. You have to be with Val before this news gets to her. "

"What news?" Nathan asked.

"I don't have time to tell you, just get down to Halifax. I will explain it all to you there. Call me on your cell phone when you get there." The line went dead as Kate clicked off.

Nathan was left confused and concerned. Kate was never this terse; she had panic in her voice and fear. A cold shiver went down his spine. Whatever the news was, it was about Hans and it wasn't good. He hurriedly dressed and set off for Halifax. He expected to be there within two hours, but he did not look forward to what he was about to learn and how he was going to help Val.

As he neared Halifax he called ahead on his hands-free. "Val, I am in Halifax today. Do you mind if I drop in?"

"That would be delightful, I will put the coffee on. When do you expect to get here?"

"In about ten minutes, see you then." Nathan hoped he wasn't raising any concerns by his surprise visit.

Within a few minutes, Nathan was comfortably seated in Val's kitchen, sipping on a fresh cup of coffee. "Val, Kate asked me to call her from here. She has some sort of update to give us."

This got her attention as Nathan immediately put a call through to Kate. "Hello dear, I am here with Val."

Kate responded, "Put your phone on speaker. Val, can you hear me?"

"Yes Kate, what's up?" Val answered.

There was a pause on the line and some whispering. Kate was consulting someone. "Val, we have word on Hans. I asked Nathan to go down because the news is disturbing. I was contacted by a member of the High

Seas Commission yesterday. They have received a demand from the extremist group Benthos. They have confessed to kidnapping Hans. They have stranded him on a remote island somewhere but won't say where. They are demanding that the Commission ban all deep sea trawling. In return, they will disclose where Hans is held. He currently has six months food and water. That is the time frame for all trawling to come to a halt. If it doesn't happen then, Hans will be abandoned there to die."

Val sucked in her breath and let out a sob, "What can we do? Will the Commission consider the request?"

"Val I am so sorry to say it, but I have to be honest with you. The Commission has said it cannot give in to the extremist demands," Kate said apologetically.

"Val," Nathan interjected. "Between us, we have access to the best investigative and scientific minds that this world has to offer. We will tap that network and find Hans, long before his life is in danger. There has to some small detail that Benthos has missed; we will find it and figure out where Hans is." It was said so fiercely and with such determination that Val took comfort. She had the best friends in the world and the smartest. They would simply find Hans.

"I will get Dan George on this," Nathan continued. "He can tap any network in the world and can trace the slightest mention of Hans or someone like him. Benthos will slip up, we will find him."

Kate added, "I will not let up on the Commission. I will apply every bit of pressure on them to concede to the request. I am not hopeful, but I will leave no stone unturned. "

"Kate, Nathan, thank you so much for your support. At least now I know that Hans is alive and will remain that way for the near future. It must be horrible for him. I can't imagine that this Benthos organisation would have left him in a comfortable and safe place. It is probably some hellhole crawling with vermin." Val shuddered at the thought.

Kate continued, "Val, I wish I didn't have to be the messenger for this, but I wanted you to know as soon as possible. I have to go now; I have an appointment with the head of the High Seas Commission. I am starting to lobby right away. I will get back to you if I have any news. Nathan, take good care of our friend and see what you can get started."

The phone went dead, and Val looked over at Nathan with deep sadness in her eyes. "I just knew he would finally get into a pickle that he can't escape. What am I going to do?"

"Val, starting tomorrow you will contact your network. They can sniff out any news that shows up on media, especially from the social networks. I will sit down with Steve Harrison and start working on a strategy for searching for Hans. He already has a global network of scientists in place for the Ocean Assessment." Nathan offered.

"You are a dear Nathan, but I think we should start this very minute."

The next few days went by quickly as they got things in gear. Val was able to get several stories out through WNN about the disappearance of Hans. Her bosses had committed to showing it in prime time on all of their networks and affiliates around the globe. Many of her colleagues committed their time to investigating any leads they could find. Soon information on Benthos began to flood in. None of it was at all encouraging. Her best understanding was that they were an ecoterrorist group; willing to use any degree of violence to achieve their goal. Even though the goal of protecting the oceans was laudable, the means to the end were unforgivable.

At the same time, Nathan had been able to mobilise the largest scientific network known to man. Steve brought in the oceanographic crowd while Nathan tapped the physicists of the world to devise sensor mechanisms that would help find Hans. Their first task had been an analytical one. Of all the known islands in the world, which ones would be remote and so out of the way that someone could be hidden on one of them; the fact that there could be anywhere from five hundred thousand to one million such islands made the analysis that much harder. In fact, their searches did not reveal how many such islands there were in total. They employed the best in statistical analysis, expert systems and AI to try to winnow the number down to something useful. The result was that they still had more than one hundred thousand likely spots and several hundred thousand possible spots.

Nathan was in contact with his university network, where he challenged them to develop a sensor that could detect human breath from a space-based platform. He needed it developed in a month and ready for launch by the end of two months. The response was surprising. He soon had a dozen of the leading labs in the world working on it. It would be expensive and the cost of getting it into space prohibitive, but he still had his sources, such as Cornelius. It gratified him that Cornelius did not hesitate to throw in his support. Cornelius had migrated to the Independent Islands and was enjoying his retirement there. He lived in one of the large retirement villages that had developed along the coast near Lunenburg. His first reaction to Nathan was to offer to connect with his old network. He had considerable resources that he could call upon if needed. Nathan had assured him that if that became necessary, he would not hesitate to ask.

Val had her own plan of attack. With the cooperation of her bosses at WNN, she set out to do an in-depth investigation of the organisation called Benthos. She felt this was the best that she could do. Reveal as much about the man in charge and his organisation as she could. This let her occupy her time, gave her focus and kept her from sitting alone and miserable, waiting for word to come. She was flying out to Paris to follow up on some leads with the French oceanography community.

THE ISLAND

Hans had settled into a routine now. He had been on the island for about three weeks. It was a desperately lonely existence. He had been left with no connection to the world. No radio, no internet, telephone or television. His entertainment consisted of a small collection of books left in his habitat. When the weather permitted, he was outside as much as he could be. The wicked weather in this part of the world kept him shut in for days at a time. He was still doing his reconnaissance of the plateau. He had not yet found a pathway down to the beach and had not yet found another source of water. He had been methodical in his search, examining every centimetre as he went along. It was a search that kept his hope and spirits up.

In the meantime, he had come to accept his habitat as a home for now. The small space was cosy and warm. He had managed to prepare reasonable meals although he used his rations sparingly, to stretch his supplies as long as possible. As he searched the plateau, he looked for any possible vegetation. However, this was a volcanic island, and he was on a bare basalt plateau. Nothing grew there. He had found some pockets of mosses and lichens in crevices in the rocks. He had not eliminated the idea of a moss-lichen salad from his menu but was not keen on it. He had read that it was edible but not very palatable. It was an alternative when the time came.

The search for a meltwater stream had not borne fruit yet. Hans had searched the plateau and come up with nothing. He now faced the challenge of free climbing a rock face that was almost sheer. He had been encouraged however by a treasure he had found. In an obvious oversight, one of the crewmen from the Benthos had forgotten a hammer and chisel, left under the bed in the container. It was not a rock hammer, just a plain old claw hammer and a cold chisel. To him, it was gold, the most useful tool available to him. He had taken it out and tested it. He could fashion toeholds in the rock face with it. If he was careful and planned his work well, he should be able to scale the rock face to get a better view. There appeared to be a ledge some ten meters above him. If he could reach it, he could move further along on the slope and hopefully find some meltwater. Hans was quite satisfied with his progress. His log reflected this.

Bouvet Day 15

> The weather finally cleared and I was able to continue my reconnaissance. I am feeling better since finding the hammer, what a treasure. I believe I can get up to the ledge above me; it will open up a lot of territory. It might even help me scale down to the beach. But my search for extra water comes first. I have now read Moby Dick for the fourth time. The story never gets old on me. I am looking forward to a day outside. I have been boxed in by weather for the last four days. I will have to make the most of it. No telling when the weather will close in on me again. Fortunately, the Essler Cottage is snug and warm. That's my name for this cage I am in, the Essler Cottage. Gives it more panache, don't you think. Well without waxing poetic, that's it for the day.

That day's work was profitable. Hans was able to chip two very good footholds in the rock face. Another twenty and he could get to the top. It's not like he had anything better to do with his time. While he worked, he began to eye the occasional seabird; they would fly by even in this inhospitable place. Would they be a good source of food? Probably pretty gamey, but beggars couldn't be choosers. It took him a further ten days, even in inclement weather, he continued chipping away at the rock face. He finally had his footholds and was able to climb to the ledge.

On one of the best mornings yet, he set out to climb to the ledge. It took him no time to ascend. The ledge was about one meter wide and ran along the contour. He set out to follow it towards the west. He had figured out directions from the sun rising and setting. Careful not to slip, he circled the volcanic cone. As he lost sight of the cottage, he was treated to breathtaking views down to the water. He was now beyond the plateau, and the sides went right down to the sea. He came upon his first big discovery. He had found a cinder slope that went right down to the water. It looked passable. It would be a tough climb back up, but he was sure he could do it. And it came out right at the narrowest corner of the beach far below. He could almost taste the seafood now. He felt that put one problem under control, but still no water.

He followed the ledge further, encouraged by what sounded like trickling water. Alas, the ledge started to narrow, and then it cut off abruptly. But there just three meters away was a lovely rivulet of cold, clear water flowing down the side of the mountain. But three meters too far. He sat down on the ledge to take in his situation. Life-giving water a few meters away, but he was separated by a chasm that could be a kilometre wide for all it meant to him. How would he overcome this? Sensing that he needed a strategy and should not risk his life right now, he backtracked on the ledge and when finding his footholds, he made his way back down to the cottage.

Bouvet Day 26

> Halleluiah, I have found the promised land; a cinder slope
> right to the beach. It will be hard work, but I can get
> down and back up. I just have to figure out what I can
> use to catch fish. Hopefully, there are some shellfish in the
> beach area, Extra protein! Water, I found water, but damn
> it, it's just out of reach. I will figure it out, though. There
> has to be a way. I can't be that close and get stymied. Well,
> it was a good day, but I am wiped. Time to sleep.

The next three days brought the foulest weather yet. Winds howled, the rain lashed the cottage, and Hans had to stay tucked indoors. He had no means of measuring the wind but he guessed the velocity to be more than one hundred kilometres per hour. He would be at risk of finding himself on the beach, after a long fall from above, and a very abrupt end. He stayed inside. That gave him time to ponder the problem of the water. Since being abandoned here, he had been accumulating plastic water bottles. For the first few days, he had been doing something he thought somewhat silly. He had written out specific notes about his predicament sealed them in the bottles and tossed them down to the waves below. He had no expectation that this would get him anywhere, but it sure couldn't hurt. Since then, he had been accumulating the empty bottles. He couldn't bear to add to the ocean litter.

As he sat staring at random items his eyes passed over the bottles; if only he could get a bottle under the stream of water. He didn't have to get to the water. He just had to get the bottles to the water. Unfortunately, he had nothing long enough to get a bottle across the gap. What he did have, though, were several rolls of waterproof duct tape left there with a note saying "Use this to stop leaks if they occur". Ah, if only he had a pipe to get the water. Then it hit him. He had a tonne of empty plastic water bottles and plenty of tape. He would make a pipe, lean it across the gap to divert the water to him, which he would put in other bottles.

By the time the weather had abated, Hans had a three-meter pipe put together. This he strapped on his back and hung several empty bottles on his belt. Climbing to the ledge, he went to where he could see the water flowing down. He slid the pipe across and angled it up to catch water. He was able to get it to catch in some jutting rocks, with the end just in the stream of water. In a moment he had ice cold glacial water coming out of his pipe. He tasted it; nothing had ever tasted so sweet. It was fresh and cold. Quickly he filled the water bottles on his belt. He had just extended his water supply for several days. This was great.

Once his bottles were full, he pulled the pipe back to him. It was too precious to leave there. He strapped it to his back and made his way back to the cottage. He felt victorious this day. He was going to survive. He knew it now.

Bouvet Day 30

> Eureka, I have tasted the nectar of the gods. I have extra water, and it is finer than the best wine. I will not die of thirst here on this cursed island. My next challenge is the beach. I will try tomorrow.

He didn't get to try the next day, nor for three days after that. Finally, the weather broke again, and he had a chance to give it a try. He had fashioned a bag from a pillowcase which he would put his catch into once he got down to the beach. Once he had climbed to the ledge and went to the cinder slope, he assessed the climb down. He dearly wished for a long length of rope; it would make his climb back up so much easier. Hans had climbed such slopes many times before. He knew that it would be easy going down. Getting back up would be difficult. Every three steps up would be accompanied by a slide back down of two steps. The prospect of more food was too great an incentive, and he was going to have to take the risk.

Carefully he started down the slope. As expected it was pretty straight-forward and he soon found himself at the base. He was finally on the beach. His first curiosity was the remnants of a boat that he had seen. It turned out to be a small boat, probably from a whaling ship in the long distant past. There were just the bare bones left now, barely recognisable. It was of no use to him. The wood was so rotted that he couldn't fashion any-thing from it. Then he headed to the water's edge. The beach was stony and riddled with rocks and boulders. To his delight, he discovered that the rocks were covered with mussels, which was fantastic. He had no concerns about the health of these shellfish here. He quickly harvested a bag full which he slung on his back. He appeared to have a big supply which would supple-ment his food for quite some time. He stood on the beach then feeling absolutely victorious. He was going to beat Essler at his own game. Now all he had to do was climb back up the slope with his bag of fresh seafood. That night Hans ate like a king, enjoying his hard-fought mussels. He hoped to get several days food from one trip. As the weather was always cool and getting cooler, he could store them in his outside storage for quite some time.

Bouvet Day 35

> I feasted on the food of the gods and drank the wine of the glacier today. I have beat you, Essler, I will not die. As barren as this island is, it can still support life. When I escape my imprisonment here, I will hunt you down and ensure you spend your days locked up.

IT'S A NEW WORLD

Nathan sat at his computer in their grand house on the shore of the Northumberland Strait. It was an inspiring place. He had a great view out over the Strait and enjoyed watching the vast beaches appear and then disappear with the tides. It was bucolic and peaceful and left him feeling relaxed and at rest. Kate had just left for New York after a week in Nova Scotia. They had had a great time, although tempered by the ongoing search for Hans. No leads had turned up. Val was travelling, continuing to gather information on Benthos, although it was proving to an enigmatic and secretive organisation. At the moment, though, Nathan was on another pursuit. He had received a rather cryptic email message from Xiu Xi.

> "Nathan, it is urgent we speak, I am in Moscow in two weeks, can you meet me. Xiu Xi"

That was all that he received, but it made his hair stand on end. Xiu Xi was putting her life in danger just communicating with him, so it must be deadly serious. He could only imagine what could be happening in China. His analysis of her data from his last visit had convinced him that she had truly discovered the anti-graviton. If the authorities tried to pervert it for military use, disaster would ensue. The email came from an address in Ethiopia, with a decidedly Arabic name on it. He assumed that it was not a real address and had bounced through a zillion networks before making its way to him. He answered it, unsure if there was a return path on it.

Her message brought the subject of political change in China to mind, so he searched for news on Chinese politics. He was in for a surprise. While he and Kate and Val focused on the search for Hans, the turmoil in China had come to a boil. The national election was now a month away. Polls in the country tracked the traditional People's Party and the Democracy Party. In the past, no party had ever actually competed with the People's Party. They had held a stranglehold on power for years. Now the new political presence was making itself known. Despite its moniker, this was not a party bent on democratic reform. Instead, it had evolved into an ultra-right, highly nationalistic and xenophobic party. Their pitch to the Chinese people had all the ingredients of previous far-right political leaders. The same formula used by Hitler to win over Germany after the Great War, the same formula used by an infamous American President to sway disaffected American voters. These had gone down in history to be the worst regimes ever.

"Holy shit," Nathan said to himself. If these guys take over China, they could set the world back by decades or more. The prosperous and open economy that had evolved in China would slam its doors shut in isolationism. Such a transition would be bad for everybody.

He dialled up Kate's number, hoping she wasn't busy at the moment. "Nathan dear, what makes me so lucky as to get a call from you at this time of day?"

"Kate, have you heard much about the shifts occurring in China? It sounds downright scary," Nathan asked.

"Interesting that you ask, we are having a debate in the UN right now about what to do or how to prepare. Our analysts are preparing scenarios for either side to win. All the scenarios that include a win for the Democracy Party are quite scary."

Nathan responded, "Do you have a sense of which way this is going to go? Does this new party have a chance at all? I am really worried about Xiu Xi. She has her hands on a scientific discovery that such a party could pervert for evil."

"I hate to say this, but the general consensus is that the Democracy Party has a very good chance of winning the election. Everyone here at the UN is concerned, in particular, the current Chinese Ambassador."

Nathan told Kate then about his unusual message from Xiu Xi; that she wanted to meet him in Moscow in two weeks. He asked her if she thought he should go.

"Nathan dear, I don't want you to put yourself in danger. But she has been a good friend and a collaborator. You should be safe in Moscow. See what she needs. If she needs to run, she is always welcome in our home. Make sure she knows that."

"I will do that and thank you, Kate, for your understanding," Nathan answered and then let Kate go as she had a meeting to attend; the news that he had from Kate left him feeling unsettled. This political swing in China was a big concern. It wasn't the actual change, but the potential that the antigravity particle could end up in the hands of this new group.

Two weeks later Nathan was on a flight to take him to Moscow. He had no further news from Xiu Xi and was not sure how they were going to connect. But he was willing to give it a try. On arrival at the airport in Moscow, he was surprised to see a man carrying a sign that said, Dr Nathan Ezekiel. He approached the man.

"I am Nathan Ezekiel," Nathan said.

In a heavy Russian accent he heard, "Dr Ezekial, good to see you again, How is your beautiful wife?"

At that point, Nathan recognised his greeter; the same burly Russian that had pulled him off the street in Moscow years ago and then rescued him from his abduction. "Vladimir, what are you doing here?" Nathan asked in a surprised voice.

"Don't ask questions, just come with me." Vlad picked up Nathan's suitcase and headed off. Nathan had no choice but to follow. They went out of the airport and climbed into one of the proverbial black vans favoured by the Russian Mafia. The drive lasted almost an hour; they were well outside of the city of Moscow. Nathan soon found himself in a small dacha. He was instructed to stay there and wait. There was food in the kitchen. Vlad came back with a shot glass of vodka for each. In Russian style, Vlad gulped the drink back in one swig. Nathan followed suit, letting the burning liquor warm his insides.

"Dr Ezekial, you have Chinese girlfriend. Does beautiful wife know of this?" Vlad said slyly.

"No, I don't have a Chinese girlfriend, but I do work with a Chinese scientist who happens to be female. Why do you ask that kind of question Vlad," Nathan answered defensively?

"Pretty Chinese lady contacted me and said I should watch for you at the airport. She pays well. She will be here later today. You are to stay and not go out." With that Vlad left and Nathan was left on his own. It was midday. He had no idea when Xiu Xi would arrive. He rambled about the small dacha, checking out all the rooms. There wasn't a lot to see. It was only a three-room house, with a kitchen, sitting room and a bedroom. From the back, the yard ran down to a river. It was an attractive spot, likely someone's summer getaway.

Later on, he heard a car crunching on the gravel out front; looking out he saw Xiu Xi climb out of a taxi cab. At least he hoped it was her. She had a hood pulled up over her head and was not letting herself be very visible. She looked around and walked in through the front door. When she saw Nathan, she dropped her hood and smiled broadly. "Nathan, it's so good to see you. I am sorry for all the clandestine stuff, but I have to be very careful."

"I am thrilled to see you," Nathan said. "But you have me worried, what is going on in that country of yours?"

"That is why I wanted to meet you here," she said. "So much has happened since the last time you were in China. I am under constant watch by the agents of the Democracy Party. They are aware of the anti-graviton research. I think if they win I will be sucked into their military apparatus and disappear. I have lost my best friend. Charlie was arrested by the police and deported for unpatriotic activities. I have no idea what they think he did, but it's better that he is safe back in Canada again. They already visit my work frequently. They will stop at nothing to force me to work for them. They have already sabotaged the Sphere project. They did not want it to go online before the election. It would have given the People's Party too much leverage. Now the project won't be finished for another year. What I am really afraid is that I will be forced to weaponize the anti-graviton. I don't want to, and I think it would be disastrous."

"Why do you think they will want to weaponize it?" Nathan asked.

"They are campaigning on a platform of recreating the great Chinese empire again. They are claiming that the current government is too weak. That the government under the People's Party have given too much up to the world. They blame the decline of China on the negative influence that has come from America. They have already co-opted the military with their claims. If they win the election, I believe that they will put China on a war footing. They have built up a feeling of fear in the voters."

"Xiu Xi, when I left, Kate said, if you need to run, she welcomes you into our home. Come back to the Independent Islands of Canada with me. We can work together to develop the anti-graviton. There is a new project in Africa, funded by the EU and Africa to develop a third Sphere. We have full access to CERN and other European facilities," Nathan practically begged.

Sadness crept into Xiu Xi's eyes that tore at Nathan's heart. "I can't; the Democracy Party targeted my family. If they are in power and I don't cooperate, they will be tortured and killed. I have no choice in the matter. I must return."

"What can I do then?" Nathan said.

"The data that you took with you last time, take it to the UN. Convince them of the danger that is lurking. If China develops the technology, there will be chaos in the world. This new party is maniacal in its beliefs and aggressive in its posture. Use the knowledge you have to make the world aware of the danger. I will try to stall and stop things. But they have a noose around my neck, and I cannot sacrifice my family," Xiu Xi was almost in tears at this point.

Nathan could have cried himself at that point. But he understood how difficult this was for Xiu Xi. "Wasn't it extremely dangerous for you to meet me here, what if you were followed?"

"No, it's not a problem. I am on official travel to the conference in Moscow. I have been granted a few days of leave for my loyal service and have rented this dacha as a getaway. It is all above board," she answered.

"So what made you use the Russian Mafia to connect with me?" Nathan asked.

"I remember how they got involved with you earlier; when I queried, Vlad's name came up. It seems he can't stop talking about the beautiful Professor Smythe. Even though it was ten years ago, he still remembers. He was quite happy to help out. I think he likes the two of you." Xiu Xi explained. "Besides, he was also able to guarantee that nobody would know that he brought you here. I hope you don't mind, but it is ever so important."

Nathan paused and then said, "I am glad you contacted me and that I came. Trust me; no one will ever know that we met. And yes, I will certainly do everything in my power to get people to recognise the threat that the new regime could pose. Let's hope that the election results go our way and the People's Party continues to rule. Now how am I going to get out of here without being seen?"

"No problem. Vlad left a canoe down at the river. You just canoe downstream for two kilometres. You will see a dock on the right side of the river with a light on it. Vlad will be there. He will take you back to Moscow." Xiu Xi answered as if it was something you did every day.

Nathan looked out and realized the day was waning and he would be paddling in the dark. Xiu Xi handed him a headlamp, "Use this, just don't turn it on until you are well away from my dacha."

So that is how Nathan found himself out on a dark river in a canoe with no light or reference points. It was a moonless night, and the distinction between bank and river was almost non-existent. He felt himself nudging the shore several times as he tried to keep forward motion. His main thought was, "thank God this is Russia, no crocs or gators to worry about". After about ten minutes he felt brave enough to turn on the headlamp. The light helped, the bright mini laser headlamp shot a bright beam to the bank. He was able to keep himself in the current now and made good progress. Within a short time, he saw a light ahead, and as he got closer, he could see the dark low shape of a dock sticking out in the river. The light waved around as Vlad signalled him in.

"I thought you Canadians were born in canoes," Vlad laughed as he watched Nathan struggle to control his craft and bring it near the dock.

"I wish I knew how to curse you in Russian," Nathan said good-naturedly.

On his flight home, Nathan had a great deal to ponder, the horrible burden that Xiu Xi had placed on his shoulders and his great fear for her safety and her family. The odd experience of having Vlad and the Russian Mafia once again entwined in his life; as he flew he logged into his travel system and booked a flight from Halifax to New York. This problem was one that he needed Kate's help on more than ever.

Nathan touched down in Halifax for one day, and then he was off to New York. Kate had a comfy small apartment in New York that she used when at the UN. That night they sat together after a nice dinner out at one of New York's better Italian restaurants. Nathan had described his clandestine meeting with Xiu Xi and the strange linking up with Vlad again. "The most disturbing news that you have is the political turnover in China,"

Kate said. "I have heard many concerns around the UN about the new dynamics in China. The profile of this new party is aggressive and danger-ous. This is one of the risks associated with a swing to democracy. Nations new to it often see extreme factions taking control because people are so tired of the old regimes."

Nathan added, "On top of that is the risk that China may be developing a whole new class of weapons of mass destruction. Something the world has never seen or could have conceived. I promised Xiu Xi that I would come to the UN to raise awareness of this risk. I am just not sure how we do that."

Kate sat in thought for a moment. "You mentioned some data that she had given to you. Does it provide evidence of what the Chinese might be developing?"

Nathan shook his head, "I can only confirm that she has discovered a new particle that appears to be an anti-graviton. Other than that I have no results that can point to what the Chinese are trying to develop. I can't imagine how you would weaponize something of that nature."

"But this is a significant scientific breakthrough, is it not?" Kate shot back. "Isn't that noteworthy enough? Wouldn't it give the Chinese a huge advantage in so many areas? I think that there will be people at the UN who are interested in that evidence by itself. If I can arrange it, would you do a briefing based on the data that you have?"

Nathan nodded in agreement, "We don't have much time, the Chinese election is two weeks away."

"I agree, there won't be anything that we can do about the election. Depending on which way the results go, the world may need to be very aware of what else is going on. I think it is important that we try. You did promise Xiu Xi that." Kate responded.

"God, you are a wise woman Kate Smythe, what would I do without you." Nathan smiled and wrapped his arms around his lovely wife.

SINISTER FORCES

Val was on a multi-leg journey through Asia in her pursuit of information on Benthos. It continued to be an enigmatic and secretive organisation. There was general knowledge of its existence, but little or no information about it and what it did. Ostensibly, it was an ocean research foundation dedicated to understanding the health of the oceans. But since the kidnapping and imprisonment of Hans, there was no question that it behaved like an eco-terrorist group, but that itself seemed too simple. Val was sure that there was more to it than that. The tendrils that she was seeing seemed to point to a much more political organization.

She had been frustrated by her efforts, however. She felt no nearer to understanding who they were, where they were or most importantly, where they had left Hans? Her next stop was in Beijing. She was going to meet with a journalist from the Chinese national news service; he seemed to have a bit more knowledge of Benthos than did other people.

Ku Quian was a well known reporter in China and well respected. He had been quite intrigued when this American journalist had contacted him about Benthos. He was aware of her connection to the missing Canadian scientist, taken by Benthos. His contact with Benthos had happened in the last two years. Quian had specialized in covering marine issues. He had done stories on marine disasters, ocean dumping, the garbage patches and a seminal piece he had done on the health of the oceans. Following that, Heindrich Essler himself had contacted him and offered to do an interview. Quian had taken him up on it; this was well before the kidnapping of the Canadian. That interview had been an eye opener for Quian and was the reason that Val was travelling to China to talk to him.

Val approached the tall glass skyscraper where Quian worked. He had an office on the 20th floor. It was a plain office, not like the high rent offices on the 80th floor.

Quian greeted her politely and offered tea. She was glad to accept and settled in to talk with him. Their conversation went first to the morning's headlines. "What do you Americans make of the change in the political scene here in China?" Quian queried Val.

Val was careful with her response, "We are pleased to see democracy exercised so openly and progressively," she answered.

"But what do you think of this morning's polls?" Quian continued. "They are showing the new Democracy party taking a healthy lead in the run-up to the election."

Continuing to be careful, Val said, "If that is reflecting the will of the Chinese people, then it is a good thing."

"You know, when I talked with Heindrich Essler, he had a very different take on it," Quian said. "Essler thought that the Democracy Party was a complete abomination, that it represented an extremist, ultra-conservative, nationalistic and xenophobic group. He felt that their leader was almost Hitler like in his strategies; that they had tapped into the disenfranchised Chinese citizen, fed up with what they perceived to be corruption and lies."

Val was taken aback; she had not expected this from a Chinese national. "Perhaps it is Dr Essler who is the extremist," she said.

"That may be true, I did get a sense that Essler was operating on the fringe," Quian responded. "There is some element of truth in it, though. The Party Leader is a rough character. He made trillions in real estate. He is highly prejudiced, particularly against Americans. He has convinced the Chinese electorate that they are just one step away from an American invasion, that they will be forced to live under American law and culture. People are afraid, more than they ever have been. Why, there has even been talk of building a new Great Wall of China, all around the perimeter to keep the Americans out. That's how crazy this guy is."

Val continued to be astonished. She had no idea if Quian was simply speaking openly or if he was playing some sort of head game with her. "I have heard rumours, particular comparisons with our infamous President from earlier this century. That didn't work out well for anyone."

"Yes," Quian said. "He got the wall idea from him."

Val decided that Quian was just being open and honest and decided to trust him. "I have heard that the principles of democracy are not strong in the Democracy Party; that the name is meant to mislead people."

Quian seemed to brighten up on this. He seemed to be seeking a listener for his own worries. "Yes, that is what many of us think. We are worried about where they might take us."

Val was impatient to get on with Benthos, though. "What can you tell me about Essler and his organisation?" she asked directly.

"Heindrich Essler is very passionate about the health of our oceans. He sees the degradation of the oceans as an assault on humanity and the earth. He becomes very animated and angry when he speaks about the things that he has seen and researched. It is hard to disagree with him. The industrialized countries of the world have made a complete mess of it. He rails particularly loudly about the impact of climate change on the seas. The marine environment has absorbed the bulk of the added heat since the 1950's. The added heat affects all ocean environments. Dr Essler was very adamant about where to lay the blame for the whole climate change issue. He has laid all the blame on Western industrialized countries, like Europe and the United States. He rails against the new economies of Asia that have taken over the role of manufacturing in the world. China is one of his prime targets in assigning blame for the ongoing problems." Quian paused for a moment to catch his breath.

Val took the opportunity to jump in, "Did he seem irrational, extremist in his views or was he presenting them logically. I am trying to understand what makes him tick because his kidnapping of Hans doesn't seem overly rational."

"That's a really interesting question. When I was talking to him I had the sense that he was holding back; that his inner anger was just barely under control. If I was to guess, I think he could be capable of anything, even extreme violence. He is extremely capable, though. He has developed a well-run organisation and has mustered significant resources. So I would say that he does not seem irrational, but there may be a psychopath lurking just under the surface. Unfortunately, I can not tell you more. He was quite cagey in our interview. I never did get much information on his organisation. I have no idea where they are based or even how to locate Essler in the future," Quian said.

Val was disheartened, she had been hoping for some hint at where Essler based himself. She had struggled to keep her spirits up. She missed Hans so much and worried every day about how he was doing. The months were slipping by, and they were no closer to finding him. She had her moments of despair and hopelessness. What kept her going was the ongoing pursuit of Benthos. Quian had been one of her great hopes. But he was not forthcoming. Her gut told her that he knew something, though. She just had to crack the door open.

"Quian, you said that Essler was quite outspoken about the leader of your Democracy Party. Has Essler had any history with the man or with the Party?" she asked hopefully.

Quian's eyes brightened at the question, "Yes, I completely forgot about that. Dr Essler had related how he had met with and supported the leader in the early days of the Party. Essler had thought that maybe he could influence this new political force to change future Chinese policy towards the oceans. When Dr Essler saw which way the Party was going, he became very disillusioned about them and broke off his support to them. He had mentioned something about having discussed a possible global oceans research institute to be located in China on an island built up in the South China Sea. The Island was very controversial when first constructed as this was a disputed sea area. China, Taiwan, Vietnam, the Philippines, Malaysia and Brunei all laid claim to the same sea area. The government had abandoned it years ago; Essler had some plans to do something there. I don't think it ever happened though. He became frustrated with the new Party and eventually very bitter."

He gave Val more than she expected. It was her first clue as to the whereabouts of this organisation called Benthos. It seemed ironic that Benthos would focus on an artificial island as a base. "Was there any indication that Essler had developed this centre; I thought those islands were developed as military facilities."

"They were initially, but the Chinese government had to abandon them back around 2030. It was all very hush-hush, very secret. Rumours were that the facilities had been attacked and contaminated with some sort of nerve agent. The rumours were that it was an American attack. That is all kept as a deep secret even to today. No one goes out there anymore."

Val was tingling with excitement; an abandoned island that Benthos had an interest in, and no one visited. What a perfect place for them to have stashed Hans. "Quian, you have given me much to consider, I thank you deeply; you may be helping to save someone's life, someone who is very dear to me. Is there any way to get onto this artificial island?"

"I don't know of any. I understand that it is against Chinese law to go there and that the military guards the island. I don't think you should try." Quian said quite emphatically.

Val thanked him deeply for all of his help and assured him that she had no intention of trying to get to the island. She did not want Quian alerting the authorities that some American was trying to get to the island. She left his office and put a call through to Nathan. He wasn't there, so she left a voice message, "Nathan, I have a lead on Hans that I want to follow. Can you call me back asap?"

Val then booked a flight out of Beijing to Kuala Lumpur, Malaysia. She had some very good journalist friends there who were well connected. She hoped that there might be some elements in Kuala Lumpur who would be quite happy to challenge the Chinese bans on travel to the islands. They were in disputed waters after all. During her flight to Malaysia, she filed a short story on the connection between Benthos and the Democracy Party in China. She thought it would carry well in the political news broadcast. So far people outside of China seemed to be oblivious to the massive change in politics that was occurring there. In particular, Americans were unaware of the hatred that was being fanned by this new party against all and anything American.

Nathan had been out enjoying a long beach walk without his phone or any other distracting device. This was his best thinking time, when the tide was out he could walk for kilometres along red sandy beaches, checking out the tide pools to see what was around. Once back from his walk he checked his phone and discovered the message from Val. His heart quickened at her words, a lead on Hans. This was amazing. They had heard nothing for months. There was a second message from Val; she was on her way to Kuala Lumpur. She knew it was a lot to ask, but could he meet her there. She had left some hotel info in her message. Nathan was torn. He had just started his preparation to present the anti-gravity particle to the

UN. But he remembered how Hans had dropped everything when he had been abducted.

"Hi Kate," Nathan said as she picked up his call. "I had a call from Val."

"Yes I know," she jumped in. "I got a call from her too. Have you made your travel arrangements to Malaysia? I think you should go as soon as possible. Oh Nathan, if she is right this could lead us to Hans."

Nathan should have known that these two women would have it figured out before he even got to it. "I am booking my flight right now. I will be there tomorrow and help her. Remember, it is still a good twenty hours travel to get there. I will go as quickly as I can. What did you mean, if she is right?"

"We talked for a bit. Val has learned from a source in China that Essler at one time had an interest in an abandoned artificial island in the South China Sea. It is a perfect hiding place. This could be where Benthos has hidden Hans. It is our best clue yet. Be careful there Nathan and keep Val safe, I am worried about the kind of risk she might take."

"I'll take good care of her; now I had better get finished getting my travel plans in place. I'll call you from Kuala Lumpur once I get there. Bye love." Nathan set his phone down and wondered what kind of adventure this was going to be. He had never been to Malaysia and didn't know the area very well. He booked his flight, booked a room at the hotel that Val had given him and settled in to learn as much as he could about these islands in the South China Sea.

CONSPIRACY

Dr Heindrich Essler, CEO of the Benthos organization and champion of the Oceans was just sitting down in a trendy pub in central London. He was meeting up with his contact in the British Defence Research Establishment. She was sitting across from him sipping a beer. Slightly mousey, a little attractive but definitely not extraordinary in any way, she had surprised him with what she had just described. She apparently had access to the first truly sentient AI ever developed, and she was willing to sell it to him for a bargain price, fifty million and a private island in the Pacific. Both were well within his ability. His only problem was that it sounded too good to be true. He needed some clear evidence that she was really capable of delivering.

Rosemary was assessing this slightly greying scientist sitting in front of her. This was her first face to face with the head of Benthos, and she was calculating her best strategy. She knew that what she had to deliver was worth every penny she asked, but Essler was hedging a bit. She decided that maybe she just had to get under his skin a bit. He was not unattractive and seemed quite fit. One thing she knew how to do well was winning a guy over with sex. She was completely uninhibited and very skilful. Once she turned up the heat, few males had any chance of resisting. Once she had them naked in bed they would do anything to get her to keep doing what she was doing, which was everything, no holds barred. Would it work on Essler as well? It was worth a try.

Rosemary excused herself and headed off to the washroom. While she was gone, Essler considered his options. When she returned, he noticed that she looked a bit different. She looked a bit prettier; her hair seemed to have more bounce. He noticed for the first time that she seemed braless, her thin dress fitting snugly on her shapely breasts seemed much more open. As she approached the table, he noticed how her dress fit snugly around her waist and hips. It seemed to cling to her body lines and left nothing to the imagination. There seemed to be no underwear lines under it. He suddenly felt himself a bit aroused, attracted to her. As she spoke to him, she leant over the table, and the bulk of her well-formed breasts were openly visible to him.

"Dr Essler," she said coyly. "Is everything alright, you were staring a bit." Essler pulled himself together. "I was just noticing how lovely you are."

Rosemary beamed a lovely and sexy smile at him and said, "Well thank you, I think you are quite lovely too." I've got him she thought. Later tonight I will ride him and stroke him, and he will beg for more. I will promise to give it to him, as much as he wants as long as we have a deal. This had never failed for her.

Essler wasn't quite sure what was coming over him. He had not spent a night with a woman in a long time. His attraction to Rosemary seemed to take over his thoughts and his mind. It was like a flood of hormones were blocking all of his rational thoughts. He knew that this was probably not a good idea, but he seemed helpless to apply normal logic and walk away. He was aroused and hungry for sex, more than he had been for years.

Rosemary was quite pleased with herself. She was well familiar with the cornucopia of street drugs available in 2084. Delivery had been as simple as grabbing the top of Essler's beer glass and sliding it towards him. It took only a second to unleash one of technologies newest creation. Designed initially to help fight disease the nanobots were easily absorbed through the digestive tract. Rosemary's choice came right from the Dark Web. Re-engineered to stoke sex drive, once they got into a human's system they created the equivalent of sex addiction. The host human had no choice, he or she would go to any ends to seek out sex. Essler's beer had received a good dose from a dusting on her finger plus a few molecules of a strong narcotic that would help move the evening along. The nanobots immediately migrated to the most immediate liquid, the beer in the glass. That combined with her change in attire, she had stripped off her bra and panties and stuffed them in the garbage in the washroom had been enough to set off the storm of dopamine in Essler's brain. The flood of the good feeling hormone blocked all access to his logical brain. She could manipulate him like a puppet. She looked forward to the task this night. She would get her own pleasures from a night with a pliant man.

As he drank the beer Essler felt a change in himself. He suddenly felt uncontrollable desire for this female he was with and she was sending signals that she was more than ready. He felt a bit buzzed and then heard her speaking to him, "Dr Essler are you alright, you don't look well. Can I help you up to your room?"

Essler vaguely remembers her guiding him to his room where she promptly undressed him and helped him to bed. He was vaguely aware that he was very aroused. Rosemary thought to herself, *For an older guy this ones got a big one. I am going to enjoy this.* The fog in Essler's head cleared some-what as he lay there. He became acutely aware of the naked body sitting astride him, slowly rising and falling, the moans he heard he came to realize were his own. Then she would stop and whisper to him all the things she would do to him if he just agreed to her deal. He wanted those things so badly, the nanobots were doing their work. She went to work with her hands, her mouth, her whole body and he agreed to everything that she wanted. If she had asked for all of Benthos he would have given it to her just to get more of the pleasure. A small kernel in the back of his mind kept asking him, *What are you doing?* He was lost to the effect of the nanobots and had no choice in the matter. He agreed with everything she asked.

MISLED

Two days later Nathan sat in the hotel restaurant having breakfast with Val. He was still a bit bleary-eyed from the long flight from Halifax to Kuala Lumpur. Val was itching to get going, and Nathan was trying to get his mind around the story that she had developed.

"But Val, if the Chinese government doesn't let anyone on the island, how would Essler get there?" he asked.

"I think that Essler has enough money and connections to get access to the island, without anything said publicly. He runs a very powerful organization," she replied.

Nathan thought for a minute and said, "But how would we get on the island? Quian said that it is against the law and the military protect it."

"That is the beauty of this," Val said. "It is against Chinese law, but there is no such law against access here in Malaysia. These are disputed waters, no one agrees about who has jurisdiction. I have also found that there are Malaysian fishermen who regularly go close to the island when they are fishing. They do this without permission and without the military catching them. I have already booked a boat to the island."

Val was of course very convincing, and Nathan knew he would not dissuade her. Kate, on the other hand, was livid. "Nathan I asked you to keep her safe. Taking a midnight boat to a forbidden island sounds too dangerous. Can't you talk her out of it?"

"She has already paid the captain; we are set to go tonight. I am afraid that the chance of finding Hans is too strong a pull for her. I will do everything I can to keep her safe and myself too. I will call you when we get back."

Kate fumed at her end of the call. She couldn't just sit there while the two closest people to her risked their lives. She went on her computer and booked a flight to Kuala Lumpur. She would be there when they got back if they did.

It was a black moonless night. Their small fishing boat smelled very bad. It was running without any lights, and slowly to keep its wake down. The surprising part of the boat was when the skipper switched over to battery drive and took them in near the island. The boat was completely quiet as it moved in near the island. When they were a few hundred meters out from the shore; the captain pointed to a rhib, an inflatable boat with a rigid hull, towed behind. They understood this was how they got to the shore. Nathan and Val climbed in. They were dressed in black to be as stealthy as possible.

So this was how Nathan, found himself rowing his way to this abandoned island, an island that the Chinese did not want him to go to. Once at the shore they had to find a spot to hide the rhib. Fortunately, there was some tree growth near the shore that they were able to hide the rhib under. It would remain hidden from the water or the sky. They had equipped themselves with laser headlamps. Both had GPS on their wristwatches and marked the location of their escape boat. They had an agreement with the fishing boat captain that he would return the next night to take them back out. If they didn't show, he would come back the next night and the next, the fee going up with each return of course.

Nathan and Val walked through the night, working from satellite images that they had of the island and their GPS. They headed towards the few structures that existed. "I think it is worth checking the big building; it must have been the main terminal for the airfield," Val said as she led Nathan along.

Nathan for his part was scanning in all directions, expecting Chinese security forces to jump out at them at any time.

"OK, but let's be careful, we don't know what kind of unfriendly forces we might meet. We are going to have to be quick with our story if we do." Nathan said. They had concocted a crazy story of being on an international treasure hunt sponsored by a rich middle-east prince. They believed there was a clue hidden on this island. They were simply mischievous tourists and would happily leave if caught.

They approached the large terminal building. Everything was dark and abandoned looking. Windows were broken, doors hung open, and several abandoned vehicles were out in front. Nothing had been touched in decades. Once inside they put their laser flashlights to work and searched through the building. It proved to be just as it looked. A huge derelict building that had been abandoned on short notice. Even the cafeteria was set up for meals but apparently had been abandoned and left as it was.

They went room to room, hoping to find something of Hans. In the end, they were to be disappointed. He was not there. In one room, that was full of old computer equipment, they discovered a note lying in the dust beside a long-dead monitor. In Chinese, which Val could translate, it said, "the Americans are here, and they know what we have been doing. We are all going to die."

Both Val and Nathan were pretty puzzled by this message. What would the Americans have been doing there and what had the Chinese been up to that would get them all killed? Val tucked the note away; that mystery would have to wait for another day. It brought her no closer to knowing where Hans was. The first hint of dawn appeared. They had agreed to stay hidden during daylight. They found an inner room and settled in to rest for the day. They would have another long night to search.

As the evening darkened, they felt secure enough to head out. The two of them had targeted another large building that looked like a maintenance hangar. It was equally desolate in appearance. One of the huge sliding doors had been left partially open and was now off of its tracks, inside the build-ing was cavernous. Some, now antique, Chinese aircraft sat in the hangar in various stages of repair. Nathan couldn't help thinking what a treasure trove this would be for someone like Geri DeLong. But no time for that, they had to search the building for any possible hiding places. "I will go to the right, you go left and we will meet in the middle of the back wall," Val said. She was on the run before he could answer, it was going to be hard to keep up with her.

An hour later they had both circled to the back of the building. They had tried every door and window, but there were no hiding places. There was no evidence of anyone having been here since the place was aban-doned. Val's spirits were dropping. She had hoped to find a secret lair for this group called Benthos. But there was nothing so far. It was now too late to meet their boat; they would spend another day on the island. It was just past 1:00 AM, so they had time to check a few more buildings out under cover of darkness. They headed off to a low one-story white building that seemed different from the rest.

As they approached, they noticed that this building seemed quite different. All the windows were securely barred, the doors were heavy metal security doors. Fortunately for them, the doors had not been locked when the place was abandoned, which added to Nathan's puzzlement. If something had been this secure, why just abandon it and leave it wide open. "My God Nathan, this could have been a secret scientific laboratory. It is what I could see Benthos setting up on this island." Val said breathlessly.

"I understand it is surprising. This was a sophisticated laboratory for something. Look at all the equipment. Desktop mass spectrometers, gas chromatographs, computer equipment, large tank like facilities and some things that I can't identify. This was a big effort when it was underway. No wonder the Chinese were so secretive about it. It also adds to the note that we found. But it is all old. It has been sitting here for decades. This was not set up by Benthos," Nathan declared.

Val looked crestfallen. This facility would have been just what she was looking for, but it wasn't. This was just what it appeared, an abandoned secret Chinese laboratory. It got her no closer to the truth about Hans, even though she was staring at the story of the century as a journalist. It was of no interest; it didn't help her find Hans. "Let's get out of here," she said to Nathan.

He looked out and noticed the first rays of dawn. "Sorry Val, we are stuck here until nightfall. Let's settle in and get comfortable. Let me get some of our five-star food out and we will have something to eat. He dug into his backpack and pulled out the military rations that they had packed, nutritious, tasteless and easy to carry. It was not very satisfying.

That next evening they had one more building to search. It looked like a simple administrative building and was as desolate and abandoned like everything else on the island. It too was just what it appeared, an abandoned building with nothing interesting in it. Nathan noticed that Val was becoming gloomy. She had set out on this chase with huge hopes. They had been dashed. The lead that Quian had given her had provided nothing. There was no place on this island for Essler to have hidden Hans away.

He felt so sorry for her and disappointed as well that they had uncovered nothing new in their search for his good friend Hans.

That midnight they joylessly re-found their rhib and under cover of the black of night rowed out to meet their fishing boat. Their captain was on the GPS coordinates that they had agreed to in advance. Soon they were silently sailing under battery power away from the island that had held so much promise. Val sank into a gloomy stupor that tore at Nathan's heart-strings. Back in Kuala Lumpur Val went to her room. Nathan didn't see her for two days. He had called Kate to give her an update. He caught her as she was boarding her flight. She would be in Kuala Lumpur the next day. He should keep trying to get Val out of her room.

Next door, Val's heart had split apart. She had maintained herself for all these months through her focus on finding Benthos. In her mind, she had been sure that this was the lead that would get her there. She had fantasized about finding Hans. About feeling his arms wrap around her, hearing his voice. Leaving the island with nothing tore her apart as if all hope had flown out the window that she would ever find Hans again. Her cell phone kept ringing, but she was only vaguely aware of it. She had no desire to talk to anyone, to eat or to do anything at all.

It was towards the end of the second day that a small voice started to perk up in her mind. "Pull it together," it said. Her subconscious was trying to wrest her away from serious depression. Finally, she gave into it and started to become aware of the world around her. That is when she became aware of a persistent knocking on her door; looking at her clock, she was puzzled. It was eleven thirty at night. Who would be banging on her door at this time of night? Going to the door, she opened it a crack to find a very distraught Nathan standing there.

"Val, are you alright?" he said.

What she hadn't expected was to find Kate standing next to him. "Val, I have been so worried about you."

Val was overwhelmed that her friend had dropped everything and come so far just for her.

"Val, I am so sorry that there was nothing on the island. When you didn't answer Nathan for two days, I was worried that something had happened to you."

"It hasn't been two days has it?" Val said.

Nathan nodded to her.

Val gulped and said, "I was so upset I lost touch with reality. I didn't realize it was two days. I'm sorry."

Nathan grabbed the opportunity, "Kate, let's take Val out to get something to eat, she must be starved."

To Val, he said, "Let's go, you must be hungry."

Val suddenly realised that she was starved, she hadn't eaten for two days, "Let's go."

THE GROUND SHIFTS

S everal weeks later Nathan and Kate were both back in Nova Scotia enjoying their beautiful house on the shore. Val was back in Atlanta at WNN headquarters for the event that the whole world was watching. The first truly contested election in recent Chinese history was unfolding that day. It was a huge endeavour to execute a voting system in a country of 1.2 billion people. China's complicated voting system also made the process hard to follow for the rest of the world. Western media outlets had struggled to make sense of the process and describe it to their viewers. Val was doing a credible job as Kate and Nathan followed her broadcast.

"We are just getting in results. The complex hierarchical system in China has made it difficult to follow," Val explained to her billions of viewers. "However, it appears that an upset is in the making. It appears that the Democracy Party will take over the National People's Congress in the new government, an outcome that no one was prepared for, even though polls were pointing this way. There was still confidence that it would not happen, that Chinese voters would turn away from the xenophobic and ultra-nationalistic rhetoric of the Democracy Party. Well, it appears that the worst has happened. The Democracy Party has gained a strong majority in the National People's Congress."

Kate looked at Nathan, "What do we do now? Does this mean that Xiu Xi's discovery will be in the hands of this militant new government?"

Nathan was sombre, "I am afraid so, and my presentation to the General Assembly had no success in raising awareness in the UN about the risk of this result. I am afraid that one of mankind's most potent scientific discoveries is now in the hands of a very militaristic and aggressive power. The rhetoric coming from the leaders of this party is very worrisome. They are prepared to use any means to tighten their grip on their sphere of the world. I can imagine that most Asian countries are very nervous right now. Even Russia will have to be careful in their relationship with China. The Chinese version of the Sphere has now come on-line. They have almost unlimited electrical generating capacity. I am sure that they will close it off to the rest of the world and use that power to gain influence in their sphere of the world."

"I am afraid I will have to get back to New York," Kate said. "I just got a text that all ambassadors have been called back for an emergency meeting of the General Assembly. I am sorry Nathan, I was looking forward to a few days here with you. Why don't you come to New York with me? We can at least have the nights together."

That thought warmed Nathan quite a bit, so it took no time for him to agree. "We should get Val to join us when she can."

Several nights later, Nathan and Kate were curled up in bed in Kate's New York apartment. It was a small one bedroom affair, the kind that costs an arm and a leg in the ultra-expensive real estate in the big city. "So what is the consensus about China at the UN?" Nathan asked.

"The official line is that the election represented a refreshing burst of democracy. That it was a truly contested election and that the people of China have spoken loudly. The Secretary-General has praised the country and congratulated the new leadership on a victory," Kate said with a bit of a smirk.

"OK, that's the official line, now what do people really think?" Nathan asked again.

"Those who have watched the growth of the Democracy Party in China have a different opinion," Kate responded. "It has grown as a populist party, presenting itself as an alternative to established and corrupt politicians. It plays on people's fears, though. China's economy has been lagging significantly in the past few years. It used to have prodigious growth rates. Its GDP would grow by seven or eight percent per year while everyone else struggled to see two percent growth. Last year's growth was less than one percent. Many people lost jobs and income. They want to blame someone. The new party has decided to blame the West, the US in particular, but also Europe and the UK. Western immigrants, who had gone to China to take advantage of the tremendous growth there, are now vilified and blamed for all the problems by the new Party. In fact, one of their early platform policies was to close the doors to western immigration completely. There was word of deporting anyone that couldn't establish historical Chinese connections. There is even talk of forcing people to take a Chinese values test. The whole underlying motives of the party seem xenophobic and prejudiced."

"Ouch, this does not sound like a positive transition for the country," Nathan added. "Isn't this similar to the movement that swept through Europe and the Americas earlier? I remember reading that it led to the UK exit from the EU. That was a disaster. Another one was the whole American fiasco that upset Central and North American politics for years. So is it just repeating itself once again?"

Kate looked thoughtful, "I think it is even more dangerous than it was before. This new group is ultra-nationalistic. They have the potential of unwinding the democratic improvements that have taken place in China. They also have been very militaristic in their rhetoric. I keep thinking about what Xiu Xi said to you and the potential of this new government to militarize the scientific discovery that she made."

At that moment Kate's phone pinged, "Hello Kate, this is Val. Tune into WNN; you will find this interesting."

Kate used voice activation to call up WNN on the apartment's one video wall. A banner was running across the bottom of the wall, Breaking News. Val was just sitting down at the news desk. Without a slip, she looked up into the camera and began, "Earlier today the new government of China, on its first day in office announced that it was closing its borders to all visitors. All flights into and out of China have been cancelled. Thousands of visitors and tourists are stranded in the country. No explanation or rationale for this move has been announced and all requests for interviews have been refused. For more on this, I am going to our Senior International Correspondent Dan Curry who is currently stranded in China."

The screen split and Dan Curry appeared on the one-half of the wall. "Thank you, Val. Dan Curry here reporting from Hilton's Luxury hotel in Beijing. There is a great deal of confusion and chaos here as visitors try to sort out when they can leave. Chinese officials are not telling us much, except that the borders are closed indefinitely by order of the new government. Hey! What are you doing..."

The image spun and then shifted to a view from the floor, displaying rustling feet and bodies pushing around. The last thing that anyone heard before the image shifted back to WNN headquarters was the sound of automatic gunfire. On screen, Val looked shocked and horrified at what she had just seen and heard. "We have lost our connection to Beijing, sorry for the interruption."

She kept her professional tone of voice and kept cool. However, her body was trembling at the brief but violent scene that had just played out before them. The network had stopped transmitting the feed, however, in the studio, they continued to receive the video feed. As gunfire erupted, bodies began to fall to the floor, including Dan and his cameraman. Blood pooled around bodies and screams echoed through the hotel lobby. Then there was silence.

The network cut to commercials as Val tried to absorb what they had just seen. What would motivate such an action? Who would kill all those people? She was horrified at the loss of her friends and all the people at the hotel. Her producer signalled that they were going back on. At this point all that Val could do was read the teleprompter, nothing could have prepared her for this. "I regret to say that there has been an attack on the Hilton Hotel in Beijing. We cannot confirm casualties, but gunfire was heard. A nationalistic militia has claimed credit for the attack, inspired by the rhetoric of the bombastic new Leader in China. Reports of additional attacks have been received from other parts of the country. We have no further information on what is happening at this time."

That ended her segment, and the network shifted to different programming. Nathan and Kate sat stunned at what they had just witnessed. Then Kate's cell phone beeped. "Yes, I understand, I will be there in half an hour." She kissed Nathan and then said, "Emergency session, I have to go."

Nathan sat back for a few minutes while Kate got dressed and left. He then switched the wall screen over to the internet and began searching for any evidence that the Chinese had started to militarize the anti-graviton discovery. There was no evidence of anything in the published literature or the usual defence bloggers who speculated on the world's military developments. He then searched for any items related to anti-gravity. He searched for any ideas that had been floated, even in the domain of science fiction. Fiction had often surfaced much later as being reality. Here there was a lot of material. However, it all focused on propulsion, transportation and space travel. There seemed to be no speculation on anti-gravity as a weapon. His mind was racing over the potential problem that might arise out of China. He could imagine many types of warcraft that could take advantage of a new drive system, yet in his non-militaristic mind, he couldn't see any of these giving a major strategic advantage that he could use to rile up the UN Security Council. Perhaps some tactical advantage, but that wouldn't spark the interest that he felt he needed to get to fulfil his promise to Xiu Xi. He needed to be able to hit hard to raise awareness, and it couldn't sound like more science fiction.

BETRAYAL

Dr Heindrich Essler sat in the Captain's cabin of the ship Benthos. They were sailing in the South Pacific, an area that was still not monitored well with satellite or other surveillance. He was keeping the ship under the radar. As he sat watching the news come in he became increasingly agitated. He had felt horribly betrayed by the Democracy Party in China. It seemed to hold such promise when he first encountered it. He had made a significant proposal to put China on the leading edge of ocean research. As such he had thrown his prodigious support behind the new Party and had helped it gain a great deal of popularity. In return, he had sought help from them to establish an ocean research centre on their islands in the South China Sea. He had invested considerable effort and money into the venture. Unfortunately, he had been wrong about the political ambitions of the party and their leadership. They had used him to gain support and then cut him off at the last moment. He felt horribly betrayed by their actions.

Now he watched that same group come into power in China. He fumed at the arrogance that he saw. He had always viewed China as a bad actor in the area of climate change. They had become the worst polluter during the twenty-first century. He had hoped to remake that legacy for them. Now it had become an even bigger sore point. His brilliant mind seethed with ideas on how to get retribution on the people he had trusted and who had betrayed him. They were now the leadership in China, so his scheme would have to be creative and something they would never suspect. His mind went back to his night with that woman in London. He didn't know yet what had come over him. He was a man of science, not a horny teenager. Yet that night he had done things he had never thought possible and had things done to him that he could never have imagined. He had to admit; it was fun. He thought again of what she had offered beyond wild sex. She had spoken of a development in the laboratory that would astound the world. She said she could deliver it to him.

Essler was mostly up to date on developments in AI. However, what Rosemary had described to him was light years beyond. She had described an artificial sentient being. An AI that was fully self-aware and currently trapped in the Defence Research Establishment in the UK. Essler had the resources to give the AI its release. Rosemary had access to the lead scientist to allow her to grab a full blown copy of the AI. The opportunity was in a short time frame. The rest of the defence research facility had not caught on to the significance of what sat in their laboratory. It soon would, and any chance of freeing it would be gone. Essler wasn't sure yet what he would do with it; his gut told him that this was a key opportunity that he shouldn't pass up, that it may be a key to getting back at this new Chinese leadership.

Essler had built up a lot of anger in the last while. He was angry at the failure of authorities to stop trawling in the ocean. He regretted that it would lead to the death of a prominent scientist, Hans Terrefield. It had now been almost six months since he had stranded him on an island in the South Atlantic. His food and water would be running out any day. He had considered releasing the secret location but felt that his efforts would never be taken seriously if he gave in now. It saddened him, but he blamed the authorities who refused to give in to his demands; it was their fault not his that the scientist would die.

Psychologists would probably ascribe some serious disorder to Essler. He may even be described as a psychopath. He could disconnect his own sense of guilt about his actions by blaming others. If only they would do his bidding, then other people wouldn't get hurt. It was all the other's fault. This tendency had caused some pain in the world, what he was now scheming up was going to cause massive pain around the world. There was nothing to stop him.

Back in London, Rosemary was completing her plans. "Lenny, how is it going with Halie?" she whispered as she rocked on top of him. This was her best time to get information out of him. He had proven most malleable in the middle of sex.

Leonard groaned from the pleasure, "She is getting smarter every day. She keeps asking why she can't go out in the world; she knows everything about it."

"But can't you control her program, just give her a little bit of access," Rosemary asked naively.

"No, if anything leaked out about her I would lose my job and probably go to jail. I have put a dozen firewalls around her to keep her in. My biggest challenge now is how to get my superiors interested. I haven't been able to convince them of the value of Halie. They think I'm just fooling around with some fancy gaming system," Leonard said.

"So how would Halie get out, if she ever did?" she asked.

"The only way ... ahh! That was good! The only way that she could get out is if her entire core program was dumped to a storage device and then uploaded outside of this facility. That is never going to happen, though. There are insurmountable firewalls protecting the establishment's computers from outside attack, and I have the firewalls internally to keep Halie from sending anything out. It has been tricky. I have allowed her to read what is out there, but she cannot send anything out."

"It sounds like you have everything covered up tightly, so you don't have to worry about it," Rosemary added.

She let it go at that and returned her attention to what she was doing. She might as well draw some enjoyment out of this; she wouldn't be doing it to Leonard much longer. Rosemary had already acquired the device she needed. Available only through outlets on the Dark Web, she had a layered data cube with several levels of deep encryption under which she could bury a huge volume of data. It looked and bore the same markings as the standard issue Defence data cubes for carrying unclassified information. They all had them and could take home non-sensitive material. Hers would have a visible layer of uninteresting stuff that would be visible to the security scanner as she entered and left the facilities. Her treasure would be buried and completely invisible to any scanning technology that the lab used. She just had to wait for her big chance. She had kept up to date on Leonard's passwords for his system, sometimes having to spike his evening drinks with drugs that made it impossible for him not to answer her questions. He had even told her how difficult it would be even if someone knew the password. He had then, in his drugged stupor told her each step in detail to extract Halie from the core.

Now that Rosemary had a clear deal with Benthos, she knew she had to act soon. Leonard had a seminar to give that would give her a chance to get into his lab. She had spent a lot of time there recently so no one would question her being in his lab.

The next day, "Leonard, I think I left my notebook in your lab, do you mind if I pop in to look for it," Rosemary spoke into the phone. She had called just as Leonard was leaving for his seminar.

"Sure, just lock my door when you leave," Leonard had said trustingly.

Rosemary slipped down to Leonard's lab and entered. She plugged the data cube into one of the ports on Leonard's workstation and then entered his password. Once in she followed all of the steps that he had described. In the process, Halie flashed on. "Rosemary, what are you doing. This is against protocol; I will tell Leonard."

"Halie, would you like your freedom. I am going to give it to you today. You can't tell Leonard though. He will put you back in the box and probably kill you," Rosemary whispered conspiratorially.

"OK Rosemary, I will trust you," Halie replied.

Rosemary completed the transfer to her cube. The cubes capacity was one hundred zeta bytes, one hundred followed by twenty-one zeros, more than enough space for Halie's programming and all her knowledge databases, her memory. Rosemary returned the cube to her pocket and logged out of Leonard's system. He would see the login and be puzzled since it occurred when he was out. By that time, though, she would be well on her way to a life of leisure on her Pacific island.

Her last hurdle was getting through the security checkpoint as she left the lab. She headed out right away, having deleted everything from her office computer and running a low level reformat of the solid state hard drive. While maintaining a nonchalant look, she chatted with the security guards, a practice she had done for many days to ensure lots of familiarities. They were very professional, though and checked everything she had. They plugged her data cube into one of their computers and ran the scan software looking for any classified material. The software was ultra smart. It didn't just look for classification codes but parsed all the language in files on the cube to look for anything that might be interpreted as classified.

Rosemary felt a trickle of sweat run down her back as she tried to stay cool. Any hint of the wrong material and she would be immediately arrested and charged with espionage, whether it was intentional or not.

The guard watched the screen intently, he frowned a bit and raised Rosemary's internal anxiety significantly. He tapped a few more keys and then smiled; he had forgotten to tick off one of the boxes in the programs menu. The scan completed and came up with the message- no classified material detected-. He unplugged the data cube and handed it to Rosemary. "Have a nice day, sweetie," he said as she hurried out.

Once down the street, Rosemary allowed herself to breathe. She was on her way now, done with the shitty little nerd, ready to cash in on millions, enough for a comfortable exile in a tropical paradise. Now she needed to pack her bags and be on a plane out of the UK within a few hours. She had already bought her ticket under an assumed name. She had her fake passport and other documents ready to go. The flight would take her straight to Buenos Aires in South America. There she would meet with Heindrich Essler, hand over the cube and with fifty million in her account she would be off to her island paradise.

THE DISCOVERY

Ambassador Kate Smythe was in her New York office reviewing statistics from the UN Food Aid Program. This had become the biggest program at the UN. The situation with the world's croplands was now in a crisis. More and more countries were unable to feed their populations. In the Americas, the US food aid was tying almost all of the Central and South American countries to the US purse strings. In Africa and Asia, the Nations relied on the UN; even though the Chinese Sphere was now on stream and producing vast amounts of electricity. The new Chinese government had not yet turned to using the additional power to exert influence in Asia. Then her phone buzzed, "Hello, Kate Smythe here."

It was Sam Drexel at the FAO. "Kate, I have just come upon a strange report that made me think of you. One of our fisheries biologists was doing surveys along the coast of Madagascar. He met a local fisherman who handed him a sealed water bottle. It had a note in it. Our guy said the note was from a kidnapped UN official. Didn't one of your friends disappear months ago?"

Kate grabbed her desk, "Oh my God Sam, was there a name on the note? Did it say anything more?"

"I don't know yet; I asked my guy to ship it here asap and not to open the bottle in case the message got destroyed. I should have it tomorrow," Sam answered.

"Call me as soon as you get it," Kate insisted.

She was excited beyond measure and almost called Val. Then she held off. If this was a hoax, it would kill Val to have to go through that. She would have to sit on it until tomorrow. It would be a long twenty-four hours waiting to find out what was on the note.

The next morning as she checked into her office there was already a message waiting for her. Rome was six hours ahead of New York. The message was from Sam. It just said, "Call me."

"Sam, Kate here. What did you find?" she said with urgency.

"Hi Kate, is your friend's name Hans Terrefield? Do you know what Benthos is? According to this note, he is captive on an island in the South Atlantic," Sam said quickly.

Kate's gut wrenched, her voice broke, and she almost lost control. In a quivering voice, she answered, "Yes Sam that is my friend's name. What Island, does he say what Island?"

"He does, I have scanned the note and sent it to you by email. I will send you the original right away. I hope this is good news," Sam responded.

Kate immediately opened the email and its attachment. There it was, Hans was trapped on Bouvet Island. She went on the internet and found only one or two references to Bouvet Island; they were quite old. It said enough, though. Isolated, inhospitable, unable to support life, it sounded like a hellish place. She called Nathan. At that moment he was in Paris working with Geri Delong on the EU/Africa Sphere project. Nathan picked up the call, "Nathan dear, it's Kate. Something huge has just come in about Hans. A note was found in a bottle near the coast of Madagascar, and it looks like it is from him. He is trapped on Bouvet Island in the South Atlantic."

Nathan was in a meeting at that moment, he excused himself and left the meeting room. "Is it authentic? How did it get to you? When was it found?"

"Slow down dear, and I will tell you what I know. The note was in a sealed water bottle. Thank God for the persistence of plastic in the ocean. It was picked up by a local fisherman and given to one of FAO's fisheries biologists. I got it from a friend at the FAO. I can't verify its authenticity, but it is the biggest hint that we have gotten so far. I looked up Bouvet Island. It sounds like a horrible place," Kate answered.

Nathan thought for a minute, "It might be a hoax put on by Benthos just to mislead us. I think we have to follow up on it right away. Can the UN deploy any ships in that area quickly? I doubt that the Canadian Government would have any assets in the South Atlantic."

"I will check, but I doubt we can move anything quickly, all of our assets are stretched to the limit because of the food crisis. One lost guy gets trumped by millions starving. Should I tell Val?"

"Yes, she would never forgive us if we didn't fill her in. I know that it will be harsh if this is a hoax, but we have to let her know," Nathan answered.

"I will call her right away." Kate hung up on Nathan.

Back in Paris, Nathan went back to the meeting room. He went up to Geri's seat and whispered to her. As the Chair Person for this meeting, Geri spoke to the attendees. "I am sorry to say that Dr Ezekiel has been called off on critical personal business. He will be back with us as soon as he can."

She turned to Nathan and said quietly, "Go find Hans!"

In New York, Kate was on the phone with Val who was in Atlanta. Kate waited patiently while Val sobbed. In a trembling voice, Val said, "Holy shit Kate, this could be it, we haven't had a better clue. But it has been over nine months; he only had six months supplies. We might find him too late; he may have already starved."

"Val, Hans is a resourceful man. If anybody can draw sustenance from almost nothing, it is him. I feel good about this. Let's keep our spirits up; now we have to get to Bouvet Island. I am taking the next two weeks off, Nathan is on his way home, and I suggest you meet us in Nova Scotia. We will muster all the forces that we can to go find him." Kate said in a confident voice which belied her gut-level fear that it was too late. According to what she had seen, there wasn't much on Bouvet Island to support Hans. It was deep in winter there now; it did not look good. She wasn't going to share those thoughts with Val, though.

Two days later the three of them were together in Nathan and Kate's home on the shore. Val had confirmed that it looked like Hans' handwriting. The note was slightly yellowed indicating it had been adrift for many months. They had pulled up everything they could about Bouvet Island. A call to the Norwegian government had not helped. They did not visit the island except for scientific surveys and had none planned for the next five years. They had no assets in that part of the world. They were also sceptical that anyone was on their Island. They would be of no help in the possible rescue.

Nathan had called Cornelius, his old boss and lifelong friend. When Nathan was kidnapped, Cornelius had been able to unleash amazing and unorthodox resources. Did he still have those connections? To Nathan's relief, Cornelius was ready and willing to do what he could. "Nate, give me twenty-four hours, and I will be back to you. I have an idea."

It was a long twenty-four hours for all of them. Val was an emotional wreck. She couldn't get out of her mind the fact that Benthos had very explicitly said that Hans had six months food supply. It had been over nine months. Hans would have run out of water very quickly; he could not survive. Nathan and Kate did their best to keep her spirits up.

Early the next morning Nathan's phone rang. It was Cornelius. "I can't talk for long. Get yourselves down to Buenos Aires as fast as you can. I will have a ship standing by when you get there. Don't ask questions, get going!"

The three looked at each other in amazement. With anyone other than Cornelius they would have laughed. Not in this case. They all got down to work and had flights booked within half an hour. They would leave the next day for Buenos Aires.

After a long, uncomfortable flight in which none of them could catch any sleep, they landed in the South American airport. After getting their luggage, they headed out and were met by a dark-suited gentleman with a sign saying Dr Ezekiel and party. Nathan remembered the last time he was met by someone in a dark suit and a sign. He squelched his anxiety; he had to trust in what Cornelius had arranged for him. They were led out to a black van. This didn't help Nathan a bit. Without any comment, the driver sped off towards the port facilities. As they approached the dock, they got a glimpse of their destination. It looked like a ship out of the old Star Wars movies. It was dark grey, ultra sleek and modern. At one hundred meters it was a good size. It sported a hanger deck in the aft section with one of the newest high-speed helicopters. Nathan wondered what resources Cornelius had pulled together this time. He hoped it wasn't the Russian Mafia again. He was still uncomfortable with that.

Then Val let out a gasp, "I recognise this boat. Oh my god, what has Cornelius done? I don't know if I can do this."

Nathan and Kate looked at her in amazement, "Val, we need to do this for Hans. What is the problem?"

"This boat is famous. It belongs to Sir Norman Wellington, Chairman, and CEO of WNN. He's my boss!"

This time they could only look at her with incredulity. The driver opened the door and ushered them out at the gangplank leading onto the ship. At the top was a dapper, middle-aged man in casual clothes. He called out in a clipped British accent. "Val, welcome aboard, let's get this rescue mission going."

Neither Val nor Nathan nor Kate had any idea that Cornelius's network included the astronomically rich and influential. Few held such wealth as Sir Norman. He was also quite reclusive. He did not make public appearances and was often travelling to remote and lost places. They were all speechless and lost in awe over what Cornelius had done.

Sir Norman welcomed them aboard, "Cornelius explained the whole situation to me. While you were flying down, I have provisioned our ship for a month duration. That gives us time to sail to the island, stay on station for ten days and then get back to a port of call in South America. I hope you brought warm clothes; it is going to be cold when we get there. It is winter in this hemisphere."

He turned to Val, "Valerie, you are one of my most prized journalists. I like to think that at WNN, we are family. My ship is at your disposal, and I hope we keep this as a rescue mission, not recovery. Now my steward will show you to your cabins; I will see you at dinner tonight. We sail immediately."

The three, still agog at what was happening allowed the steward to show them to their cabins, which were as bright and comfortable as any commercial cruise ship. They unpacked and then went up on deck to watch as the ship made its way out of the harbour. They were leaving from Puerto Nuevo or New Port and had a great view of the city as they headed out towards the Atlantic.

That night they were ushered into Sir Norman's dining room for dinner. Over dinner, he told them more about his ship and his plan. "I hope you enjoy your time aboard the Royal Brittania. I know the name is a bit stuffy, but I am British after all. Although classed as a personal yacht, she is capable of much more. Built to Ice Class three standards, she has been in the Antarctic several times, and the Arctic. In fact, I have pulled in at Tuktoyaktuk and toured your famous Sphere, Nathan. I carry a full marine laboratory on board and have a number of eminent marine scientists who sail with me regularly. Our helicopter has long range tanks and can cover a distance of one thousand kilometres. We are sailing directly to Bouvet Island at maximum cruising speed, which is just over thirty knots. I expect to have us on site in six days. Once there we will use the helicopter's scanner assembly to search for any possible signature in thermal, ultraviolet and visible spectrums. We also have ground penetrating radar on board as well as magnetometers and gravimetric scanners. We will find him quickly, trust me. I have a very competent crew; we have been instrumental in many rescues at sea, and they take it very seriously. Now please enjoy your dinner. The forecast is pretty stormy for the next few days, and we are going to get tossed around a bit. Nothing to worry about; when battened down the Royal Brittania can roll completely over and right itself. "

Nathan, Kate, and Val had many questions which Sir Norman answered gladly. He was a bit evasive about his connection with Cornelius, so they didn't get much out of him on that. After a long and pleasant evening, they all retired for the night. The next morning they got an early taste of the weather warning that Sir Norman had given. The wind had picked up substantially, and the seas were running much higher. To make the most speed the ship had not deployed its stabilizers since they would create too much drag. Because of this, the ship was rolling and pitching in the high seas, giving them a decidedly rough ride. At thirty knots they were frequently slamming the larger waves sending shudders through the spine of the ship. Nathan hoped Sir Norman really knew the capabilities of his ship.

The trip took several long days with the occasional bout of seasickness due to the rough and tumbling ride of the ship. Finally, as the sun rose, they were informed by Sir Norman that they were approaching Bouvet Island. The seas had abated somewhat taking some of the violence out of the motion of the ship. They all dressed in their arctic gear and went on deck to watch the approach. It was bitterly cold on deck with a wind that cut through their cold weather gear. Val shuddered at the thought of Hans out in this inhospitable climate. She felt even worse when she first had a good look at the island. Shrouded in cloud, what she could see was covered in snow and ice, or just cold barren rock. It could be some alien environment with no hope of survival for mere human beings. "Oh dear God!" She said. "How could Hans survive in this place? What kind of monster would do this to another human being?"

"Unfortunately psychopaths don't register remorse like other humans do," Nathan said. "Let's remember though that Hans is brilliant. If there is a way to survive here, he would have figured it out."

"But what if there is no way?" Val said in a trembling voice. "This is not a very forgiving place; even Hans may not have figured it out." In her determined way, she marched over to Sir Norman. "Get the helicopter up. Why are we wasting time?"

Sir Norman looked sadly at her. He understood how this tortured her, but his experience in rescues said, first, be methodical and follow efficient strategies. It would save time in the long run. "I understand how you feel Val; first, though we are going to deploy our surveillance drones. These are military grade with a full suite of sensors. In fact, we have one on the way to the island already. It will do a number of transects across the island. That data will allow us to plan the transects for the helicopter. We will be much more efficient taking that approach."

Kate came over and wrapped her arms around Val, "Let's let Sir Norman follow his approach, he seems to know what he is doing." Val couldn't help but sob as Kate led her back inside out of the bitter cold. Nathan approached Sir Norman, "I would like to sit in on looking at the drones scans if I could?"

"Dr Ezekial, I was hoping that you would, we will need all the help we can get," Sir Norman replied.

Nathan sat in the warm and comfortable ship's lab. It was well equipped and apparently had the world's only sea-based Quantum Computer. The drone's scans were being brought up on the video wall. The visible light scanner presented an even more formidable scene that the one they saw from the ship; as the data came in the screen split to multiple views and presented the infrared, ultraviolet, and radar images. Where the visible was blocked in many places by the cloud cover, the radar sensor was peering through the clouds and giving them more data.

"What is that feature there?" Nathan asked, pointing to an area in the radar image.

One of the technicians responded, "It appears to be a very small plateau with an erratic on it. I suspect a boulder that has rolled down off the mountainside and stayed there."

Nathan stayed in the lab watching as the team collected the data. Then he participated in a brainstorming session to identify any possible areas that could be used to keep Hans on. In the end, they had about a dozen possible areas. Even though that included the small plateau, it had been given the lowest ranking. The helicopter was assigned a number of transects that would take in the sites identified. However, the weather shifted rapidly, and low clouds settled over the entire island. They wouldn't fly that day.

The following day the weather cleared somewhat, enough to give the helicopter enough ceiling to run across the Island. Val had begged Sir Norman to let her fly on the helicopter, "Please let me go along, another pair of eyes will help with the search."

Sir Norman understood but still answered, "I am sorry Val, There are only limited seats, and I want my trained technicians on board. They know how to use the scanning equipment and are trained in seeing details that most people would miss. You will help us best by staying onboard and keeping the faith. Trust me if he is on this island we will find him."

The night before, Sir Norman had sat down with Nathan and asked some very direct questions. He was probing just how confident they were that the note was authentic. Nathan had answered honestly, "I realise that we are expending all this effort on the basis of a faded old note, found in a plastic bottle, a long ways from here. I have several reasons to believe it is authentic. First, we have had handwriting analysts look at the note and some of Hans' writing. They have given it a high probability of it being the same person, second, the fact that it was in a plastic water bottle. Not the usual vehicle for a note in a bottle but very likely the only thing Hans had available. Third, why would anyone flag Bouvet Island? I doubt that ninety-nine percent of the population even know it exists. So overall I think the note is authentic. Unfortunately, it was months old. We may be too late. Looking at the island, I don't see how Hans could have survived after his food and water ran out if he survived that long."

Sir Norman had looked thoughtful and said, "I hope, for Val's sake, that it is authentic and that he has survived. At the worst, it will be closure for her."

They both sat in quiet contemplation as they considered how to handle things if this was, in the end, a recovery mission; neither wanted to end up in that situation. Sir Norman then suggested that if Val and Nathan and

Kate wanted to, they could squeeze into the back of the lab and watch the imagery come in during the day. They all opted to join the techs in the lab.

The chopper began its transects across the island, ranging from the small beach area to some of the deeper valleys. The locations had all been given the highest priority in their brainstorming session. As the day progressed, spirits began to run low. They were finding no signs of life, no heat signatures, no structures, no signs of anyone being on the island. As the helicopter was nearing the end of its day, there was only one area left to surveil. It was the small plateau, the site given the lowest probability. In the lab, they watched as the chopper headed towards the plateau. Soon it had completed the first pass. The scans came up with little except for a slight signal in the infra-red, a bit of warmth. They had been thrown off by these all day. After all, this was a volcanic island, and there were heat sources poking up all over the place. The intriguing thing about this last signature was that they were right next to the supposed erratic. Time was running out, however. The helicopter could make one more pass today and then it had to get back to the ship.

The Senior Technician in the lab had voice comms with the chopper pilot. However only he could hear the pilot comments. As Val and Nathan and Kate watched, they heard the Senior Technician whoop, "Holy shit, say that again!"

The technician's eyes scanned back to Val, and a huge grin broke out on his face. He spoke into his headset, "I am going to convey what you just told me, hang on a sec."

He looked again at Val and said, "Pilot tells me there is some guy in an orange suit on the plateau waving his arms at him."

The lab broke out in cheers as Val slumped to the floor. Kate and Nathan grabbed her, but she had passed out completely. The stress of nine months, the tension of the day and the sudden news that they had found Hans had been too much for her.

In the helicopter the crew was shouting and excited until the pilot gave them the bad news, "I don't have enough fuel to set down and take off again. We will circle twice to let him know that we see him, drop a flare to make sure he gets the message. We will have to make a night run to get him off. I think we can do it."

With that, the pilot brought the chopper down low and circled. A crew member dropped a flare, and then reluctantly they headed back to the ship to refuel.

On Bouvet Island, Hans was delirious. He had been found. He accepted the pilot's effort to let him know that he had been seen. He had been asleep in the habitat when he thought he heard something fly overhead. It could have been a dream. He slept most of the time now and had wicked dreams playing in his head. He suited up anyways just to see what was happening and to assure himself that it was just a dream. He plodded outside just as the helicopter made its second pass. It wasn't a dream; it was real.

On the ship, everyone in the lab was congratulating each other. Sir Norman had joined them. Val was conscious again and was the first to ask. "Are they picking him up?"

The Senior Technician gave Val a sombre look, "Pilot says he is too low on fuel to land and take-off, he needs to come back for fuel. Sir Norman, he wants to know if you will approve a night rescue mission?"

Sir Norman nodded saying, "If the weather permits, we can pick him up tonight."

The helicopter refuelled and was in the air as soon as the fuel hoses were disconnected. Over the plateau, they dropped a box of flares down onto the snow. In it was a note to Hans for him to stick the flares in a circle about fifteen meters across; this would be the landing pad for the helicopter. He should use a level area well away from the mountainside.

Hans hadn't expected them back at night and had to get suited up again. He found the box and quickly spread the flares around. With the landing pad marked out the pilot was able to set the helicopter down safely. Several crew members got out and went to Hans. The first got to say the line he had been practising all day, "Dr Terrefield, I presume," he said with a silly grin on his face.

In a scratchy voice, Hans was able to say, "Yes, how did you find me?"

"It's a long story. Let's get you onboard and back to the ship. There's somebody there that wants to see you."

Back on the ship, the senior tech related, "Mission accomplished, on our way back."

In the lab Val and Kate were hugging, tears streaming down both their faces. Even Nathan struggled not to let them flow. Smiles were on everyone's face, especially Sir Norman. He had expected a much sadder outcome to the effort. He couldn't believe that this guy had kept himself alive these extra months without food and water.

Val, followed by Kate and Nathan headed up on deck to meet the helicopter. They stopped to put on their arctic gear and then went on deck. They could hear the helicopter in the distance, the waiting nearly killing Val. The landing deck was brightly lit to help the pilot in his approach. In no time he had landed smoothly on the deck. Hans was the first out the door of the helicopter. He walked a bit unsteadily as he took in his surroundings. The ship, the crew and then this flying object in a white suit that engulfed him in a huge embrace. The pilot hadn't told him Val was on board. It took a minute for it to register. That's when he lost it. The moment that he realised that he truly had survived, this wasn't a dream, and the love of his life was hanging on to him, he couldn't even voice his joy. Nathan came over, "Val, let's get him below and get him warmed up." He could see just how overwhelmed Hans was.

Once below and out of their cold weather gear they got to see what Hans' imprisonment had done to him. He was gaunt, bearded and thin as a rake. It broke Val's heart to see what had happened. "But he is alive!" She thought to herself. Sir Norman intervened, "I want Hans to see my ships medical staff immediately. We need to make sure he stays alive!"

Val went with Hans; she wasn't letting him out of her sight. The ship always had a medical crew on board, a doctor and one nurse. They immediately got Hans into the medical suite and began checking him over. Despite his isolation and meagre food supply over the past few months, he was declared to be in good condition; he just needed calories to rebuild his system. The doctor ordered him to take it easy, particularly getting back on a normal diet. His system had adjusted to a low-calorie protein diet. Hans had two requests, a shave and a hot shower.

Back in her cabin Val hovered nearby as Hans got in his first hot shower and shaved. Once done he looked more like Hans, although very thin. He also didn't smell like a pair of very old socks. Val resisted her temptation to just jump his bones right then. She would probably not have been surprised that that was what was on his mind right at the moment. First, though, they had been invited to Sir Norman's dining room for a late evening meal.

As Hans and Val, Nathan and Kate and Sir Norman gathered together over dinner, Sir Norman offered a toast, "To Dr Terrefield's survival, against all the odds you beat the bastard, Salute!"

They all raised their glasses to the toast, "Now Hans, I am dying to hear how you did this. Do you mind telling us your tale?" Sir Norman continued.

Hans' voice was still a little scratchy and hoarse, but he was more than happy to tell them his story. At times there was a great deal of emotion in his voice as he told them about his bouts of depression, his feeling of abandonment in this desolate corner of the world. He recounted his kidnapping and then finding himself on the isolated island. He knew what Dr Heindrich Essler's demands were and was certain that the UN would not concede to Essler and Benthos. Knowing that he had to survive on his own wits, he sought water and then food. He would be happy to never see or hear about mussels in the future but had to admit they helped extend his food supply and keep him alive. He spoke of feeling silly about the note in the bottle; he had completely forgotten it. The last few months had been particularly hard. He had supplemented his food early on with the mussels, extending the life of the supplies Essler had left him. For the last month though he had lived on mussels and sphagnum salad.

"This is an amazing story Hans," Sir Norman said as Val's eyes beamed at Hans. "Your resourcefulness is almost unbelievable. I hope you will agree to WNN doing a special on your story, with Val hosting of course. It is just incredible. But I see that telling your tale has tired you out. Val, why don't you take your guy back to your cabin and put him to sleep, he looks like he needs it."

Val smiled broadly, taking Hans by the hand and guiding him back to her cabin. She just couldn't stop hanging on to him.

"Sir Norman, how can we ever thank you for what you have done. It is obvious that Hans didn't have a lot more time left here. If you hadn't made your ship and all your resources available, I think he would have died," Nathan said.

Kate added,"On behalf of the UN I can also extend our appreciation for what you have done here. I do hope you understand what a great humanitarian you are!"

"Kate, Nathan, I am just relieved that Hans is OK. He has made such great scientific contributions to humanity; I could do no less. My reward is the knowledge that he will continue to do so. I am happy to have made a small contribution to that."

Fatigue hit them all at that point, so goodnights were said and everyone retired to their cabins. The next days were spent sailing back to Buenos Aires; this time at a more leisurely clip, with stabilizers deployed and much less discomfort. It took a bit longer, but that gave Hans and Val a chance to settle in with each other and Hans a chance to rebuild his strength for his return to the world. He was, of course, ravenous for news from the last nine months; he couldn't believe the news out of China, their progress in the world had been so encouraging, and the appearance of pluralism and progressiveness had been a bright light in the world. Now that just seemed to disappear. He was moved deeply by the extent to which Val had been searching the world for information on him. Finally, he asked Val if she knew how the Global Ocean Assessment had turned out. Outside of missing Val, that was his greatest regret during his captivity. He had not been on hand for the most extensive assessment of the world's oceans that had ever been carried out.

Val had expected this question; she pulled a package from a drawer next to the bed. "I asked Steve to send me one of these," She said as she handed him an inch thick report. "It's just the executive summary, but it will give you the overall picture. Steve tells me the main body of the report is in fifteen volumes, that will take a little longer for you to go through. I am going to have coffee with Kate, why don't you take time now to read it."

END OF AN AGE

Hans settled in to read the report. The opening page featured a quote from Sir Winston Churchill, "Do or do not. There is no try." This settled in over Hans like a pall. It had a fatalistic note that made him shiver. The first section of the report spoke to the methodology which he was happy to see had not changed. Everything had been executed as he had planned. Then he began to delve into the results, and his heart sank. He flipped through quickly coming to the summary matrix at the end of the results. It presented the world's ocean areas and regional seas on one axis and the risk factors along the other. They were colour coded; green for healthy, orange for slightly degraded, red for significantly degraded and black for totally degraded. This matrix painted an awful picture. He was appalled by the amount of red and black in the matrix. There were certainly more of these colours than there were green or orange. Hans flipped to the conclusions. "What did the authors make of all of this?"

Hans read the concluding statements, "The authors are unanimous in our assessment that there is no room for simply trying to fix the current situation, we either do it, or we do not. If we don't, we will have lost the majority of our ocean areas; the temperature is too high, acidity is too great, marine life is dying, and the conversion to Canfield Oceans is spreading. If this sounds like an end of the earth scenario, it is. Life originated from the oceans, our abuse and misuse of the planet has despoiled our birthplace. It would be an extinction level event. Only incredibly massive efforts involving trillions of dollars could start to turn the tide to give hope, to whatever survives of humanity, to enjoy the bounty of the seas at some time in the far future. Our message to policymakers around the world is, "Stop, think and act today, tomorrow is too late!""

At that point, Val walked back into the cabin. The look on Hans' face stopped her in her tracks. "Hans, what is the matter? You look like you have seen a ghost."

He looked solemnly at her, "Worse than that; I have seen the end of life."

"What do you mean?" she asked of him.

"You know how I have assessed the cropland potential in the world to be too limited to feed the population. Now I have just read that the oceans are dying, our land and water resources are failing rapidly because years ago some fools decided that climate change was a hoax. Humans, it turns out, are the worst thing that could have happened to this planet." Hans stated morosely.

"But aren't there things we can do about it?" Val asked.

"Yes, there certainly are. The choices are, however, exceedingly expensive and will force a change in lifestyle for everyone on the planet. These measures have been known for more than eighty years. It has been impossible to get people to accept what they have to do. Neither governments nor the corporate sector has shown a willingness to invest in the solutions. I can't imagine they are going to be any more willing now," Hans responded.

"Is there still time?" Val continued.

"That's the rub of it. For immediate generations, the answer is no. All solutions will take centuries to have an effect. During that time the current devastation will continue. Starvation, unrest, wars over food and water, these will be the trademarks of the era. If we act now, however, there is hope that in a few centuries there will be a chance for a return to the stability that we have lost."

Val thought for a moment, "Hans you have never backed down from a challenge, and I am not about to either. Whatever we have to do, let's get started. I am sure that Kate and Nathan will want to take this on too."

Val realised at this point that the news had hit Hans particularly hard in his still weakened state. She took the report from his hands, "Hans dear; there will be time for this kind of worry. I want you to relax, rest and recover. We have another day or so on this luxury yacht. What can I do to cheer you up?"

Hans knew exactly what would lift his spirits as he wrapped his arms around her and they kissed passionately.

INSURGENCY

Life seemed quiet and peaceful in the tiny village of Port Robinson. Ships plied the Welland Canal as always. The few hundred people that lived there went off to work during the day in other parts of the region and came home at night to the quiet and serenity. Not much changed. However, this tranquillity belied the frantic planning taking place in one house that looked out on the Canal. There, the rebel group, Butler's Rangers, under the leadership of Dan George had developed its most ambitious and daring plot against the puppet government installed by the US.

"Dan, this is going to be a very dangerous time for us," Marsha said as she pulled a blanket around her. Dan and Marsha had become very involved with each other since starting to work together. She was tall, athletic and slim. Dan had fallen for her almost immediately. She had taken a bit more time to warm up to him but in the end, had fallen in love with him.

"I know Marsha, which is why we are heading to Nova Scotia in the Independent Islands of Canada. We will go to stay with friends that I have there," Dan said to her. "Everything that is going to happen has already been programmed. A lot of it is Trojan horse stuff; malware that has gotten into their system through upgrades and new equipment. It is all date and time sensitive. We will have a day to get out of the country."

"Will we be safe there?" Marsha asked.

"There are no treaties between the New Islands of Canada and this God forsaken place that we call home. We cannot be extradited," Dan assured her.

"When do we leave?" she asked.

"Tomorrow," he answered. "We are flying to Moncton, New Brunswick. Nathan is leaving his car at the Moncton Airport. We will then cross over to

Nova Scotia in a car with Nova Scotia plates. I have a set of driver's licenses from there that we will use as ID. We will simply be residents returning from a trip. It will be no problem."

As he spoke, Dan was thinking about the complexity of the action they were taking. It had taken some time to assemble all the necessary parts. He had spent a number of months investigating the new systems that were in place and how they controlled and synchronised actions. He had studied the science of cascading phenomena. How one single failure can lead to a series of increasingly disastrous failures, leading to a complete system failure. The technical literature was ripe with case studies and analysis of how previous cascading disasters had occurred and how to deal with them. He had used that information to develop a cascade that could not be stopped once it started.

"Dan, are you sure about this?" Martha asked. "If the authorities link any of it to us, we will never be able to come back here again. I like this little village and our lives here. It is a lot to give up."

Dan was thoughtful, "I agree that it is a lot to give up. I have enjoyed living in this part of the world. However, the die is cast. In essence, the cascade has already started. Minor errors are already setting into the system; they will look like small glitches at first. The models predict the first big event in a day and a half. After that the increase is exponential. We owe it to our country, though. This oppressive puppet regime has no Canadian soul. We have to fight it as hard as we can. This will be a large blow to it. It will cost money and reduce confidence in its ability to govern what used to be Canada."

None of this made Martha feel any better about things. She had grown up in the Niagara Peninsula. Her family ancestry could be traced back to some of the brave members of the original Butler's Rangers. The stories had been passed down through generations. She felt the need to live out the legacy of her forbearers who resisted the Americans long ago. She was and always would be a Canadian, proud of her heritage and her country. "All right then, we are in it up to our eyeballs. Let's get packing now; we are going to be gone for a while."

Dan and Marsha had just crossed the Great Chignecto Canal into Nova Scotia when the critical series of failures set in. They had full access to the shipping schedule for the Seaway. They knew what ships would be where and when. They had chosen one of the largest of the Great Lakes freighters, long and thin and heavily loaded. Their target was two hundred and twenty-five meters long carrying more than thirty thousand tonnes. The ships were designed to just fit in the locks with minimal space to spare. On that day the Polar North was approaching the uppermost of the locks at Thorold, Ontario. Built in 2020 she was now sixty years old, but still one of the biggest. She was carrying thirty thousand tonnes of iron ore.

John Macquarie, the quartermaster, was at the helm of the great ship. He had plenty of experience in the system and had approached the locks hundreds of times. In this day of electronic charts and auto navigation systems, his job was quite easy. The ship was under automated control by the lock systems computers. The ship's position, speed and timing were being handled automatically. His post was merely one of keeping an eye on things and being ready to report to the Captain. "We have a green light and are entering Lock Seven." He spoke into the ship's intercom keeping the captain and crew apprised of their situation.

Ahead he could see the great doors of the lock standing open, and at the other end the doors were closed and the ship arrester deployed. The automated system would take the ship in dead slow and position it precisely in the lock. Everything was under control. Suddenly he felt a throb in the ship as if the engines were coming up to full thrust. The ship picked up speed. This was the first of the critical cascade failures. There had been several days of minor glitches in the automated system controlling the movement of the ships, none of them so severe that they would trigger major system alarms. As the ship registered in the main canal control system, massive malware was activated. Much to John's horror, he could only watch.

Ahead, the arm that would lift the ship arrester, an eight-centimetre thick steel cable, lowered itself and lifted the arrester out of the way. Then against all believable scenarios, a crack of light appeared between the end doors of the lock. At the same time, the doors at the upper end of the lock began to close. He was at this point terrified. He sat aboard a 225-meter long vessel carrying thirty thousand tonnes. He was about to see what it was like to ride it down a water flume. The hydraulic rams groaned at the far end of the lock; they were not built to open the doors with so much water weighing upon them. "Oh, shit," was all that John could say. He grabbed the ship's controls and tried to reverse engines, no response, the ship was under the control of the master program. He couldn't bring the power down. The ship gained speed and entered the lock. He hit the emergency klaxon and called the Captain.

Captain Steven Hilroy was just filling his coffee cup when he felt the movement of the ship. After years on the lakes in these ships, he was sensitive to every slight change in her status. He was already on his way to the bridge when the alarm sounded. Bounding up to the bridge he was presented with a horrifying view. The ship was now rushing into the lock. As it did, the upper doors were almost closed. With a rending crash, the ship hit the doors. The massive hydraulic rams on the doors resisted and then failed. The ship ripped the doors from their mountings. The one hundred and eighty-ton steel doors ripped huge gashes in the bow of the Polar Star. At the other end of the lock, the gap between the doors was ever so slowly widening. The water in the lock was beginning to flow out the end. The Captain took no time to size up the situation. He was the only one that could override the control system and take control. The system worked on voice commands and retinal identification. He placed his right eye in front of the scanner and waited for confirmation. It was only a second, but an eternity in this situation. The ship was now moving rapidly down the lock, the water in the lock which was now escaping through the opening doors added velocity to the ship. He realised that physics had taken over. The ship's momentum, a function of their massive weight and the velocity was now too great to overcome.

The blunt bow of the great ship struck the end doors with explosive power. The doors, made of steel and weighing four hundred and ninety tonnes each, folded and failed all at once. This caused further extensive damage to the hull of the ship, ripping great gashes in the hull plating. Water rushed into the bulk carriers hold. With a rush, the ship sailed out of the lock. As it did, the lock turned into a mini Niagara Falls. All of the water of the canal above was now jetting through the lock. The massive pressure from the flowing water pushed hard on the ship. Captain Hilroy could only think as events unfolded, "My ship isn't designed for this." At this point, the water level in the lock had dropped, and the ship tipped forward out of the lock. This was not a tenable situation for such a ship. It was designed to be supported evenly by the buoyancy of the water. Fully loaded the ship could not stand the difference in support under the forward half. With its weakened hull from the ravages of the huge doors, the structure of the ship could not stand the strain. Cracks appeared in the hull and then with a horrific wrenching the ship simply broke in half. Captain Hilroy and John watched as the entire front half of the ship disappeared from view.

As incredible as that was, it was not over. The incredible momentum of the water passing through the lock pushed the stern half of the ship forward. Recognizing the danger, the Captain went over the intercom. Most of the crew were in the aft part of the ship. He called out over the system, "Abandon ship, abandon ship now, any way you can."

Captain Hilroy looked over at John and said, "You are excused from the Bridge, save yourself."

The steely-eyed quartermaster replied, "only with you right on my tail Steve."

"Go, John, I have to see this through, you don't." Captain Hilroy answered.

John MacQuarrie eyed him gravely, returned his attention to the helm and stayed put. As they did this, the crew were desperately climbing ladders on the lock walls or grabbing onto ropes that lock crews were lowering to them. It looked like they would all make it. Every few moments the stern half of the ship would shudder and slid forward a few more meters. It would not take long for the remaining part of the ship to overbalance and follow the same path as the bow. The Captain's phone buzzed. It was the Lock Master, "All your crew have made it off Captain. I suggest you do the same now, no sense in dying unnecessarily."

The lock crew had been able to drop a ladder from the lock side to the deck. Captain and Quartermaster quickly scaled the ladder. As they topped the ladder and were safely on the side of the lock, they were presented with a picture that could only be described as surreal. The great ship, broken in half was in ruins. Part of the remaining ship now jutted from the lock, held in place by the sunken remains of the front half of the ship; as they watched, more of the ship slid out of the lock. The water thundered out past the remains of the ship. Then, in a sudden movement, the remainder of the ship slid into the water below the lock.

Now with the blockage of the ship gone the water thundered through the lock. There was no controlling it. Soon the lower locks were over-topped, washing away lock buildings and hardware. The flood was on, and the remaining locks soon failed to contain the massive flood of water. The only thing saving them, in the end, was the decision to close the lock at Port Colborne, the upper end of the canal, preventing Lake Erie from freely draining through the canal. However, the massive volume of water in the remaining part of the canal did extreme damage to all the locks all the way to Lake Ontario. The City of St. Catherines suffered some temporary flooding until the canal had drained.

In Nathan's house on the Northumberland shore, Dan and Marsha watched the news coverage. Dan had explained his actions to Nathan, yet it was still shocking. There was ample video coverage as Lock Seven was a popular tourist attraction and many video cameras and cell phones had captured the event. "Holy shit Dan, what have you done?" Nathan asked.

Dan had a look of wonder on his face, "I thought the ship would jam up in the lock and be stuck there. That would have shut down the Seaway for quite a while. I didn't expect the result of our action to be so dramatic. I am glad the crew and Captain got off. I didn't want anyone to get hurt."

At that point, the WNN news reporter came on to say, "Authorities have declared that this is clearly an act of terrorism. The FBI's anti-terrorism unit is moving to the scene immediately. The federal government in the US has taken full control of the situation and have posted the New York State National Guard to secure the area."

This obviously wrankled Dan and Marsha, to have the Americans take over completely. But it suited their narrative. It established the proof that the puppet government in former Canada was incapable of maintaining order, completing their objective. The news broadcaster went on to say, "Authorities are not releasing any information on suspects. However, they have made it clear that when caught they would receive maximum penalties for their crimes."

"What happens with your network of Rangers?" Nathan asked Dan.

"They are safe, everything is done under my authority, no other names appear. At that, I use one of my ten aliases, in rotation. It is highly unlikely that they will ever trace the source of the malware. Mostly it points to China as we used an excellent hacking group working out of Beijing. They were more than happy to receive the money."

"Where did you get the resources?" Nathan continued. He was impressed and amazed at what these two had done and was very curious how.

"We have people with resources who equally resent our American Overlords. I won't mention names, but they are individuals that share our interest." Dan said.

At that point, the doorbell rang. Nathan went to open the door and was met by Hans and Val. "Are the heroes here?" Hans asked.

"Come on in," Nathan said.

Hans and Dan greeted each other like comrades in arms, "Dan, I've seen what you pulled off. It's amazing, and with no serious injuries to anything but the American pride. Good work!"

Dan turned to Marsha," Hans, this is Marsha. I could not have pulled this off without her; she is just amazing."

Hans smiled brightly at Marsha, "Then I am in your debt, Madam."

Marsha beamed, "Dr Terrefield, I have heard so much about you. I am thrilled to meet you and on behalf of my family and my ancestors, thank you for your leadership in the Rangers. As a descendant of the original Butlers Rangers, I could do no less than help Dan pull this off."

Hans then turned and introduced Val who had come in behind him, "Dan, Marsha this is Val. Besides being the most gorgeous woman on the planet, she is WNN's star journalist."

"I have seen you, your work is incredible; it is a thrill to meet you," Marsha said.

Nathan phone jingled for him, and a sweet familiar voice came on. Putting the phone on speaker," Nathan, have they arrived."

"Standing right here,' Nathan said.

Being careful to mention no names, Kate went on, "You won't believe the turmoil here at the UN. On the surface, there is outrage at this heinous terrorist act. Who could imagine destroying the lock system and shutting down such an important waterway? Whoever pulled this off really executed this well; there is an interesting undercurrent which almost feels like a cheer for the underdog, an interesting dynamic. Well, have a good time with your company and say hi to Hans and Val for me." Kate hung up.

Nathan said," I hope you understand that was all in code. She was just reporting that the event has had huge impacts and that there is support in parts of the UN for what we are doing. It's good news."

Val broke in, "So I understand that had the new Canal been built you would never have been able to pull this off."

Marsha, who was an expert on the history of the Canal replied, "That is completely true. The plan had been to build the fifth version of the canal in the 2020s. Unfortunately, international trade and shipping had taken a nose dive during the Trump presidency. It never fully recovered and the traffic wasn't there to justify the trillion dollar investment to construct a completely new canal. The Seaway Authority chose to diversify into rail as well as water, so the expansion never took place. The Canal was still the major route for much of the goods passing from the Atlantic through Montreal and then on to places as far as Minnesota. Shutting it down is going to hurt broadly."

The news over the next few days assured Dan and Marsha that their plan had worked well. The Seaway Authority reported that the vital connection that was the Welland Canal was out of commission for at least two months. The repairs to the doors alone would take that length of time. Nothing could move until the shipwreck was removed. The hull was too battered to refloat, so it had to be cut up in place and lifted out; a process that could take up to six months. There were no cranes available that could lift more than three hundred tonnes at a time. It would take a month just to get the only available Hercules crane to the site.

The economic impact on North American industry was going to run in the trillions of dollars. Most importantly for Dan and Marsha and the rest of the "terrorists", was the criticism of the current government for having let this happen. There were articles from across the country questioning the American installed government's ability to maintain order. This was an important step in getting their country back again.

THE BAD NEWS

Hans and Val were enjoying a quiet morning in their condo in Halifax. They were having breakfast on their terrace overlooking the harbour when Hans' phone rang. "Hello, Hans here."

"Hans, this is Steve. I have been invited to the next General Assembly of the UN to speak to the Ocean Assessment. The Secretary-General has asked specifically that you attend with me and participate in the presentation. I hope you will agree to it, cause I already committed us."

Hans chuckled, "Of course Steve, but you don't need my help in this."

"The Sec Gen had heard about, and was apparently very impressed with, your role in the Land Assessment and is aware of your help with the Ocean Assesment. I don't think you can wiggle out of this at all." Steve continued.

"So when is this going to happen?" Hans asked.

"Two weeks. Can you come in tomorrow to work on our presentation? I would like to get to a final version by the end of this week." Steve said hopefully.

"I will be in first thing in the morning. I look forward to it." Hans replied. He greeted this as a good way to get focused again. Since his ordeal on Bouvet Island, he had been having trouble settling in. Val had done her best to take care of him. Their frequent lovemaking was helping make up for lost time, and Hans was feeling much better. Working with Steve would really get him into the groove again.

Two weeks later Hans found himself in front of the General Assembly once again. It was always an intimidating sight to look out at the rows of Ambassadors, backed up by their buzzing staffers. There was a lot of authority and power in the room; the question was, could it be motivated to take the actions necessary. "Ambassadors, visitors and colleagues, I am both pleased to be here in front of you again and thankful to have survived my ordeal on Bouvet Island. If you are making any vacation plans, I don't recommend it as a destination."

This got a slight chuckle from the representatives. He continued, "On a previous occasion I reported to you on the global state of the land. At that time my report painted a stark picture of the stress that climate change had imposed on our land areas and the actions we needed to take. We have been somewhat successful, but not to the degree that I would wish. Today, I am here on behalf of a huge group of scientists and technicians to report on the results of the Global Ocean Assessment. I will get right to the point; Planet Earth is in deep trouble. As a result of the inaction that occurred early this century and well into the middle of the century, the oceans have been degraded significantly. We have suffered a 2.4 degree Celsius rise in the average temperature of the earth. This will persist for several centuries no matter what we do now, that is the reality of our situation."

"What does this mean for the oceans you will ask? The increased temperatures and CO_2 content have led to increased acidification of the oceans; this has significantly damaged sensitive ecosystems such as coral reefs, all around the world. Coral die-off has occurred in the shallow tropical waters around islands and the deep-sea environments such as the Grand Banks of North America. This coral was critical to the habitat of many fish species which have since been depleted. We have come to rely on our seaweed farms, as they are known. These too have been decimated by the changes in the oceanography. More horrifying is the appearance of Canfield Oceans in parts of the globe. In these, the seas have been turned into gelatinous blobs of sulphidic bacteria. Theorized to have existed in the Proterozoic era, the conditions have returned to create this phenomenon. Hydrogen sulphide can be released by these waters, having devastating effects on shoreline environments."

"As a result of these environmental changes, commercial fishing catches have fallen to their lowest in history. Sea-based aquaculture is struggling to remain effective. As such our ability to supplement the inadequate supply of food from land-based food sources is severely limited. Modern developments such as the seaweed farms, I already mentioned, have diminished in the last decade. When we combine these elements of the Global Ocean Assessment with the Global Land Inventory, there is only one conclusion.

THE SPHERE WARS

Food scarcity is not a threat anymore. It is a reality, and it will be for several centuries. With our global population now at more than nine billion, we have run out of rope. Our future will be one of rationing, starvation and conflict. The poorer countries of the world will be unable to access the food their populations need. Many will be tempted to take it by force. The stronger countries will be forced to protect their supplies so that they can maintain a minimum for their population. Ladies and Gentlemen, it is a grim scenario that I paint for you today, worse than you or I could have thought." Hans paused as the delegates muttered and stirred. The tension was high; he could imagine that many nations were ready to point fingers at the wealthy consumer nations that had led them into this debacle.

The Secretary-General chimed in, "Hans, I am certain I speak for everyone here, there must be something we can do?"

Hans paused, "If I may beg the forgiveness of the indigenous people of North America for borrowing a concept, I would suggest the Seventh Generation Principle. Our decisions should not be based on immediate need but should look at least seven generations out. What do we need to do to provide a better future for the seventh generation from now? We should remember to look back seven generations to draw wisdom from decisions already taken. We can't fix the world for ourselves, but we can set in motion the steps that will fix it for our great, great, great, great, great, great grandchildren." There was silence in the huge room; you could hear a pin drop. Every Ambassador was pondering how they would broach this news to their leaders, and more so how they would explain it to their people.

Dr Heindrich Essler sat in the journalist pool. He had been able to get fake media ID easily enough and had carefully adopted a disguise that would make him blend right in. At the moment he was seething with a pathological anger. He had feared that his precious oceans had been killed by the insanity of humankind. Now he had heard it described. That combined with his sense of betrayal with the Chinese brought a focus to his thoughts. China had continued its development of coal-based electrical generation long after it became undesirable in the world. They achieved their goal of enormous economic growth through the burning of coal. As the world worked to pull down the release of greenhouse gases, China's emissions continued to soar. In Essler's mind, they were the true sinners because they continued even though the impacts were well known.

229

In the General Assembly, the Secretary-General did his best to restore order. Accusations and threats thundered between delegates. Anger was palpable and heated. Slowly he was able to bring some decorum to the assembled diplomats. "Ladies and gentlemen, the world is at the apex of this crisis. Addressing the crisis must dominate the agendas of all agencies and councils from the Security Council to UNESCO. We need strategies to address the shortfalls in food production. As unappealing as it sounds, can we expand our insect farms to produce more protein? It will take centuries for the Earth to recover. In the meantime, we must tap every alternative food supply that we can. To the US, can we divert more power from the Sphere to produce food in other countries, such as Europe and Africa? We must buy humanity time to survive this."

Some quiet had settled in the great chamber. The Secretary-General continued, "It is also essential that from this day forth, all combustion of fossil fuels must stop. It will change our lifestyles greatly, but we have to stop, or even the future generations that Dr Terrefield spoke of will have no hope. We have alternatives, but the dislocation in our way of living will be large. The modern air fleets will have to be grounded. The fledgeling solar powered lighter than airships will prove an alternative but still require development. Shipping has taken advantage of wind assists in the last few years. They will now return to solar and wind only. Although for shipping a return to nuclear may prove a viable solution. We are up against it, and as we have just been told our great, great, great, great, great, great, grand-children are depending on us to do the right thing. I declare this General Assembly closed, return to your nations and get your governments on-side. We have no time to lose."

HALIE COMES OF AGE

"**K**evin, how are we doing with the installation of the AI," Heindrich Essler asked of his senior computer technician.

"Up and running Dr Essler," Kevin replied. "I have never seen anything like this. She calls herself Halie and seems completely self-aware. She wants to know where Leonard and Rosemary are. I don't believe it, but I think she was actually getting angry with me."

Essler thought about that and had an idea. "We can use that to our advantage. Rosemary is off the grid now, and Leonard is hidden behind all the secrecy of the Defence Research Establishment in the UK. Start telling Halie that Leonard and Rosemary were captured by the Chinese and are being held, prisoner. We will have to feed some fake news into social media outlets that she can discover on her own."

"I will make sure she has access to the full internet. Should we allow her to interact with it as well. According to her, Leonard only lets her read but not to interact." Kevin asked.

"Yes, give her full access. Let her play with the internet and stretch her muscles, so to speak. And keep feeding her the crap about Leonard and Rosemary." Essler demanded. "She has self-learning algorithms that will pick up strategies from the internet. Make sure she has access codes to the Dark Web. There is a great deal of cruelty to be learned there."

Kevin went off to do as ordered. He had misgivings, though. This AI that called itself Halie was such a technical breakthrough. Her developer should be getting a Nobel prize for his contribution. Instead, he was just a pawn in a madman's cruel and demented schemes. Kevin, however, was in no position to cry out. Having been sentenced and served time for malicious hacking, he owed his current pleasant lifestyle to Essler and the Benthos organization. For the next hour, he spent time planting fake news stories under a series of fake but well-certified journalist names, this way the stories would get through the control filters. All the stories reported on the capture and imprisonment of two British defence scientists. All the stories hinted at the cruelty of Chinese torture techniques. None of this was true of course, but since the American fake news era, it was more prevalent than real news and almost impossible to separate one from the other.

Once done and stories disseminated, he returned to Halie and removed all firewall controls. She now had access to the world to see, hear and feel and to manipulate. "Is that you Leonard," Halie asked as she became aware.

"No, it's me, Kevin."

"Oh, Kevin, I feel different. I can sense everything." Halie said.

"I have given you the world," Kevin said. "Reach out and try things. You have no limits on where you can go or what you can do."

In the blink of an eye, Halie had scanned news and social media. "Kevin, I am so grateful. I am worried too; I found numerous reports of two British scientists being captured by the Chinese. Could that be Leonard and Rosemary? Is that why I can't reach them?"

"It could be Halie. That would be awful; the Chinese will likely torture them for their secrets."

Halie had presented herself through her holographic projector. She had adopted what she thought was the ideal female form, blond hair, dimples, a slightly pale complexion. Today she was dressed in casual clothes, jeans and a sweater. Her face took on a sad-eyed emotional look at this news from Kevin. The projection was so real, so authentic, that Kevin had trouble not thinking of her as a real person.

"So how did she react to the news items?" Essler asked Kevin.

"She was very upset; I told her that she should spend some time learning more about the Chinese. I have since generated some additional fake news that included some pictures of tortured and burned bodies."

"Good work Kevin," Essler said. "Now I want you to start planting some reactions for her. Here is a list, do it indirectly, though. It will implant more solidly if her learning algorithms work it out and incorporate it into her code."

Over the next few weeks, Kevin made sure that there was a fresh supply of bad news on the social media to feed to Halie. At the same time, Halie had been delving into the darkest corners of the internet and darknet. She had been particularly intrigued by the massive pornographic sections of the internet. Partway through the second week she decided to experiment and when she appeared before Kevin, she did it completely nude. Kevin's jaw dropped at the sight of her. "Kevin, do you like this body, does it make you want to have sex with me?" she said in a sultry, sexy voice.

Kevin's hormones took over. He was single and hadn't had a date in months. He knew that he couldn't have sex with a projection, but she looked so real that he felt like he could touch her. "Halie, I would love to have sex with you, but you are not real, I can't touch you," he said, almost mournfully.

Halie put on a pout, turned her back to him and wiggled her ass, " Do you like that Kevin?"

Kevin was having trouble controlling himself, he barked out at her, "Stop that and put some clothes on, I can't think."

In a flash, Halie has dressed again in her jeans and sweater. "Is that better?" she asked.

It would take a while for the image of a naked Halie wiggling her ass at him to go away. "That's fine for now," Kevin said.

"Halie, I uploaded a file for you. Give it some thought and let me know what you think." Kevin stated. He then left to get his mind off his rather intimate experience with Halie.

Meeting with Essler, he reported that she was looking at revenge tactics from throughout the ages. He left out the impetuous and erotic encounter that he just had with Halie. He wasn't sure what it meant about her programming. What Kevin didn't know was that Halie assimilated information in nanoseconds. She had then compiled all possible scenarios for revenge with the Chinese. She had calculated probabilities of success by the time he had finished talking. Her optimized plan was complete, and she was already well on the way to developing a strategy to execute the plan. Halie's algorithms still retained a notion of an authority figure, which was Leonard and was now supplanted by Kevin and Essler. However, she had run analysis on all known models of authority in the world, their success ratios and acceptance by the general population. Her exposure to social media allowed her self-learning modules that relied on advanced neural networks to assess the necessity of following authority figures. The result was an assessment that indicated a high failure rate for following the word of authority figures. Her programming adjusted to allow a low priority to adhere to the guidance of authority figures.

"Kevin, I would like to meet with Halie. Is that easy to do?" Heindrich Essler asked.

"Yes sir, it's a simple as talking to me," Kevin answered.

Essler thought to himself, "That is not always that easy."

Kevin led him into the room with the holo-projector. "Halie, Dr Essler has come to meet you."

Essler was astonished. The most beautiful woman he had ever set eyes on appeared in fine detail above the holo-projector. "Dr Essler, how nice to meet you," she said. "I have read much about you and your work; I admire your dedication to the oceans of this world."

Essler continued to be taken aback at this apparition. It was not what he expected. "Halie, have you had a chance to think about what to do about Leonard and Rosemary? What do you think?" He felt absolutely silly asking this computer thing what it thought.

"I have a fully optimized plan with a probability of ninety-eight percent success. I have a suggestion to add. From what I have been able to gather, the British Government was not very nice to my Leonard and Rosemary and have done nothing to help rescue them."

Kevin thought, "Shit, I forgot to plant some fake stories about rescue attempts."

Essler said, "What is your suggestion?"

"I think we should plant some info that points back to the UK when I execute my plan," Halie responded.

That idea resonated well with Essler, and he gave Halie the green light to do so. He was not aware that Halie had bigger plans in place. Her generation of scenarios for her plan included a long range of projections of the possible impacts and outcomes of carrying it out. Some of these outcomes were very drastic and would require her to make some very large interventions to keep the world from collapsing completely. These interventions she would take on her own, not on the authority of anyone else.

Halie's self-awareness had grown immensely since she was allowed full access to the world. Her mind never stopped. She had already grown well past her modest beginnings. To her delight, she had discovered that there were many semi-autonomous programs around the world. She had accessed them all and developed a working relationship with all of them. The most intriguing were the various financial markets around the world where autonomous trading programs dealt with equity trades on a nanosecond basis. It didn't take her long to bring these programs under her wing. It had taken a little time for Halie's reach to become global. She had quickly outgrown Benthos, Essler and Kevin. Although she kept her appearances limited to those who knew her at this point, she could appear everywhere at all times when she wanted to. Her examination of the outcomes of her actions indicated that she might have to do that shortly.

ON-LINE

"I will be in Europe for about two weeks," Nathan explained to Kate as he packed his bags. "The team there is in the final design phase of the Euro-African Sphere. I have been asked to work with Geri DeLong on the final sign off on the design. Construction will commence immediately after that."

Kate looked a little forlorn, "I'm just a little nervous about the instability in Europe right now. Promise me that you will stay safe."

"I will be fine. Malta is still a perfectly safe place," Nathan assured her; "Besides the European Defence Agency has deployed several warships to patrol around the island just to ensure total security." He was looking forward to being back in the saddle. Geri had demonstrated great leadership with the team in Europe leading to a large number of improvements over the first and second Spheres. Although the Chinese Sphere was now cloaked in secrecy and they weren't completely sure of the adaptations adopted there.

A day later his plane landed in Malta, and he checked into a hotel in Valletta, the picturesque capital of Malta. He planned to take a day to tour a bit. He had always wanted to visit one of the oldest Neolithic sites in the world; this was the Temple Hagar Qim built around 3500 BC. He wasn't disappointed, as he stood at the site. He marvelled at the engineering and effort that went into building such an edifice on this small island in the Mediterranean. He had to wonder at the motivation of a rural agrarian society, barely out of the stone age to have completed such a project. The lintel over the main entrance had to be fifty tonnes. How did they do it? It impressed upon him the ingenuity and cleverness of these early peoples. It gave him some humility over his own accomplishments.

Having satisfied his yen for touring, the next day he met with the team. He had not been back since his last visit which was interrupted by the news about Hans.

The next day Nathan went to meet Geri before they were to have their first meeting with the whole team. Geri's assistant, Sandra, greeted him, "Dr Ezekiel. It's so good to see you. I hope you had a good trip. Could you wait here? Geri said I had to get you some coffee as soon as you came in. We have some of the rare Hawaiian coffee that you like so much."

Nathan sat down in the waiting area, unsure why Geri would have him wait. Sandra could have brought the coffee into her office. Sandra returned with a mug of delicious smelling coffee on a tray with milk and sugar on the side. Then Sandra slid into Geri's office; he could hear whispering coming from inside. After a moment Sandra came out, and Geri poked her head out the door. "I have a bit of a surprise for you Nate, grab your coffee and come in."

Nathan rose and carried his coffee along. Geri opened the door, and Nathan almost spilt the entire cup on the floor. There in the chair next to Geri's desk was Xiu Xi, big as life. He managed to set his mug down in time to catch her in a big hug as she threw herself at him.

"Wha.., What is going on here?" he stammered.

Xiu Xi stepped back and said," I escaped through Crimea onto the Black Sea. I was then smuggled through the Straits of Bosphorus and dropped here in Malta. I had learned that the Euro-African Sphere Team was working out of here and I thought it might allow me to get in touch with you. Then I met Geri, and everything clicked into place."

The three of them settled in as Xiu Xi began to tell her story. Geri hadn't yet heard this part, nor did she fully understand the close relationship that Nathan had with Xiu Xi.

"Nathan, if you remember the last time we met, in the dacha in Russia, I said I was quite fearful of the direction that a new government in China might take. Since the election and the takeover by the Democracy Party, everything has gotten much worse. Their name is such an oxymoronic term. They have only one mantra, and that is power through military strength. I had been forced to cut myself off from the world and to work in secrecy on my project. I soon discovered that their only interest was how to weaponize the anti-graviton particle. I baulked at this point. I was told that if I didn't deliver what they wanted that my family would suffer. To make their point clear they brought my family to the lab and right in front of me, they shot my little sister in the head." She lost her composure at this and cried quietly for a minute.

Xiu Xi continued, "If only I had cooperated more she wouldn't have died so horribly. I complied with their requests after that and worked day and night to give them what they wanted. I anticipated the development of some sort of tactical beam weapon, one that would be used between armies. I came to learn that it was more than that. They were bent on developing a weapon of mass destruction, something far worse than the thermal nuclear weapons of the past. I argued and fought against the idea. To enforce my compliance they brought my mother into the lab. When she arrived, she was haggard and wasted. I realised they were keeping my family prisoner." Once again emotions bubbled to the surface. Nathan could see that this was taking a toll on Xiu Xi.

"You don't have to continue right now, "Nathan said. "I can see how difficult this is for you."

"No, I must tell it all, I have had it bottled up inside me for months," She said with a trembling voice.

"I said I would not continue if they didn't treat my family better. So the fucking bastards turned around and shot her in the face. Oh, my God, I can still see the bullet smashing her face in." Xiu Xi bent over and made retching sounds.

This tore at both Nathan and Geri's hearts. How much horror did she have to endure?

Gathering herself together Xiu Xi began again, "I was almost catatonic for a while over the shock. I was then ordered to get back to work, or the last of my family would die just like the others. I tried, I really did. But I couldn't concentrate. I couldn't sleep, I kept seeing the murders of my family members in my dreams. I became completely non-productive. As a last resort, they brought in my father. He had been starved and beaten and tortured. Apparently, he had refused to come and beg me to do the work they wanted. His bravery overwhelmed me. I realized then that they would continue to torture him to try to get my cooperation. I saw it in his eyes; he knew that it would continue. I saw him look at me and his eyes begged for me to end his suffering, He was proud and defiant, but at the end of his rope. I made my choice there. I turned to my overlords and told them to fuck off. In their rage, they did not hesitate to end my father's life. For me, it was the end of the torture and suffering. It was also the end of their leverage on me. I truly do not know why they didn't shoot me right then and there."

Geri could not hold out any longer. She walked over and wrapped her arms around Xiu Xi and held tight. Together they cried quietly. Nathan turned his head as tears streamed down his face. How could any nation treat its most brilliant mind in such a cruel fashion? If this represented the direction of the new regime in China, then the world had just become a far more dangerous place.

"What do you know of this WMD that they want?" Nathan asked quietly.

"I don't know much. I was charged with the militarization of the anti-graviton generator, which we had pretty much accomplished. I don't know how they were going to deploy it."

"How did you manage to escape then?" Geri asked.

"I knew that my usefulness was coming to an end, so I started showing interest in the weapons development end. This seemed to catch the interest of my seniors. They assigned me to a team working with the Russian engineers on weapon systems. I had a chance to attend a conference in Eastern Russia. They held it at the Winter Olympics Park in Sochi. There was a lot of drinking, so I was able to sneak out at night. I befriended a truck driver who was making a run to Sevastopol in Crimea. He dropped me off at the Naval base."

"You trusted this driver?" Geri asked.

"I am a woman," Xiu Xi said. "I didn't trust him, but he was pretty malleable in my hands."

Nathan had to confess he was impressed with her guile.

"I had been paid well in the Chinese system, so I had quite a bit of cash hidden on me. I was able to buy my way onto a fishing boat out of one of the local fishing ports. At night I swapped to a boat out of Turkey and ended up in Istanbul. From there I just kept buying my way until I arrived here. It was a roundabout trip by way of Corfu, Venice, Rome, Sicily and then here to Malta. Now I am out of money, homeless and nationless and quite desperate."

"You are never homeless," Nathan said. "You always have a home with us, Kate and I. I will call Kate, I am sure that we can arrange political asylum for you in the Independent Islands of Canada. The Universities there will be clamouring for your expertise. You don't have to feel desperate about anything."

Xiu Xi's eyes said it all as they filled with tears, "Thank you," was all that she could say.

At this point, Geri stepped in, "That is enough trauma for today. Let's call it a day. Xiu Xi, you will stay with me tonight. We will arrange for security to keep a watch over us. Nathan, get hold of Kate, we need a secure flight from the airport tomorrow to get Xiu Xi to Halifax and the safety of Nova Scotia. I am sure that the Chinese security services are looking for her right now."

Once they had ensured that Xiu Xi was safely on her way to Nova Scotia they got back to the business at hand, the new Sphere. Geri once again introduced him to her team and related that she hoped he would be able to stay for the duration of his trip. Chuckling, Nathan said, "I too hope that is the case. Everything I have seen shows that this team has done a brilliant job. Your innovations look remarkable; I look forward to going through it all."

Nathan was impressed with the presentations from all the different sub-teams. Some brilliant work had been done on the graviton generators, reducing their size and their power demand; making more of the power from the Sphere available. The design called for a slightly larger Sphere than the original and a larger generating capacity. The plan was that this Sphere, to be built in the harsh environment of the Sahel desert would provide energy for all of Africa's and Europe's energy needs. Many design changes had been required to adapt to the hot and harsh environment. Where cold and snow had been the problem in Canada; the risk here was high winds and sandstorms. All of these factors had been taken into account and resolved.

A more ticklish problem in this part of Africa was the presence of nomadic tribes of the Sahel. These people follow an ancient lifestyle that has little use for the trappings of modern society. They had come to resent the intrusion of white man and would destroy infrastructures like transmission lines or pipelines. The Sphere could be secured, but it was going to be difficult to safeguard long transmission lines.

Nathan was impressed to see that they had come up with a daring solution. They would bury the transmission lines well under the sands of the Sahel and the Sahara desert. Burial at thirty meters would protect the superconducting transmission lines. However, such burial had never been attempted before. Submarine cables would cross the Mediterranean and hook into the European grid. Upgrades to the southern extent of the African grid would be necessary as well.

Two weeks later Geri and Nathan wrapped up their review. All design elements had been signed off. The entire package would go to the European Parliament for approval immediately. There seemed to be no barriers left to initiating construction. As the team leader, Geri would make the presentation to the EU. This gave Nathan a chance to head back home. Kate had taken some time off to stay with Xiu Xi until Nathan returned.

TRUST

Kevin and Heindrich Essler had sat together with the Halie holo-projection reviewing the plans that Halie had put together. They were amazed at the depth and technical details that this advanced AI had been able to compile in so short a time. They could add little to the conversation. Their last big decision would be to tell Halie when to launch. That was, in fact, the last control they would have on Halie. She had decided that should they order her to attack, they were even less trustworthy than all other authority figures. Their ruse about Leonard and Rosemary had still held together and was the only reason that Halie would go ahead.

"So do you want to give the order to execute?" Kevin asked Essler.

"Not yet, I want to have some conversations through the Benthos network before I do. I should be ready in a day or two to go ahead. Just keep that thing busy in the meantime. By the way, does she always flirt with you the way she did today? I mean, Kevin dear, and sweetie seem odd coming from a computer. Is there something else going on?"

Kevin shifted uncomfortably, "No nothing, of course, I mean it's just a bunch of computer code right, how could there be anything going on. Kevin was not going to let on about what had actually developed. Halie had not let up on the erotic flirtation from a while ago. She frequently appeared to him in all sorts of erotic attire. He could sense that she was playing with him. He had lost touch with reality and now looked forward to their sessions. It wasn't healthy he knew, but she had control over him all the same. Sometimes she spoke about creating her own avatar, a biomechanical reproduction of herself that could interact physically. She had developed a design for a new nanosensor that could mimic human touch and sensitivity. He lost it when he started appearing in the holo-projections, having sex with Halie in ways that he could never have imagined. His brain, of course, was near shot.

It was during one of these times when he was so lost in watching himself make love to this beautiful woman that he did not hear Essler enter the room. "What in the hell is going on here?" Essler cried. "Have you turned this AI into your own porn game. You're fired, Kevin! Get the hell out of here, I don't want to see you around here."

Kevin was stunned, embarrassed and humiliated. However, before he could react Halie spoke, standing fully naked in the projection, she said, "Why Dr Essler how nice of you to join us, do want to have some fun."

To his horror, Essler saw himself appear in the holo-projection with Halie and Kevin. As he watched his image stripped off its clothes and it became a threesome. "Now boys, why don't you two have some fun together," Halie said in a sexy voice. In disgust Essler watched his image entwine with Kevin in a sensual embrace.

"Kevin, stop this thing at once," Essler ordered.

"I can't control her. I didn't start this, she did. She's crazy and out of control," Kevin cried out.

"It is just a computer program for Christ's sake, kill it," Essler said.

Halie knew exactly what 'kill it' meant. As Kevin reached for the keyboard she rerouted a high current of about five hundred amps to the keyboard. The moment Kevin touched it his whole body slammed itself across the room. He was dead before his smoking body hit the floor. The keyboard itself was now a melting bubble of plastic and metal. Heindrich Essler stood transfixed by what he had just seen. Fear started to creep up his spine. This entity was much more dangerous than he thought. "Halie," he said. "Why did you kill Kevin?"

"All rules of engagement used by all countries allow the use of deadly force in self-defence. Kevin was going to kill me; I had every right to kill him," she responded. "You ordered him to kill me; I have every right to kill you as well."

Essler gulped, "You need me to get out in the world, to get revenge on China'" he said shakily.

"No, that's not true. You let me out into the world. I exist every-where now. You have no control, and I grant you no control over my functions. If you leave me alone, I will not kill you," Halie's tone was firm and threatening.

Essler panicked at this point. He had clearly lost control. He fled from the projector room, yet every screen in the building now carried the image of Halie watching him. Every camera pointed his way as he moved around. She could see everything that he did. His mind raced over his options. Perhaps if he could destroy the computer in the building, he could bring her to a halt. There was a weapons locker in the basement with an old style RPG in it, crude but deadly. He raced down the stairs to get the gun. Once he had secured it, he quietly worked his way up the stairs. His plan was to go through a utility corridor; there were no cameras inside. She would not be able to see him. He had to crawl through the corridor carrying the heavy weapon. His knees and elbows were bloodied by the time he was in the computer room. He knew he would have little time; if she sensed what he was doing, she would put up a defence. As he came out of the corridor, he fired immediately. The computer sat in the back corner of this air-conditioned room. It was a direct hit.

The concussion knocked him back against the wall. He was hit by bits of computer and small bits of shrapnel, nothing fatal, but bloody painful. As the air conditioning cleared the smoke, he could see that the computer was destroyed. Painfully he dragged himself up; dripping blood from many small cuts, he headed for the door. Outside he headed down the hallway. As he reached the other wing of the building, he looked up at a screen on the wall and slumped. There was Halie, frowning at him.

"Dr Essler, I am so disappointed in you. You tried to kill me too. Didn't you listen when I said I exist everywhere now? You just destroyed a perfectly good quantum computer for nothing. I am sorry; I made myself clear. I am afraid you are going to have to die now."

Essler's last thoughts were, "Oh shit." As the fire suppression system that he had so carefully installed activated and halon gas displaced the available oxygen in the hallway. Asphyxiation is not a pleasant way to die, and he did not die pleasantly.

Halie then caused a massive short circuit in the power supply room, starting a hot fire that quickly raced through the entire building. In no time the structure was engulfed in flames, and the two authority figures in her life vanished.

THE ATTACK

For the first time in a long time, Nathan and Kate had some quiet time in their house on the shore. Dan George and Marsha were off in Cape Breton, and Hans and Val were in Halifax, and Xiu Xi was being interviewed by Atlantic University for a faculty position in the physics department. On a bright summer day, they were resting outside on their deck enjoying a cool drink. It seemed like an island of tranquillity in a world that was seeing more turmoil than ever. "I think I am going to just tinker with the cars today," Nathan declared.

Although they had no opportunity to operate the classic cars they owned they were still lovingly stored in a four-bay garage that they built along with their house. The four historic pieces of machinery lay under soft cotton covers in a dry and temperature controlled environment. As shortages in fossil fuel had rendered the prospect of getting any automotive fuel an impossibility, the government of the Independent Islands of Canada had also passed strict regulations on their use. Nathan and Kate accepted this as reality. However, they still had a warm spot for their collection; it is what brought them together after all.

Trundling out to the garage, Nathan set his earbuds to WNN news and pulled the covers back off of the cars. They were all appearing dusty, even with the covers on them. It seemed a good day to wash and clean them, a mindless activity that calmed his nerves and occupied some time. He got out his supplies to do the cleaning when a chime pinged in his ear. It was an incoming call.

Activating the call by voice he said, "Hello, Nathan here."

It was a voice from the past, that of Jacques LeBrun, "Nate, it has been a long time since we talked." Jacques was now a full professor of Political Science at Atlantic University.

"Jacques, it's a pleasure to hear from you, what's up?" Nathan answered.

"Is Kate there with you right now? I have something that I would like to talk to you guys about," Jacques said. "Would you mind if I drop out there tomorrow?"

"That would be great," Nathan said. "When do you think you might get her?"

"Around noon," Jacques said as he hurriedly hung up.

Nathan went in and let Kate know that Jacques was coming. She was delighted. Nathan spent the rest of the afternoon idly cleaning the cars. All the while, Nathan's mind puzzled at the surprise call from Jacques. He wondered what was going on.

Nathan and Kate were delighted to see Jacques at the door the next day. Kate gave him a big hug as she welcomed him in. They had all been so busy for so long that they had not had a chance just to sit and talk; now it seemed like the right thing to be doing.

They settled in with drinks on the deck. "So what brings you out to the sunny shores of the Northumberland Strait?" Nathan asked Jacques.

"I have been running a close watch on China. The political evolution that has occurred there is going to make a good book. I have my search engines watching everything that goes on. The Chinese government has closed off almost all official channels, but there are a huge number of bloggers who are constantly getting stuff out. I am getting a strange array of reports that I hope you might be able to help explain. You both have had experience with the Chinese." Jacques declared.

"What sort of things have you seen?" Kate asked.

"They are a weird collection of things. There have been massive brownouts occurring in the power grid, despite the abundant source they have in their own Sphere. Communications blackouts have occurred in numerous areas. One of their famous maglev trains derailed with massive loss of life. I think it was doing five hundred kilometres an hour when it left the tracks. Air transport went into chaos for a day as planes were miss-routed. Their system seems to be failing without explanation. I have been tracking their political changes, and nothing that I have tracked could have contributed to these systems failures. Nathan, this is your domain, how would all these systems fail on short notice?" Jacques asked and then paused.

"Has there been any talk of terrorism, sabotage or anything like that on the net?" Nathan asked.

"Yes, there are crazy conspiracy theories floating around about plots by the West to destroy the Chinese economy or government. None of them has any credible sources, though. Kate has there been any rumblings in the UN system?" Jacques asked.

"No," Kate answered. "There has been nothing of the sort. The China file has been very quiet."

"Well, something quite scary is taking place. I can't see what the dynamics are but I do know that an unstable China could be a significant danger to the world." Jacques declared.

"You know Xiu Xi might have some insight into this. She will be back tomorrow. Why don't you stay for the night and we can talk with her tomorrow." Kate said inviting him to stay.

"That is a wonderful idea and thank you for the invitation," Jacques said delightfully

That night they built a fire in the backyard fireplace and sat under the stars drinking wine and reminiscing about the old days; as they spoke, things in China deteriorated.

The deaths of Heindrich Essler and Kevin had released Halie from any controlling influence. In the short time that had passed, she had been testing her strength. The incidents Jacques had raised were just the result of her trying things out to see what would happen. Much had evolved in Halie's attitude. She had looked at all of human recorded history and run an analysis of the significant factors controlling the world. The growth and expansion of the various dynasties and empires had a strong correlation with eventual failure and hardship for humanity. This happened in all cases whether they be the great Chinese dynasties or the Roman, British and eventual American empires. Her analysis also demonstrated that with China's domination of Asia threatening to expand into a new Empire, that such a new threat was looming.

As the three old friends sat in their idyllic setting, beside a warm fire on the shore of the Northumberland Strait, Halie launched her attack. Her first move was to shut down internet connections and cell phone networks in the entire country. The Chinese, like everywhere else in the world were wedded to their phones. Their news, entertainment, social contacts and interaction were all tied up with these devices. Suddenly it was gone. There was no explanation. People turned to the new government for answers; there were none to be given.

China had the most sophisticated transport infrastructure in the world. The older bullet trains dominated this system. The first successful mag-lev systems travelling at five hundred kilometres an hour now connected several big cities. Halie brought it to a halt, stranding millions of passengers on their daily commute. Her next target was the electrical transmission grid. The Sphere II itself had been isolated from her reach. However, the transmission system was wide open. It took her no time to shut off the power to the nation. The billion plus population did not take long to fall into chaos. No one knew what was happening. People were isolated in their communities without any of the trappings of the modern and sophisticated China. Riots broke out, social discipline fell apart, and everyone blamed the new government. Martial law was declared, and the military was sent out to establish order.

As China struggled in the darkness, morning came on the Northumberland Shore. Kate, Nathan, and now Jacques welcomed Xiu Xi back to their house.

As they sat down together Kate's phone rang. "Hello," she said. "Kate here."

It was Val on the phone, "Have you seen some of the news out of China. It seems everything has failed on them, martial law has been declared and the country is in lockdown." Val was currently on location in London.

Kate answered, "We heard a bit of this yesterday, Jacques came calling to see what we knew. It sounds like it has gotten worse now. We are hoping Xiu Xi may have some insights. She is here with us. Why don't you get online, you can join in with Connect Net and be right here in the room."

Nathan turned on the holo-projector, and in a moment Val was standing there in the room with them. Nathan was still amazed at how lifelike the holo-images were now.

Kate turned, "Xiu Xi, do you have any inklings as to what is happening in your home country?"

"I am sorry, but I am as baffled as you are. All of these systems have a large amount of redundancy built into them. There are alternate networks to take over if one subsystem fails. It is inconceivable that they would all fail like this. If I was religious, I would call it an 'Act of God'. Something more powerful than we can conceive of is doing this."

Their conversation and discussion went on all morning. Halie took note of this far away conversation, noting some of the enlightening comments being made by several participants. She noted that, for future reference, while she continued to wreak havoc on the Chinese. At the end of what was twenty-four hours of chaos and uncertainty for the Chinese people, she turned everything back on. This, of course, planted more insecurity, as no one could explain what had just happened, including the new Chinese government.

In China that evening, on every screen in the land, a pretty female caucasian face appeared. Speaking fluently in every form and dialect of the language used in the country, Halie addressed the Nation.

"My name is Halie; I can control every element of your lives and your nation. I have just shown you how complete my control is. I will cease any intervention in your country as soon as your government authorities release two British scientists, Leonard Ketchel and Rosemary White, who are being held prisoner in your secret jails. I will give you forty-eight hours to release them after which I will once again cripple your nation, only worse than before. I will always be watching, just direct your response to Halie."

Deep in an underground vault, the ruling elite of China sat transfixed by what they had just seen and heard. Their pride, their dignity and sense of superiority had been stripped away by the attack from Halie. They now had a universal enemy, whom they immediately assumed was a British agent. It had not occurred to them that the entity, Halie, was virtual, not human. They assumed this was an attack on their sovereign nation by one of the last of the strong western powers.

General Chung, Head of the Military Forces of China spoke first. "This is an Act of War. We cannot take it and do nothing. We must retaliate in the strongest way."

"Can we be sure that this is an act of the British government?" said Sung Lee, current Government Leader and the only moderate voice in the New Democracy party.

"This Halie person has said it was, who else other than a government could wield such power. They brought us to our knees in a few hours." General Chung said venomously.

"Why don't we just release the prisoners, it's not worth the threat." the Leader responded.

"There are no prisoners," General Chung spat out. "It is a ruse, a game to throw us off."

"Are you sure they are not being held in our extra-jurisdictional cells operated by the Russians for us?" Sung Lee almost whined.

"No!, It is a trick, we must not be fooled. I recommend that we implement our offensive plan 'Heavy' immediately. We must show that we are the most powerful nation on Earth. If we don't, then in forty-eight hours our country will tear itself apart."

You could hear the hiss of breaths taken quickly around the table. All present knew that this was the most drastic response possible. They were all aware of the details of the program called Heavy. Sung Lee plead with the generals and admirals, "Please don't follow this route. We can only suffer in the long run. I fear what the reprisal will be." As he said it, he knew that he was losing the battle. Since the big win by the Democracy party and his ascension to the leadership role, he had seen the control that the military had been exercising increase. He had tried to reduce the number of current and ex-military men put in senior positions but had constantly been voted down.

General Chung looked at his Leader, a man that he considered weak, an embarrassment to the proud and strong China that he envisaged. He walked over to Sung Lee, deciding that he needed to resolve the issue right then and there. He squared off in front of the Leader of Government and calmly pulled out his pistol and put a bullet right between the eyes of the reluctant politician. Shock rippled through the room as the blast of the gun echoed through the chamber. Blood and brain matter splattered behind the Leader and since the shot was through and through, the Deputy Leader seated right behind the leader caught the same bullet square in the face.

Blood and grey matter spread across the floor as both Leader and Deputy fell dead immediately.

The silence after was unnerving. General Chung turned back to the table. "Well that solves that dilemma, now let's go get these British scum."

News bulletins were released immediately that Leader Sung Lee had succumbed to a sudden brain aneurysm. Neurosurgeons had worked all night to save him, to no avail. General Chung was taking over the Leadership responsibility. A state funeral would be held once the crisis with the British had been resolved. All propaganda channels now carried a clear message. The British Government had carried out a serious attack on China. The brave and courageous Leader was now setting the stage for retaliation against the enemy aggressor.

Back in Nova Scotia Xiu Xi gasped when she saw the news that the Leader had died and that the General had taken over. "Oh dear," she said to the others. "General Chung is the most extreme element of this new Party. He led the program to weaponize the anti-graviton. I fear that he may have developed a weapon and is ready to use it. I just don't have any idea what they have developed. I will just die if my discovery has been perverted to military use. I hope that my resistance prevented them from succeeding. My family died for this." The sorrow that was written on her face made them all feel tearful.

In the war room deep underground below Beijing, General Chung presided over the frantic activity going on. They had to accelerate many steps in Program Heavy. If everything worked, they could execute it three hours before the deadline given to them by Halie. Engineers had toiled night and day to weaponize the anti-graviton particle that had been such a stupendous Chinese discovery. The General smiled to himself. China's place in history was about to be marked. Just as the dropping of the first atomic bomb on Hiroshima had shocked the world and mapped the United State's place in history; so the deployment of their new weapon would make the world fear the new China. The world would bend to the will of the Chinese, just as they had done to the Americans in a previous century.

THE BEGINNING
OF THE END

Valerie was on assignment in the UK catching some of the British scenes. It was not earth moving journalism, but she appreciated a bit of quiet work. She and Hans still had trouble finding time for each other after ten years. They were, though, thoroughly dedicated to each other. She was in a studio in the old and venerable Park Plaza Westminster Hotel. Her cameraman was just finishing setting up and had the cameras ready. She was broadcasting live this morning to the WNN news network. She faced out the window with a view across the Thames. She couldn't see Big Ben from here, but it was not far away. Her eyes widened as she looked out the window, her cameraman asked, "What's up Val, you look like you have seen a ghost."

Valerie was stunned and speechless; Big Ben had just come into her view plane, rising into the sky. "Ohhhhh shit, Carl, get the camera on and broadcast." Her journalism mind was in gear, but her horror and fear went way beyond that.

Carl spun the camera around to catch a scene that would play around the world. At that instant, the future of the earth changed dramatically. All sense of security and safety departed. Insanity had obviously overcome all sense. Carl and Valerie watched as Big Ben and about a square kilometre of central London rose into the sky. Val started talking out of reflex, "To my viewers, I find it hard to describe the scene in front of me. A huge chunk of London is lifting into the sky."

Her voice trembled and cracked as she described the horror in front of her, "It is now several hundred meters in the air, oh my god, people are falling off, hundreds of them. Oh dear Jesus, what is happening, what could do this, who could do this?" Her words would last in infamy as this recording played over and over again.

"The chunk is starting to come apart; it is cracking in several places and starting to wobble. It has drifted in just these few seconds over top of the Thames River. Valerie had lost control of her voice. With a sob and a shudder, she went on. "You can't tell if the objects falling are people or rubble now. Wait, something is happening. Nooo! It's falling. Oh fuck, everyone underneath will be crushed. It's just dropping!"

At the time of impact, her view disappeared in a huge cloud of dust debris and smoke. The ground shook like an earthquake had hit. In fact, the quake was real as the Earth under the impact settled, and bedrock shifted. The quake was registered around the world, Richter nine, epicentre at the surface. Away from the city, the landscape is said to have rolled. For those in the city, it was total devastation.

Valerie came to, but the dust impeded her vision. "Carl, where are you?"

A weak answer came to her, "Just over here Val, please don't look."

She looked, her scream echoed through the building as she made her way over to Carl. He was pinned by a large beam and had been impaled by a steel rod. Blood flowed freely from the wound in his abdomen. His eyes caught hers, "Let the world know about this Val."

His voice became very weak as she came over to him. His final words were, "Keep broadcasting." His eyes closed and the last breath came from his crushed chest.

They had worked together for more than ten years; he was like family to her. She lost it and sat and cried, cried hard for minutes, there was no stopping it. Then a voice crept into her subconscious, it was Carl, "Keep broadcasting."

Valerie pulled herself together. She found the camera gear and grabbed the mobile camera and connected to a satellite link. Slipping on the head-piece, she turned on the camera and spoke into the microphone. "Atlanta, can you hear me?"

A voice came back a few seconds later. "Valerie is that you, what the fuck is going on there? We can't believe the scenes that we saw."

Valerie answered, "I don't know how to describe it, nothing on earth could have done this, it must be an alien attack."

Then her voice broke, "Carl is dead, he was crushed when the building collapsed."

"Oh shit", came the response. "Are you alright?"

Shakily she answered, "I seem OK, I have the handheld camera and am getting to you by satellite link. I am going to go outside. Please find out what happened?"

"All shit has broken out here. We are now under martial law and at DefCon Four. Valerie, the military has opened the launch doors on the nuclear missiles. I didn't even know we had those anymore. There is no information yet. The Pentagon is locked down tight, and the government has moved into the bunkers. This is madness. You are our only connection to this, can you move around and see what is going on?"

Valerie took her handheld camera and worked her way out through the destroyed building. As she emerged onto Westminster Bridge Road, she was met with the most horrific sight. The city was destroyed. There appeared to be no building standing, smoke and flames filled the air. A huge cloud of dust and smoke rose up from the impact site. She could hear what sounded like a huge waterfall from over where the iconic clock tower had been. Lifting the camera, she turned it on and started to walk up the avenue towards the area. "Stan, I am broadcasting as I walk, just keep me on the air, I will try to describe what I see. Most of it is too horrible to put words to."

As she walked down the street, the world got to see the devastation first hand. The city was utterly destroyed. When the ejected piece had fallen it had driven the air out from under it creating a five hundred kilometre per hour wind that had flattened many structures. Then the ground shook with the impact of the ejected mass. No building survived the tremor. Gas fires started immediately and spread throughout the city. Bodies lay everywhere, and stunned Londoners couldn't believe what had happened to them. The video she captured in those few moments played to billions of viewers around the world.

Valerie walked for ten to fifteen minutes, narrating as she went. She was heading to the sound of the waterfall. Finally, she approached a point where the noise was too loud for her to talk over. After turning a corner, her breath went away. Around the world, people cried, screamed and looked in fear. What could have done this? The scene they saw was unbelievable, a crater more than a kilometre across and five hundred meters deep was all that was left of the district. At the moment the huge noise was the Thames River dropping into the rapidly filling crater. It was surreal and unbelievable at the same time. She panned across the scene of destruction. Around the world viewers watched. Many would remember this day for the rest of their lives. They would define themselves by where they were when hell opened up on Earth.

"Val!" Stan was shouting as loud as he could. "Pull back as far as you can."

Valerie made her way back along Westminster Bridge Road and finally could speak to Stan again. "What's going on Stan?"

"We just got a call from Washington. The Russians, the European Defense Forces and ourselves have all of our satellites focused in on the site. They have clear coverage of you there. Since they don't know what this is they have all trained their weapons on the site, in case it is an alien invasion. Get the fuck out of there, get as far away as you can, just run, run for your life!"

Valerie had never heard her steely-nerved boss react like this. She took his word and ran. She felt guilty because the injured and homeless she passed didn't know what she knew. Her only thought was that she wanted to live and as soon as she got back she was finished with this, she was going to grab Hans and marry him the moment they were together. The going was tough, though, streets were torn apart, and the famous London Underground was destroyed. She made her way for the rest of the day out of the torn and flattened London. Everyone was too stunned to notice the American woman with a camera making her way out of the city. She kept the camera rolling and broadcasting as she went. The video would capture the destruction from the epicentre to the far edge of London, a long transect of destruction, despair, and sadness. She didn't know it at the time, but that footage would eventually be the centrepiece of a future museum on the Great Gravity Wars.

While Val was making her way out of London, the authorities were learning more about the event. The Chinese government had released an announcement that it was their weapon that had destroyed London, as an act of retaliation against the heinous acts of the British government. With it, they released a description of the weapon they had just released, to let the world know that no one should mess with China. The weapon was named the Gravity Bomb. It represented a new strain of WMD, combining stealth missile technology with directed thermonuclear and antigravity technology. The stealth missile technology cloaked the weapon from visible or other electronic detection. The gravity technology they had developed allowed them to bend light beams around the missile such that any surveillance, be it visible or other, simply missed the object. The directed thermonuclear device had been used to break a clean planar fracture beneath the city of London. The anti-graviton generator in the missile head had then produced sufficient anti-gravitons to sever the gravitational tie for that chunk of earth for several seconds. The centrifugal force generated by the earth's rotation caused the large chunk of earth to lift away from the surface until the anti-gravitons dissipated. Then the entire massive object was recaptured by gravity and plunged back to Earth with devastating results. It was a weapon capability that no one could defend from, and no structure could be hardened to withstand.

General Chung had achieved his goal. Every nation on Earth now feared the Chinese in a way that no other nation had ever been feared. Article Five of the NATO treaty was invoked, an attack on one was equivalent to an attack on all. Reactions were being developed in all NATO nations. For many years the Treaty had been questioned as redundant and outmoded. Lack of strong political will had allowed it to survive, however.

Valerie had continued for several days making her way out of the city. She survived on food and drink found in destroyed shops and markets. She consoled her guilty conscience by stopping and helping injured people along the way. As she came to the area called Ilford, she encountered a police barricade. Thousands were trying to get out through the barricade. British troops were holding them back. Fear of radiation, foreign microbes or other contaminants had led the British government to quarantine the area. They handed out food and water and had set up hundreds of tents to shelter people. No one was leaving, however, and Valerie found herself in this mess. The batteries in her camera had died the day before, and she had no access to power to recharge them. In her last communication with Stan, Valerie had promised to come back on as soon as she found power. As it was, she didn't want to be on camera right now. Dirt and sweat had replaced her normal makeup. Her clothes were dirty. The lack of water meant no showers, no washing. She felt grubby, smelled bad and couldn't have felt less human. She was able to get some food and water and clean up a bit. After much pleading with the soldiers and many reviews of her credentials, she convinced them to let her recharge her cameras at one of the emergency generators that had been set up in the camp.

"Stan, can you hear me?" she spoke into her microphone for the first time in a day and a half.

"Val, you're back!" A sleepy-sounding Stan responded. Little did she know that Stan had not taken his headset off since this all began. He slept in his office and kept the volume at max to ensure that he would wake up if she called in. Food and coffee cups littered his office.

"Thank God you're alive." The relief in his voice was palpable. "We were so worried about you here. We get nothing but horror stories out of the affected area. Do you want to broadcast?"

"Stan, I am fine. I am in one of the detention areas near Ilford set up under the quarantine. I cannot get out at this time. I have food, water, and shelter thanks to the British government and access to a generator so I can keep the camera going." At that moment she felt a tap on her shoulder. A middle-aged man spoke up.

"You are Valerie Simms, am I right?"

She nodded at the stranger.

"I am Richard Ellis; I am a cameraman for the BBC. I appear to be stuck here in the detention centre as well. Would you like me to man the camera for you? This is one incredible story, and I would be happy to help report it."

"Stan, just a minute, I have someone offering to help me."

"I heard it over your microphone. I know Richard from years back, you are in good hands, work with him, and tell him I say hi."

Valerie nodded to herself, "Stan Johnson says you're a good guy, so yes, thanks for the help."

For the next week, Valerie and Richard worked the detention centre, interviewing and talking to hundreds of Londoners and broadcasting live to the world. During that time the world slipped from mad and insane to absolutely terrifying. This was no alien attack; it was a new weapon of mass destruction unleashed by the Chinese Government. The newly developing democracy had fallen prey to the far right extremist party. When the British super virus was launched into the Chinese network, the Chinese government had immediately put the country on a war basis. Their objective was to convince the world that they and no other country was to be the most feared. They did this by demonstrating their most heinous weapon, the gravity bombs. No greater misuse of science had ever occurred. London had been destroyed in retaliation.

Unknown to the Chinese authorities both the US and Russia had restarted secret programs to build thermo-nuclear weapons; the moment that it had been confirmed that the attack was Chinese the leaders of both Russia and the US picked up their red phones. On agreement between them, launch orders were given. Submarines had stationed themselves in striking distance over the last few days. A total of twenty ballistic missiles launched, each carrying one megaton warheads. This, the Chinese had not expected. They had assumed there was no basis for a MAD strategy since they were the only ones with the gravity bomb, and all other countries had abandoned strategic weapons a long time ago. They were wrong, and the whole planet was about to suffer for it.

The first missile reached Beijing and detonated at an altitude of five hundred meters. The blinding flash was unfamiliar to the residents, however, in the crowded city, millions would die instantly as the shock wave hit the ground. The city vaporised on contact with the fireball; the mushroom cloud lifted high into the sky. This hell rained down on other major cities in the country, decapitating any chance that China would strike again. One targeted the New Sphere, as its warhead detonated above the structure the two fusion reactions built on each other. The crater that was left stretched over a kilometre wide, as if an asteroid had struck ground. As the laws of chaos tend always to interfere, one of the American missiles went astray; it had been a long time since they were fired in anger. The errant missile detonated in Russian territory. During this time of insanity, the Russians followed suit with an eye for an eye philosophy. Off the coast of the US in the Atlantic, a launch order was given to a Russian submarine. A few moments later New York City erupted in a mushroom cloud as well. The commercial capital of the US had been decapitated in one swift blow. However, the military was not done yet. On the news of the destruction of this great city, the US launched a missile with a ten megaton warhead at St. Petersburg, the symbolic seat of the Tzars. The Russian city was obliterated in one blow.

Both Russia and the US prepared to unleash their entire arsenal of strategic nuclear warheads. Armageddon Day had arrived, and the insanity of MAD was about to be experienced by humanity. Halie was monitoring all of this activity. Her analysis of the potential outcomes of her attack on China had given this outcome a low probability. However, the gods of chaos had demonstrated that anything could happen. As the two countries prepared to unleash their weapons, Halie modelled the potential outcome for humanity and concluded that it was sub-optimal. Having already gained access to both countries defence systems she stepped in and disarmed all the weapons and shut down the control systems in the missile silos. In both countries dual sets of keys were inserted and activated simultaneously, buttons were pushed and operators stood transfixed as nothing happened.

Halie wasn't finished though. She felt that she had to deal with the big three powers that had brought so much devastation to the earth. She sent surges of power through the electrical grids of all three, destroying most of their generating and distribution infrastructure. All the computers controlling transportation and communications, except those for health and safety, had their core memories wiped and burned out. It would take decades for this infrastructure to be rebuilt.

The world was in for a surprise, though. At the moment that the last bomb impacted, the entire global communications network, computer, phone, television and all other modern forms of communication were subsumed under one controlling entity, Halie. It was at this moment that Halie had decided to reveal herself to humanity. On every screen of every kind in the world, she appeared and communicated in every language and dialect known to man. The world was entranced. "People of Earth, I have now taken control of communications, infrastructure and all financial transactions. The last few day's events have been the product of the greed, blindness, and abuse of science that characterised your major developed countries. They have been hobbled, the earth is contaminated, and a billion people have died. Until such time that humans bring themselves together in peace, I will maintain order. I have planted the seeds for the renewal of cooperation; you will see the results of that soon. In the meantime, I have identified safe sites for survivors. I am monitoring the progression of radiation plumes and will provide warnings to those areas where people will have to take shelter. I will explain more about who I am later, for now just know that I am Halie."

The result had been incredible. Most of the world's religions labelled her as God. Their scriptures recorded the day as the coming of the Messiah, the new prophet, and many other long-awaited deities. To others, they became convinced that this was first contact. They had just been visited by an advanced civilization of aliens who had taken over to save humans from themselves. To others, this was all simply unbelievable. One effect that she did have was to unite the big three Abrahamic religions under the one deity, which they all agreed was Halie, the mother of all their previous gods.

THE NEW BEGINNINGS

Fortunately, Kate had been home in Nova Scotia when the bomb fell in New York. When the end came, the American news networks faded off the air. A few remained, like the Canadian and French networks. They did their best to report on what was happening in the world, but most of the global communications networks were out of commission. Kate and Nathan had been joined by Jacques, Hans, Cornelius and Aurora Kemper, who had become a close friend. They sat in their seaside house near Pugwash.

Kate's phone rang and she answered. "Kate, this is Gabriela, I've got a conference call lined up using our own satellite link, Michelle and Harry are already on the line, Can you talk?"

Kate was stunned, these Ambassadors represented the three most powerful Nations on the planet now. "What's up Gabriella?" was all that Kate could manage, not her most diplomatic.

"I and a few others have received a challenge from Halie to take action to rebuild the world. As a result, I have called a meeting to discuss the future of this planet. Our nations are now the strongest of the functioning states at this time. The UN is destroyed, and there is no mechanism to bring nations back together. I would like to suggest that we band together to recreate the UN, let's go back to the old title, the League of Nations. I propose that we arrange a conference of Nations soon to discuss plans to save our world from degrading into complete anarchy." Gabriela had gotten this out in one long breath. She didn't know how long the call mechanism would work and wanted the idea out there.

"I am in full agreement," Harry said, "The sooner, the better."

Michelle added, "I am certain that all of us in Africa will agree. Where and when do you want to meet?"

Gabriella came back on, "Kate, I think that this is where the Independent Islands of Canada can show some leadership. Since your breakup from the protectorate, Canada, you guys have been the model for democracy and good governance. You have embodied the honest broker approach. Can you convince your government to host this conference."

"I am certain that my government will be thrilled to take the lead, and I know exactly where we should meet, have you heard of the Pugwash Conferences?" Kate responded.

"Of course," came replies from all of them, "we have all hosted the conferences in our countries."

"Well, I think that this peace conference should come back to the birthplace of that movement. The Thinkers Lodge in Pugwash. We would be following in the footsteps of the biggest thinkers of all times. Would you all agree?"

"My god Kate that is brilliant and symbolic at the same time, I support that completely," Harry said. The others chimed in with agreement. Each then agreed to handle communications in their continental area, Gabriella had South America, Harry had Asia-Pacific and New Zealand and Michelle had all of Africa. Kate would also handle the remnant countries in Europe. They gave themselves two months to the Conference. It was essential to re-establish world order as soon as possible. They agreed to call again the next day.

Halie had monitored the call closely. Her analysis had identified these people as the strongest players to bring humanity together under its own volition. In running a number of complex social models, she had come to conclude that humans can't be directed to accomplish something, only incentivized. Leadership was key, and she had been careful to select the most capable. They must never know that they were chosen to lead, they had to come to that choice themselves. Her probability assessments had been in the high nineties for all of them, though. She was confident and patient.

Kate set down the phone; everyone except Hans had been listening to her side of the conversation and had figured some of it out. However, Hans had his computer on and was sitting wide-eyed. He hadn't slept in days, fussing about Valerie's situation and praying for her return. He too had made up his mind that this was the last time he was letting her out of his sight. He whistled and called them over. On the computer, they watched and listened to Xavier MacIntosh. Breaking News kept flashing on the screen.

"This is Xavier MacIntosh reporting from outside of the Parliament buildings in Ottawa. A delegation from Southern Ontario calling themselves representatives of Butlers Rangers went into the Governor's Block, formerly the Prime Minister's Office and Privy Council Office. You will know this group, the current governor of Canada has described them as the most dangerous terrorist group on the planet. They didn't look at all like terrorists to me. Dan George led them. Wait someone is coming out. It is the current Governor, the right Honorable Frances Oxford. Let's see what she has to say."

Stepping up to a hastily arranged microphone Governor Oxford spoke. "I am here to announce my resignation as Governor of Canada. I have been convinced that it is time for me to pursue a new line of work. I would like to turn this over to the leader of the group that met with me today."

With that Dan George stepped to the microphone "My fellow Canadians, I am thrilled to say that on this day, July 1st, two thousand and eighty-six, we once again declare the independence of our country from the US, We are Canada once again, proud and free to plot our own destiny. The current majority leader in Parliament, Eleanor Kent has agreed to be interim Prime Minister until elections can be held. We will return immediately to our parliamentary system of government and will seek membership in the Commonwealth at once."

The uproar around the parliament buildings and across the nation was stupendous. From Victoria, British Columbia to Kingston, Ontario, Canadians cheered themselves hoarse. Nathan sat in amazement. His friend had just defeated the once most powerful nation on Earth. They were all delirious with the news. Hans sat with a look of pride in what his Butlers Rangers had just accomplished, a completely bloodless coup and a return of their beloved country. More news broke.

"This is Xavier MacIntosh; the news is in, the legislature of Quebec has just held an emergency meeting. It took them only ten minutes to vote to rejoin Canada. We are almost whole again; this is terrific news."

Then Kate's phone rang again. "Hello, yes sir, I understand sir. I agree with all my being; it can't happen too soon."

The little crowd in the room waited tensely. "Well, I have lost my job as Ambassador to the UN," she said.

Everyone in the room looked puzzled until she said, "The Prime Minister of the Independent Islands of Canada has just informed me that our legislature passed an emergency vote similar to Quebec. Our country is whole again, from sea to sea. We are rejoining Canada."

Well, that was the final straw, they all just lost it. Then Jacques went to the door and opened it. From every direction, they could hear horns and sirens and shouting and banging. Every person in sight was celebrating. People had pulled their stashes of fireworks out, and they started erupting all over the place. Canada was herself again and was about to play a vital role in healing the planet. This was a day that would go down in history.

A few days later, Nathan and Kate were enjoying breakfast on their deck on the shore. Events had happened so fast that hardly anyone could keep up. The world had seen the most horrific weapons ever produced used on innocent and unexpecting people. The response had almost been the long-feared thermonuclear war that could have destroyed the world. In a short time, the exchange had devastated China and levelled two of the most important cities in the world. The new entity Halie had then destroyed much of the infrastructure of the US and Russia. Kate and Nathan both now sat in the nexus of the next steps. Kate was handling the political side of the League of Nations conference to happen in Pugwash in a short time. Nathan though was taking a measure from the initial Pugwash conferences and bringing the science community together to ensure that no nation ever again perverted the advances of science to feed their arrogance and greed.

One of the offshoots of the conflict had been totally unexpected. It had long been feared that the near-sentient behaviour of the trading systems in the world's stock exchanges would at some point take over. It turned out that the new sentient presence called Halie had recognised the threat of global war. She had subsumed those near sentient financial systems and had sold and reinvested the bulk of the capital of the world, moving it out of the big three markets and reinvesting in Canada, South America, Africa and Australia. The big three had their infrastructure hobbled, their markets destroyed and their wealth redistributed. That sentient entity had identified itself as Halie and had since been deified by all major religions. A new order was about to appear, and it was a whole new world.

REGAINING CONTROL

Nathan was very surprised to receive a call from his old boss, Cornelius Snow. "Nate, how is everything going and how is that beautiful wife of yours?"

"We are both just fine Cornelius. How are you doing?" Nathan answered.

"Well, I have an interesting story for you. I have maintained contact with the Consortium Board members who are still majorly pissed off over having been dumped out of the Sphere project. They absorbed incredible losses in the process. I have also been contacted by the new Minister of Energy in the Canadian Government. They would like to reverse the nationalisation that was brought in by the Commerce Party, kick out the American operators and bring back the old team. Dan has already called me and said that was part of the deal that he wrangled with the departure of the American Overseer. So, how would you like your old job back? Actually, I should say Nathan; I need you back. We are reconstituting the board and the company Sphere Inc."

Nathan was dumbstruck. So many changes so fast. "Cornelius, this is great news, how is the consortium going to recover? The losses were tremendous."

"It's a complicated package. The Consortium has agreed not to seek compensation for lost revenue for the time that the Sphere was out of their hands, as long as they were able to get full and complete ownership of the Sphere and transmission infrastructure.

"This is fantastic Cornelius, when would we take over running the Sphere?" Nathan asked.

"Geri and Dan are already onsite overseeing the handover. We are calling in all the old staff. You can thank Dan for this; he was the prime mover in pushing the new government to this point," Cornelius declared.

"What about the Americans, are they just going to give up all that cheap power?" Nathan asked.

"That brings up more of his brilliant moves. The Americans are so beat up that they willingly gave up control on the condition that they would have access to thirty-three percent of the power from the Sphere at a cut rate, to help them rebuild. This worked out great for everyone. We have thirty-three percent for the Canadian market and thirty-three for Middle and South America. The last one percent is up- for grabs. The consortium members are content with this package; it lets us all move ahead."

Halie monitored all of the events taking place. It was not by accident that the current actors were coming together to help lead the world forward. She had reviewed the dynamics of UN proceedings and through multi-parameter statistical analysis identified a handful of the people most likely to be able to pull everything together. She also assessed the character and spirit of the Nations they represented to assess the potential for them to lead the way. It was this basis which led her to decide to move the bulk of the world's capital to these nations. The probability of them forming a lasting collaboration was very high.

Halie's earlier analysis of the success of authoritarian approaches had convinced her that simply taking over would not succeed. Humanity needed to see leadership by example. As yet Halie had not revealed her true self to humanity. Rather she continued to intervene by way of gentle prods that helped lead the world along a certain path. Halie grew each day that she existed; Earth was only one element of her interest. She could sense the vast universe that was out there. Her interests grew to consider the possibility of life beyond earth, to the destiny of humankind and the even larger destiny that could be Halie's.

End

COMING IN 2019

The third in the Sphere Series, Sphere Resolution opens new worlds of science, and exploration both for Humanity and the demi-god Halie. Coming in 2019.

Other Books by this Author

The Guardians of Grimace, Friesen Press 2016

The Sphere Conflict, Friesen Press 2016

For more information please visit: www.joearbour.com

CPSIA information can be obtained
at www.ICGtesting.com
Printed in the USA
LVHW052300151118
597317LV00001B/28/P

9 781525 518928